"Hardaker will put a spell on you with her sleek and haunting prose."

Silvia Moreno-Garcia, bestselling author of *Mexican Gothic*

"Imaginative and uncanny, *Mothtown* is a gripping tale of grief, love and metamorphosis."

Carys Bray, author of *A Song for Issy Bradley*

"*Mothtown* is an immersive, shapeshifting book, a haunting meditation on grief, loneliness and our yearning to belong. Caroline Hardaker writes with a poet's sensibility, conjuring a world both vividly familiar and alienating, mapping the landscapes around us and the struggles of the human soul with empathy and beautiful prose. Strange and moving in the best way, this story will stay with me for a long time."

Sophie Keetch, author of *Morgan Is My Name*

"*Mothtown* is a tale about discovering how to belong. Hardaker doesn't write a book you simply read, she delivers a book you experience."

Nils Shukla, *The Fantasy Hive*

"Haunting, atmospheric and wonderfully uncanny... a novel unlike any other"

Grimdark Magazine

"Caroline Hardaker's latest novel explores the pain of transformation and the beauty of becoming one's true self."

Books, Bones, Buffy

Composite Creatures

Caroline Hardaker

MOTHTOWN

ANGRY
ROBOT

ANGRY ROBOT
An imprint of Watkins Media Ltd

Unit 11, Shepperton House
89-93 Shepperton Road
London N1 3DF
UK

angryrobotbooks.com
twitter.com/angryrobotbooks
Mothamorphosis

An Angry Robot paperback original, 2023

Cover by Sarah O'Flaherty, illustrations by Chris Riddell
Edited by Rose Green and Travis Tynan
Set in Meridien

ISBN 978 1 91520 273 4
Ebook ISBN 978 1 91520 277 2

Printed and bound in the United Kingdom by TJ Books Limited

9 8 7 6 5 4 3 2 1

To the starwatchers. The wanderers. The dreamers.
And for Ben, for seeing me through this whole thing. All the
things.

AFTER

~

Something solid drives through my gut, like a wall of water, and I'm a ghost. Split down the middle.

No... a human knot, plummeting down rocks and bony roots until I hit earth. My head cracks against something sharp and my skull splits, from my ear to the nape of my neck. Something like smoke pours out, but wet and warm. It curls up and around my face in a red veil. The earth licks and holds me still like a great wet tongue.

All is quiet. For a moment, all is quiet.

But from the silence, a shrill ringing builds in my ears. A scream, like an eagle testing the sky. Like I'm inside a brass bell. Trying to shift my joints is like bending the branches of a tree, so I push into the mud, sending feelers out to understand the state I'm in. Count my body parts, one, two, three. Grass tickles inside my left ear. My right palm rests on a rock, slippery and black. My jumper is twisted and pulls against my throat. Burnt orange knit, little brass sparrow button, splattered with black. My head throbs, and the hollow twists and weaves like the ocean.

There's no time.

Light flashes through my fringe. *Too long. Why didn't I shave it close, in case I had to run?* I brush it from my eyes and smear a clod of cold mud across my forehead. Behind and above, something delicate snaps and a shower of pebbles tumble down the crag face into the ditch.

They're here.

I turn my face into the earth and force every muscle to move. Every bone screams as I rise. Little details embedded in the earth are floating from side to side – pebbles, dangling bracken, my fingers in the soil, as if there's a lag behind my eyes. I cover my face with my hands, and when I pull them away, they're cupping blood. My palms are deeply lined, scored with pain. They look so old. When did I get so old? Why did I wait so long to run?

I retch into the ditch and my throat rips as easily as wet paper. All is red. This is worse than the ache; this is tissue tearing beyond repair. I grab my neck and make everything tight.

Pin it all closed, hold it together. I've made it this far. I can breathe. Move.

From my knees, I claw up the ladder of jutting roots. The black soil feels like clay. My legs drag uselessly behind, as if I'm a thick, sallow worm, heavy with water.

One, two, three more and I'm over the ledge. Rolling on my back, a lilac sky shifts behind swaying branches. *I can't lie here. I can't go back. It's too late. I've done too much.* And then, a whimper in the quietest part of me: *I never thought it'd be like this.*

I fight back a sob and push myself upright. Moving makes me gag, but I hold it down. Some long, deep breaths still the trembling forest. I scan the trees up by the cliff face for the two shadows, but whoever they've sent is either hiding or still too far up the mountain to see. I'd only caught a glimpse of them, dressed in faint grey, blending into the mist. Something was pinned to each of their chests, something that reminded me horribly of a timer.

Their eyes were black. Almost entirely black.

I must've fallen around thirty feet from the rocky ridge, but it's impossible to see the spot where I slipped. My stuff is gone – my yellow backpack, my kit, everything – either stuck up the crag or it's tumbled down further than me and out of sight. All is obscured by trees, standing so closely that their roots are in knots and their branches grapple for space between them.

Using a boulder as leverage, I scramble upright, but when I put my right foot down it won't take my weight. My ankle is hot and loose, as if all the bones are lost. Should it hurt? My trousers are heavy with mud, and a thick but uneven coat of moss has attached itself to the fabric. I try to knock it off, but it's stuck – as if I'm the stone each clump was born on. I prise the lumps off with my nails.

I need to get my foot going, so I test it on the ground again. It's then that I realise I'm wearing brown brogues, the type with serrated edges and little holes cut out from the leather. At least two sizes too large, the heel hangs away from my ankle, and the laces dangle undone, thick and slimy like wet black liquorice.

They aren't mine.

A second avalanche of stone comes rolling down the other side of the hollow, so I turn and lurch through the forest. The thin silver birches are densely packed, and I grasp them tightly to ease the weight on my leg. From there, I enter a crush of pines and my knitted jumper catches on the branches, but I press on, praying that I'm not leaving a hairy orange trail for them to follow. Here, the ground dips again, but this time I use my good leg to slide down the pass, using the roots to control my fall.

I must be sliding for miles. *How far down does the mountain slope?*

It's a long time before the ground starts to level out. Here the trees are plugged further apart, and through them I can make out a wide field of dry yellow grass, sticking up in short, round tufts like anemones. It's open ground and I might be seen, but I need to know where I am. I rub and squeeze my knees like my father used to do when he rose from his chair and needed to move quickly.

On my feet again, it takes a few tries before I find a branch long enough to hold me up, and I slowly creep out from the cover of leaves. I'm in a wide valley, split in half by a stream which froths white at the edges. At this side of the valley is the steep slope of white trees, and at the other is a range of tall brown crags, coated in dead brown grass like hair on a giant.

Being here is to shrink.

If I look along the valley, I can just about make out mounds of mauve veiled by mist. Hill and valley, repeated into the horizon.

Thank fuck. I've seen this before. The map Michael showed me, but never let me keep. Faded brown ley lines on a tea-stained sheet of paper, so old it felt like tissue. Like Bible pages in church, it had to be held with care and apprehension. Michael had let me touch it, even peer in close to memorize the route, but that was it. At the end of each lesson, he always rolled it back up in foam and locked it in the lowest drawer of his desk. It was too faint to even photocopy, but then something in Michael's eye told me that he wouldn't have allowed copies, even if I'd asked. He kept all the maps, the secrets, and the keys.

Michael had told me of the silence here in the valley. He

said to me, "It's like the air is turned inside out." Already, I wish I could go back and tell him it's not like that at all. Write a research paper about it. Tease out the truth, that really, it's far more like being in an oil painting. The quiet comes from the absence of movement, of life. Each breath you take is the swill of a creaking ship, and you are electricity, bristling with noise. I clap softly, testing the sound.

Reassured for now that the two shadows must be still far above and seeking me in the trees, I step out into the open glen and dip my free hand into the water. It runs red, but soon it's glassy again. I plunge my other hand in and then lift the water to my face. Rubies drip from my chin. I wait for them to turn crystal before straightening up and searching left and right for my next steps. Michael's finger had traced a route along the valley with the crags on the right; I'm sure of that. Which would mean that here I should turn left.

I set off, trying to place a little more weight on my right ankle each time. It still feels strange and wet and hot, but I don't want to look at it. I have a feeling that if I inspect it, I might not want to hurry. If I tried to forget it, maybe I could move on quicker. Heal faster.

I carry on up the valley, careful to step in the brush and avoid the shining pebbles. My ears are open, listening for the slightest crack or creak from the white forest to my left, but Mothtown is silent, the breeze not even enough to rustle leaves. It's hard to believe it could ever have been a town, with its naked hills burning beneath the stars. It's wild twists of woodland. The loudest quiet. The only sounds are the light trickling of water on stone and the wet drag of denim on denim. The deep goose of the water is kind and easy on my eyes.

I had no idea the place would feel like this. Obviously I

knew it was remote, but with that, I'd imagined the valley to be a host to wild things that loved the light of the sun but hid from people. But the sky was a wide grey blank, a dirty chalkboard with no clouds, no birds.

In one of our first lessons alone, I'd asked Michael if it was a town, as the name suggested. He sat back in his leather chair, brought his hands together in a steeple over his mop of gelled blonde curls and said, "No. If anyone ever lived there, they're long gone. No one's lived there for thousands of years. Anyone who did is now buried beneath a cairn. These days, Mothtown is home to a high population of native moths. Fluttering around in communities. Flutter... or flap – is that what moths do? These are rare ones, big and beautiful. The sort you don't see out in the open, or in places further south." Michael's eyes glared at the dirty cream lampshade on the ceiling. "I *believe* that's the reason."

The analytics in my mind clicked into gear. I wanted detail. "What sort of moths?"

"Why would that be important, Mr Porter?" Michael leaned forwards, his eyes small and squinting. "Besides, I've never been there. I haven't seen them myself. But no living man knows more about Mothtown than me, so my words are golden."

I imagine the crags to my right covered in sleeping grey moths, their markings blending with the cracks and crevices. But no – even I can see that it's bare, violent, dead rock, and little else. Not even a sprout or sprig of green. In fact, now that I'm here, there seems to be no life at all. Every time I take a breath, I'm stealing, and every time I release it, I'm polluting. The idea of being utterly alone had once invigorated me, but I'd never before imagined how it would feel to be completely surrounded by quiet. No, more than that. The complete absence of life. And in the stillness of the world, I bristled. Chaos.

Michael told me that nothing that stays here for long, survives. But that's OK, I don't plan to be here long. I can do this quickly. It's in my blood. My whole life has led to this moment.

Not too far ahead is a tall white stone, about twice my height. It's lodged in the middle of the stream so that the water runs around it in thin trickles. As I approach it, I realise that the lower third of the stone, so up to my stomach, is blotted with white paint. At first it looks like random streaks and splashes, but slowly the shapes become clear, and I see that the patterns aren't accidental at all. They're handprints. Hundreds of them, layers upon layers. I get close enough to reach across and press my trembling palm onto one. My metacarpals protrude through my skin. Did it always used to be so thin? The spread of my hand matches the upper levels of prints perfectly, but as I try the ones further down the stone, my hand covers two of the white shapes easily. They must be children.

How?

I close my eyes and see us as children, finger painting with mud, flicking little copper coins into a cup, and I struggle to catch my breath. My throat rubs raw with each gasp, so I try desperately to breathe slowly through my nose instead. This doesn't make sense. *Who were they?* This isn't a place for children. This is death's house. How would a child even get here? Michael wouldn't have sent children, no. That wouldn't be right. Someone that young – they could never make this choice. I trace one of the handprints with a stubby fingernail and discover that it's not actually paint. Whatever it is has permeated the stone over time. So perhaps they're from years ago, centuries perhaps, before Mothtown became what it is now? Yes. That would make sense. Maybe it was the native community here that originally found the door, and sent a message to the world that this was the way out?

Behind the standing stone, the stream forks to the left, back into the white forest, and to the right, slightly up and over a tight nest of stones. I force my mind back to Michael's map. On there, the stream was unbroken, and ran straight and true to the edge of the paper. It was as faint as everything else, but I'd traced it with a finger time and time again. The stream was the east to west compass. It didn't deviate.

Fuck.

Neither path seems right, but then again, I'm acutely aware that I'm standing in the open beside a focal point that could attract eyes from anywhere with an open view of the valley. I have to choose. I look up at the crags, jutting from the ground like teeth. The door is up there somewhere, and I'll be just as exposed on higher ground. If this is the quickest route up there, then it's the only way.

I limp across the narrow rivulets and squeeze through the stones, sometimes by sitting and swinging my legs over, and sometimes by sticking my branch in the gaps and pivoting over the most jagged. Luckily, the stones don't stretch far, and I can see the plateau where they break into a flatter stretch, where wild yellow grass with fluffy tops grows. It looks like it might reach past my shoulders.

Only a little bit further.

Michael had promised that once I reached Mothtown, it wouldn't take me long to navigate its hills and valleys to reach the door. The way out. Two days, at most. Perhaps I could even make it today, since I'd technically cut time by taking the faster, 'falling' route down through the woodland.

My two shadows would have to turn back, return to their pale house with empty hands and dark eyes.

For the first time in as long as I can remember, my face breaks into a grin, before the ground falls away beneath me. I slide like a heavy stone into black water, and my head is sucked beneath the surface.

BEFORE

1.

You want to know how I disappeared?

Here I am, surrounded by things bearing my name, brass things under bell jars, instruments glinting like silver starlight. Dust-that-is-not-dust still drifts down to us from the rafters. Your hair is white. Feel it, dry like chalk. This is my ash. Sticking to things freshly cut. Things burst.

It's a lot to take in. I thought it'd all be blue. Light, airy blue, like the sky you scribble when you're little, when the sky is always that same pastel shade. Fresh cotton in the lungs. But the walls, watching me with jade irises, they're just like his special room. And that's – that's strange, isn't it? That it's so similar. The velvet curtains. The arms of red leather. I'm squeezing them in case I float away, but this is real now, isn't it? It's all real?

What do you want from me? How would I even begin to explain... I know where I was, and what happened, but the last three days – they're a blank. I don't know. I don't know. I'm tired. Blood still trickles down my chest, avoiding the part where my heart flits. Too fast. Moth-fast. Why is there so much broken glass on the floor? It crunches beneath my feet.

Start at the beginning? All right. I see it differently now. I have new eyes.

Some stories start with running. And some end with it. But my legs never were up to much – spindly, all knee-lumps and no muscle. I run like a spider. When I was very young, every summer Mum would present me with a pair of shorts like it was a special treat. After pulling them on, I'd crawl down the stairs like a beetle, searing my knees across the carpet. Emily would lean down over the arm of the sofa, her face peering at me like a bright, wide moon, before shaking her head and turning back to the beautiful people between her magazine pages. Mum and Dad would just ignore me, occasionally muttering under their breath, "Bloody hell, David, you're a hazard." But if Grandad was there, he'd bend down to my level, his face wrinkled like an old apple, and whisper, "What are you today, Bumblebee? Take me with you." I was the only one who saw the way his eyes glittered behind his glasses, like they were made of hundreds of jet fragments, all flicking around independently. With one finger, he'd loop my curly fringe around and around into two spirals, dangling like a pair of pale gold antennae. Then, I'd whisper whatever creature I was and he'd click like a cricket, or twitch, or fold his arms across his chest like a praying mantis. Sometimes he'd pull me to him first, just so I got the full itchy experience of his favourite orange knitted jumper – the one with the brass sparrow button on the collar – before releasing me back to the floor, my cheek scorched.

Grandad smelled like iron. Like something unearthed and laid in the light.

I used to think it strange that one place can be home to one person, but not to another. Grandad's office at the university was my cave. Lamp-lit bell jars, apparatuses with round pieces of glass that distorted the light, and yellowing certificates that couldn't have been as old as they looked framed in bronze. Being there was being inside Grandad's head. Every day after primary school, I'd sprawl on the sofa and watch loose spider threads drifting in the draft from the old windows, while Emily went to theatre practice. But if it was cancelled and she came to the office with me, she'd choose the awkward wooden stool in the corner, eyes on whatever book or magazine she'd brought with her. She carried her home in her pockets, whereas mine was the smell of old leather, dust, and the tapping of Grandad's computer keys.

Most often it was just the two of us.

Grandad's office was where wonders happened. Everything had a story, a place. Everything was important. Most of it I couldn't ever have appreciated for what it was because I was so young. It was beyond me. A sculpture that reminded me of a fortune cookie but made of silver mesh, framed certificates the colour of spilled tea, a row of plastic models mounted on a wooden plank that reminded me of twisted letter 'H's, and a huge glass model that sat on a little plinth so that it was the first thing you'd see when you walked in. Panes of glass in different thicknesses, separated by air and suspended like the layers of a cake. And piercing all of them were two glass straws, all bending in their own unique way. Blue and orange. Grandad did explain to me once in his own way what it meant, as he weaved a shoelace between the straws. "You're blue, and I'm orange, of course." He smiled and traced a finger up the blue straw. "And this is you travelling through time, each glass is a heartbeat. And this," he threaded the shoelace through the gap, "is an alien travelling at the speed of light. Look how much wiggling and weaving he can do in the time it takes for your heart to go 'thump'!"

But my favourite things in the room were the mirrors. There were mirrors everywhere – on shelves, on his desk, between books, and mounted on the walls. If you sat in his desk chair and looked to the left or right into the mirrors mounted there, there'd be thousands of you, falling away into the tiniest speck. If one of Grandad's meetings overran, I'd wait for him on that chair, spinning as thousands of Davids dangled their skinny legs, their pale and wispy hair blowing in the breeze from the window. One time, Grandad caught me doing it and stood between the mirrors with me, staring into the depths of our reflections. He didn't speak a word, just gazed into my eyes through the glass as his cheeks ran with tears.

Grandad seemed to think a lot of things that made him feel things. He mostly worked in silence, but would repeatedly look over at me as if about to speak but then change his mind. I'd catch him watching me out of the corner of my eye, as I pretended to read one of his books. Normally we'd be left alone in his office, but down in the courtyard, men and women in white coats bustled from place to place, their heads down, eyes on the prize. I couldn't even imagine what they talked about, but I liked that. I liked the mystery. Grandad's office was the heart of a creature that moved of its own will. Why would anyone want to be anywhere else?

But now, when I go back there in my head, it's always the last visit I see.

One Friday, when I was ten years old, the telescope was set up at the small, blacked out window in the corner. It reminded me of a long black cannon from one of the war films Dad sometimes watched, apart from the white label on the side, printed with 'Property of the Institute of Dark Matter.' It was late afternoon and the November sky was already turning indigo. I pressed my eye to the lens but formless black oozed back at me. I gestured to the telescope then up at the sky.

"What is it, David? You want to see?"

Grandad heaved himself up from his desk and took three trembling breaths before joining me on the wooden bench. As he fiddled with the silver knobs, I watched the papery skin stretch around his jaw. The hollows where his little half-moon glasses sat beneath his eyes were as purple as new bruises. Dad had said we shouldn't point them out to Grandad or ask about these things, just to accept them as part of Grandad now. I didn't like it. It was as if he was starting to rot, the inside being eaten by something I couldn't see. But I was sure Grandad would've talked to me if it was something he wanted to share, so over the last year or so I watched him transform silently, from my soft and round-faced friend to something new. A wrinkled and gnarled creature, emerging from an egg.

Grandad sighed and leaned back. "I don't think there's much to see, Bumblebee. It's too cloudy. The skies are clearer where I'm going; I'll take some good pictures for you, OK?"

On the floor beside his desk was a stuffed yellow rucksack, almost as tall as I was. Once, Grandad had sat me down on the floor and told me what each pocket was for. The chest support. The load lifters. A strap for a water bottle. A lock and key. We'd take a tour of the world through the bag; each corner contained a memory from his research trips. He never left without it. He called it his 'trusty companion.' When it was bursting at the seams, that meant Grandad would be going away, and no one knew how long it'd be before he returned. Days, weeks, months. And when he did, he always looked smaller. When I'd mentioned this to

Emily she just scoffed. "Don't be stupid. He's the same as he's always been." But I knew he wasn't, even if no one else saw it.

"Can you take me with you?" I whispered.

Grandad smiled, his teeth yellow, and wrapped an arm around my shoulders. "If I could, I would. I promise. Maybe one day, when you're bigger. I'll show you what I've found."

"You always say that. I'm bigger now."

Grandad squeezed me closer and whispered in my ear. "You want to know a secret, Bumblebee?"

I wanted to show him that I was still annoyed that he wouldn't take me with him so I turned away, but I couldn't help but smile. He did that to me.

"I've found something."

My breath sounded almost as loud as his whisper. My heart began to race. "What?"

"A secret, David. But it'll change life as we know it. Especially for me. And especially for you. People like us. But I need to explore it before I break it to the world."

I looked right into his eyes, then. Black and twinkling. They were more alive than I'd ever seen them. It was incredible. It was terrifying.

"And you will be the first person I tell when I'm back. I promise."

"But why now? Will you miss Christmas?"

Grandad sighed and rubbed my shoulder. "I might. I don't know."

"Can't you wait?"

"I have to do it now," he said. And then his voice dropped to a low whisper, "Because Midwinter is coming."

"Why?"

"It's very special, David. It's like a curtain." His eyes

glittered. "Between endings and new beginnings. Death and life. But keep this to yourself. Don't tell your father. He'd just get upset." And then he shook his head and chuckled.

He'd said death and life. It didn't make sense to me. Grandma was dead, I knew that. It was permanent. She wasn't coming back. But he'd made it sound like a door that could open and shut. For the only time in my life, I couldn't meet his eye. I wanted to know more, but I was afraid to ask. It made me feel odd.

A knock at the door and our magic broke. Grandad whipped around, his mouth pinched. A small man, with thick black glasses and a shiny bald head, strode into the office. He looked about my Dad's age. A wedge of paper folders was pressed against his side. "Frank, you need to go. Their patience has run out." He didn't seem to care that I was there, but I could tell that Grandad did. He stood up and approached the man, whispering in response, "I'm going. My bag's packed."

"And what about the rest?" The bald man's voice reached every corner of the room. It was rough and musical at the same time. He raised his eyebrows at the rucksack. "I can't guarantee that everything will still be here when you come back. If you want any of this," he gestured to the room, "saved, this is your last chance to pack it up."

"Don't you worry about that. It won't be a problem."

The man scoffed. "It IS a problem. Already. It's all meant to be gone." His eyes locked onto the rucksack, leaning against Grandad's desk. "You know I'm going to tell them what you're doing. I have to. You can't use University resources for this. It's not right."

"OK. It doesn't matter anymore."

This seemed to leave the small man at a loss for words.

He shook his head and looked at me, still as a shadow in the corner. "Frank, he shouldn't be here either."

"Get out, John."

They stood face to face for a few seconds while neither moved, like in the Westerns my Mum watched on Sunday afternoons. It seemed an impossibly long time before the bald man shook his head, shrugged, muttered, "You're lost," and stormed from the room. I was just about to congratulate Grandad on winning the duel but something stopped me. The space between us hung strangely, as thick as water. Grandad was motionless, even his usual slight sway on his knees was gone.

"Grandad?"

He didn't move. His breath rasped. I slid from my stool and fought my way through the fog to reach him, to give him my hand. By the time I reached him, he'd started to hum under his breath. A tuneless burst of notes that sounded more like language than song. Bumps and clicks. I knew what to do. By the time I touched his fingers, I was humming too, mirroring the soft sounds as best I could. Grandad looked down at me then, his mouth hanging open as if he'd just remembered I was there. Or that he'd just discovered me, like a prospector discovering gold.

"I'm here," I whispered. Even though his face was silhouetted by the brass lamp behind him, his eyes glittered like the moon in a puddle. His cheeks were wet.

"Don't worry, David. It's all right." His hand on my arm was shaking. "We've got each other, haven't we, Bumblebee?"

"What did he want?" I whispered.

Grandad leaned his face into my hair and sighed. "He isn't ready to see my discovery He's stuck in old ways, David. Not like us."

Shortly after this, Dad arrived to take me home. By then, Grandad was back at his desk, making notes in a red hardback book while I lay on the old leather sofa, bumping my finger along the leather spines on a shelf above. Dad burst into the office, setting up a swirl of dust that caught in the lamplight. My chest tightened as I took in his sweating brow, his downturned mouth. He didn't even look at Grandad, just eyed the yellow rucksack and then gestured to me with his good arm.

"Time to go, David."

I quickly swung my legs down from the sofa and pulled my trainers on, leaving the laces loose.

"You said you were staying in the house today. Aren't you meant to be out of here by now?" Just like the bald man, Dad's voice was too loud for the room. He didn't fit.

"Just finishing up, William."

Dad sighed. "And this," his voice was softer as he pointed to the rucksack. "How long will you be gone for this time? It's the dead of winter. You shouldn't be going, given the news–"

Grandad cut him off. "Of course I'm going. Don't be so ridiculous–"

"You're not fit."

Grandad froze. Dad's face softened in a way I wasn't used to. I didn't like it. "I wish for once you'd listen–"

"You're not telling me how to live my life. This is MY life. How dare you?"

Dad's keys jingled in his pocket as I pulled on my coat. He beckoned me over and guided me out of the office by my shoulder, allowing me one last look over my shoulder at Grandad, who gave me three of his alien little clicks. His chin was tilted aloft, the corner of his lip creased in a smile. He was asking for something, gesturing in our special language, but before I could click my reply, Dad closed the door and marched me down the dark and silent university corridor.

Dad buckled himself into the front and I slid into the back seat beside Emily. Her eyes were painted purple, and she was slouched low, her black hair wrapping around her face like seaweed. Clutching her flute case close across her chest like a shield, she glared out of the window at the darkness. The streets were empty, other than a lone walker or person at a bus stop. Lampposts flashed past the window as we headed out of town and back to the village. Many of them were plastered with overlapping posters bearing faces, but we moved too fast to see them properly. Mum never let me look at the faces. If she saw me trying to, she'd yank my sleeve and bark, "Don't, David. Look at the pavement." Face to the ground, I'd imagine the cracks were widening into chasms, ready to swallow me whole.

The car radio crackled with static, and Dad twiddled the knob until the newsreader's monotone voice became clear. "Twelve bodies have been discovered on the slopes of Bidean nam Bian in Glencoe this afternoon, most likely belonging to the 'Leeds Twelve' who were reported missing by their families three weeks ago. Early reports coming in suggest that the bodies were found in two locations, on either side of the mountain, and like all the others were carrying unidentifiable scientific apparatus…" Suddenly, her voice cut off and was replaced by music. Dad coughed into his fist and caught my eye in the rear-view mirror for a second before focusing his attention on the road again.

I'd seen photos of the Leeds Twelve on the news at home. All smiling. I only got to hear these things when Mum and Dad weren't around, because they always switched off the TV when these reports came on, or when the scheduled shows were replaced by a special report on the disappearances. In lots of ways, the Leeds Twelve weren't any different to the other missing people reports. But one man, who had had a round face, curly hair, and little glasses reminded me of a young Grandad. His name always stuck in my head: Martin Bowness. I wondered if he still looked like Grandad, or whether – like the others I'd heard kids talking about at school – he'd been found floating down a stream, as stiff as a log, his eyes masked by the last autumn leaves. Or perhaps he'd been discovered spread-eagled on a grassy fell, scorched black by the sun. Or, like I'd heard through the fence between my school and the senior school, perhaps what they'd found no longer looked human at all. Transformed into a thing that was neither here, nor there. An unnameable thing. Maybe they'd never know if it was the nice man with the round face and curly hair. Maybe all they'd find were his glasses in a puddle of something… *Black, dripping.*

I shuddered. Squeezed together in the back of the car, I could feel Emily's heat through my coat, so I edged closer. I knew she was long gone, away from the car. Even if I'd said her name, she wouldn't hear me. She was still enough to be a portrait, but her face twitched with thinking. It's like when you stare at the soil long enough so that it comes to life, and suddenly you become aware of all the wriggling things, the crawling legs. They're everywhere, and how could you not have seen them before?

You see, Emily was always there, even when she wasn't. As far back as I remember, I was trying to say 'Emily.' She'd been in the world five years before me, and though she could've been jealous when I appeared, she never was. She wasn't someone you could displace like that. She was the nucleus. The spine that holds the cat together. And I was her shadow. I imagine she sang and danced around my cradle before I even learned to see, just so I would love her most. Summoning me to her, determined to be my solace, my captain, and my tormenter. She was everything. Grandad understood – and when we were visiting somewhere and it all got too much he'd whisper in my ear, "Watch how Emily does it, take note. Copy her." I was never really sure what he wanted me to do, so I'd just let my eyes rest on her, trying to envelop myself in the control she so effortlessly held on to. Even now at fifteen, clad in black and slumping low in her chair, she held the room. If we stood outside, the wind carried her voice so it sounded like it was everywhere. When we walked through the village to the bus stop, all the green things rustled with her steps and her hair shone like it'd rained, even when it hadn't.

In the village, she stuck out like a crow. We didn't have lots of neighbours, but everyone knew everyone's face, even if they didn't know your name. And they watched Emily. They wanted to know what was happening inside her head. I would see them, their wrinkled faces pressed to their windows as we stepped off the school bus and she absentmindedly half-ran, half-walked down the middle of the road. Most of our neighbours were bent double and balanced on sticks, their eyes squinting and lips pursed as if it hurt to stand. But stand there they did, with nothing else to do until life arrived. Some had their armchairs pushed up behind the window, like prisoners ready for visiting time.

Is this right? Is this the sort of thing you want to know?

My first memory? My first memory. It's of Emily. Of course it was Emily. Seeing something shining in her that made me feel dark in comparison. You see, Emily had another gift. She lived and breathed a secret that she didn't know she had. She was a master decoder, a code-breaker. A chameleon. A natural.

She was also Dad's favourite.

I used to watch as they played these little games together without speaking. She'd sit on his knee and he'd touch the end of her nose. She'd touch his nose and make a little noise, and then he'd flick her chin and make a different noise, and on it'd continue. I had no idea what they were doing or how each of them knew what to do next, but it normally ended with Emily curling in a fit of giggles and Dad pulling her into his broad and balanced chest.

I tried to make him play with me like that once, but he pulled my hand from his ear and boomed down at me, "Don't do that, David. That hurts." Looking up into his face gave me no clues as to what to do next. Something had happened to him when he was younger that'd left him with a permanent look of concern, a one-sided frown. I sometimes caught a spark in his eye when he raised his voice, a bolt that lashed across my face like a black whip. Dad never moved his face much, choosing to keep his thoughts hidden beneath his furrowed forehead and stubble. I'd watch Emily stroking his beard this way and that, as if petting a cat, and I wondered if I'd have a beard one day. If one morning I'd wake up and it'd just be there, like my hairline had shifted overnight, and whether I'd have to go to the hairdressers every day to tame it. The ones booming with loud men, laughing, moving, commanding their spaces like kings. I wanted to know what Dad's face felt like. Were the bristles sharp like hedgehog spines or soft like fur? I'd stare at his beard as it caught the light through the window, to try and understand the truth.

I watched everyone. I still do. Mum said it was why my eyes were so big and "goosey." Like grey glass, letting everything through. Emily said they were so pale that they made me look like a ghost.

I watched Emily on the way back from my last visit to Grandad's office, when I was ten. I watched to learn how to move without thinking. I watched to learn how to make your home the space inside your skin. I watched to decode why she slumped so low in her seat, and I watched to understand what she could see in the dead of winter that was so inviting.

It was around that time when we started seeing homeless people in our village. "Vagrants," Mum called them, her nose wrinkled. But I thought of their flapping layers the colour of earth, and the way they stooped and walked like boulders come alive, and I called them mudmen. Our neighbours watched them warily through the glass as they trudged up the street like armoured beetles, laden with stuffed plastic carriers and sleeping rolls. More than once, I'd seen them pull out a wrinkled map with faded black lines on it, about the size of a sheet of printer paper. They'd never keep the map out for long, as if exposing it to the air degraded it somehow. Sometimes, after folding up their map and tucking it away into a deep inside pocket, they'd stop at the side of the street to inspect the abandoned bouquets and belongings that bordered our road like offerings. Big blue

bunches, stitched-back-together teddy bears, framed photos of families, always smiling. But all of them abandoned and left to rot until all that was left was the bones of stems, the rain-sodden fur. These things didn't appear on Poplar Avenue around the corner, or Church Gardens down in the valley. In fact, it was only our street, leading down to the broken fence at the end. Mum never looked at them directly. Even when she tended the flower beds at the front, she'd work as if her hands weren't plunged into layers of withered gifts. I did ask Mum once what they were, but she just waved her hand and gave me this strange tight-lipped grin that made her look like a scarecrow. "Just people trying to make the place look nice, that's all."

Sometimes men and women wearing bright lanyards around their necks came to take photos of the mounds, their huge cameras flashing like lightning. About once a month there'd even be smartly-dressed men and women talking into microphones, gesturing towards the rows of rotting gifts like they were holy relics.

And when evening came, the ones who brought the offerings came. Always dressed in black, they'd stand for hours, staring at what they'd laid down. Their faces were always grey beneath the streetlamps. Withered and waxy. I imagined that their hands were cold to the touch. Villagers never approached them, and simply drifted by them as if the black figures were as formless as shadows. One evening, I watched as a tall woman in a long black coat laid down a ring of blue roses. Beside her, a little girl in a navy dress pressed something white to her chest. It looked like one of the shirts Dad wore when he went to work. I went downstairs and described them to Mum, pointing out of the living room window to the curb where they still stood, but she shook her head and scrunched up her face. "Don't be silly David," she said, "I haven't seen anyone like that at all."

But the mudmen were different. I kept them to myself. I watched them from my bedroom window after school, always heading down the slope towards the broken fence and away towards the cow fields. They never came back, either. They only ever travelled one way. Always in the deep grey light at the end of the day. Always alone.

Ours was a village where the curtains never closed, but no one touched.

2.

After that last visit, I waited for Grandad every day. Every night I came back from school I willed him to be there waiting for me on the sofa, a tiny steaming cup of black in his hand. He might have a few new cuts and bruises. He might even have a sling or a foot in a cast. But I'd squeeze next to him on the sofa, and he'd tell the story of what happened in a way that made the pain OK. Exciting, even.

While Grandad wasn't there to pick me up, Mum agreed to finish early at the church and take me home when the bell rang. For three weeks, I raced into the living room only to discover it empty, and then trudged upstairs to my bedroom. Mum never said a word when I did it, just watched from the front door as she slowly peeled off her layers.

I had things to do. You see, while Grandad was off discovering things, he'd given me work to do too. Each night, I'd retrieve the black leather notebook he'd given me and read through the symbols of our special language. The Verbatinea, he called it. He taught me that word. He said it meant a special type of language, just for us, so we used it as a name for our clicks, tuts, and hums. My book was only a copy, filled with my scribblings, and Grandad had the original in his house – the 'Key Verbatinea,' he called it. Only we were allowed to write in that book, and only we were allowed to speak it. No one knew what we were doing when we made our little sounds. Mum and Dad just thought it was a game, but Emily knew there was more to it. Her eyes would flick between my lips and Grandad's, mouthing silently to herself.

But that one evening, three weeks after Grandad had finished packing his yellow rucksack and left again, I was determined to come up with a new word myself. The first thing I'd say to him when I next saw him. Something that'd show him that I was an explorer. Every half an hour, Mum would burst in, her lips pursed and eyes wide. Sometimes her hands shook and pulled at the collar of her shirt, other times her curly hair stood practically on end, as if primed to discharge electricity. There was always some excuse; "David, do you want a drink?" Or "David, tea's ready in an hour." I was so used to this that I didn't even look up. I knew what she was doing, and the sight of me sitting on the bed would be enough for her to relax for another short while, before she'd go and check on Emily.

But this time, she didn't come. I didn't even notice until almost an hour had passed and the house was still silent. I sat for a few minutes, and felt my own chest tighten. Something wasn't right. I tucked the Verbatinea away in the top drawer and padded out onto the landing. There were no voices, no movement, only a muffled voice coming from the TV in the living room downstairs.

Light as a cat, I slipped down the stairs one a time. I was halfway down when the news reporter's voice became clear enough to hear. "...No sign of the eight missing individuals, only their equipment by the edge of this remote lake in Wales; Cwm Pennant in Golan. Early reports suggest that along with several coats and miscellaneous items of clothing, bundles of hair were also discovered at the scene, potentially belonging to more than one individual. Who knows for how long divers will continue to search the waters and whether this is again one of the latest examples of–"

"David!" Mum's face peered up at me through the bannisters. Her face was round and red like a balloon. "What are you doing? Don't listen to this. Emily, Emily!"

A sigh drifted from the living room. "Yes?"

"Take David for a walk to the shop on the corner. Get me some magazines. Any magazines. Whatever they've got left, OK? Just for twenty minutes. No longer. Your Dad should be back by then."

A few seconds later, Emily appeared around the corner, still wearing her parka over her school uniform. Next to Mum's, her face was drained, expressionless. "Come on, Davey."

Mum waved us off at the door and I watched through the living room window as she raced back to the sofa, her hands pressed over her cheeks. As we headed down the main street, Emily's breath fumed like smoke from a dragon. No matter how hard I puffed, mine remained invisible. On either side of us, neighbours sat in their armchairs looking at their TVs. None of them had closed their curtains, and all of them were alone. I had the odd sense that I was at a museum, passing by wax exhibits. There were no new offerings along the curb this time, though the cellophane from the piles of dead bouquets twinkled under the lamplight.

Emily broke the silence. "Don't worry about Mum," she whispered. "She's just... worried. That's all."

"Why? She doesn't know those people on TV. She doesn't ever know any of them."

Emily shrugged. "No, but she's worried she will one day, I suppose." She stopped by the old pink house with the black front door on the corner of our street. All was dark within, and the windows looked like they were steamed up on the inside. The night was cold, but even from the other side of the garden wall, the pink house felt colder. That house was dead.

Emily leaned on the wall and swung a leg over.

"Don't!" I cried, grasping her sleeve. "Don't."

She smiled, her teeth gleaming in the lamplight. "Oh come on, what? Are you scared now?"

"No. But it's not… right."

"It's empty now, Davey. What difference does it make? They're not coming back. How long has it been, two years?" She looked up to the upstairs window. "Both of them. They were only young. They looked young, anyway. No one ever talks about them now, do they? It's like they never existed."

"I don't remember them," I whispered.

"Really?" Emily smirked, still staring at upstairs.

"No."

"That's what everyone says. But I do."

Both of Emily's legs were over the wall now. I fought the urge to pull at her parka, to yank her back over onto the street where life was. I balled my fists in my pockets and made my feet heavy.

"I wonder how long they looked for them?" Emily said, softly. "They were some of the first. I wonder if they ever found them?"

"Dad said they'd moved."

Emily sighed and swung one leg back over the wall. "You believe that, do you Davey?" She spat. "They didn't move. But you know that, don't you? Despite what Mum and Dad try to hide from you." She looked me up and down in a way that made me uncomfortable. "They think you're too little, but you're not. You're watching everything with those big, wet eyes."

It had started to rain. I looked back up the street to our house, our path illuminated by the TV in the living room window. A horrible acidic taste crept up my throat. "Will they be rotten wood now, Emily?" I whispered. "Or tangled weeds on a hill? Kids at school say they're not human anymore. Half gone. Like that bundle of hair, on the news."

"You do see everything." Emily rose and wrapped her arms around me and suddenly, everything was warm. "Good," she whispered.

Dad came home late again that night. For the past week we'd hardly seen him, both of us having gone upstairs after dinner by then. She was meant to be doing her homework, but the sound of her tiny TV reverberated through the wall between us. I didn't mind. It made my room feel like part of a beehive, as if all the walls were alive. It muffled the angry shouts from the kitchen downstairs just enough so that I couldn't hear the words. Most of Mum and Dad's fights blended together. They were so repetitive and meaningless. But this time, something about the tone of their voices caught my attention and I opened the bedroom door a couple of inches to listen. What I heard next would never be forgotten. Even now, so very far away, I still remember it word for word.

Dad first. "I can't believe it."

"Why did he do it?" Mum's voice. Shrill. "It's selfish. What are we meant to do now?"

"I... I don't know."

"Did they say anything else? What are we supposed to do?"

"Just a letter. I can't–"

"He must have said something to SOMEONE. Before this."

They were both quiet. And then Dad, sounding shaky. "They didn't say."

Silence. Then Mum again. "It's so selfish. I *knew* he was selfish."

"Stop, Paula."

"How dare he do this to you? What're we supposed to tell people?"

"Stop."

"What's on the back of the letter?"

Silence again. But this time it was the sort of silence before a volcano erupts. I was hardly breathing at all.

"For fuck's sake – what about his house? His office?" Mum's voice kept getting higher and higher. "Are *we* meant to sort it all out?"

"It doesn't matter now."

"What about those bloody blue people? They don't deserve to get everything. They were knocking on him every day, and they did nothing. Shouldn't they take some responsibility?"

"Paula!" Dad was yelling now. "Give me one fucking minute. Please."

Then silence, followed by some muffled notes, like words spoken into a jumper.

"I'm sorry," Mum said. "I'm sorry. I'm just so angry. This didn't have to happen."

"So am I."

Through the wall, the sounds of the TV stopped and were replaced by the roaring sound of a hairdryer. I took some deep breaths and scrunched up my face, feeling like I was going to be sick.

The next night, Mum and Dad sat Emily and I down in the living room. Dad sank into the leather armchair while we sprawled on the floor. Mum perched on the edge of the sofa, staring at Dad and twisting a handkerchief around her fingers. She sniffed.

Dad rubbed his hand across his chin. Emily's mouth hung slightly open as she looked between Mum and Dad. Mum stared at the empty fireplace. Her face was a very strange colour.

Dad coughed a little, wiped his mouth, then told us that Grandad was dead.

Then a few things happened at once – suddenly, but slowly. My stomach squeezed. My head floated free of my shoulders, just a few inches. And the whole of the sea lashed against my inner ears. I felt these things, but distantly. It was like I was outside of my body, observing them happening to someone else. I couldn't think. My mind had been severed from my body and now I was a ghost. Despite this, I didn't take my eyes off Dad. I couldn't, even though Emily had started to moan in the seat beside me.

Dad told us that Grandad had been in hospital for the last week, but they hadn't wanted to frighten us. Grandad had had a stroke, just like Dad when he was younger, but a lot worse and that his body couldn't cope with it. Couldn't recover.

By now, Emily had started to sob, but I just felt confused. Dad looked at me as if I was doing something wrong, so I squashed up my features in the middle of my face like a fist. But he continued to stare, his brow furrowed. Emily looked up at him. "Can we go see him? Like we did Grandma?"

"There's nothing to see. He's gone." Dad shook his head,

his eyes fixed on me. "Grandad's gone, David. Don't you know what this means?"

I nodded, my mouth tight.

"What does it mean, then?"

Emily turned and pressed her face in the gap between Mum's knees. Mum stretched out her handkerchief and lay it over the back of Emily's head like a shroud.

I stared Dad hard in the face. "It means he's not coming back."

"Mum…" Emily whispered, her arms wrapped around Mum's legs. "I wish we knew where they went."

"No one knows that, Em. We've just got to hope it's somewhere better than here. And we'll all be together again one day."

Emily took three sharp breaths inward. "Did he miss Grandma too much? Is that why?"

The air in the room changed. Mum's face was white marble. Dad's eyes were closed. The skin around his chin shook a little. *He wouldn't like this. Emily should have known not to mention Grandma.* I looked down and it was raining on my knees. No one said anything for what seemed like an impossibly long time, and then Dad got up and left the room without a word.

"He's still not ready to talk about that, rabbit," said Mum as she blew kisses into Emily's hair. "But yes, Grandad will have wanted to be with Grandma."

I couldn't listen anymore and floated up the stairs to my bedroom, my legs like jelly. Once my door was closed, I fell to my knees beside the bed. How could Grandad be dead, yet feel so very much alive? I'd only just seen him a few weeks ago. I could still feel the knit of his jumper, the bones of his knees. The brass sparrow button that Grandma had sewn onto his collar still glinted in my eye. Our language still sang in my head. And now, what? Dad said he was dead, but life didn't feel different to before he said it. They were just words.

No. Grandad was too important to just not exist anymore.

This isn't how things were supposed to go.

Questions in all shapes and sizes fluttered around inside my head, yet none formed a solid shape. I felt around my eyes for a sign that I was like Emily, but my skin was still dry. I clutched what hair I could between my fingers and pulled hard. It felt as soft and insubstantial as smoke.

No. This was a truth that I couldn't swallow, and it rolled around my mouth, heavy on my tongue. I knew I should be sad, but I wasn't. Instead, I felt empty, as if something had been scooped out and not replaced. But in that hole, *something* lived and breathed, and was flapping for attention. So I lay back on the carpet and tried to let the truth of it settle, like boiling water coming to rest.

3.

Are you still listening to me? Yes. I see my eyes in your eyes.

It's strange, but if anyone ever asked me to picture Grandad, it would always be him sitting in Grandma's armchair. Though his office was where we made our magic, that chair was where his layers fell away. A flowery yellow chair, splashed with red and lime green. Everything else in that living room was wood or the colour of wood, but Grandma's armchair stuck out like a tropical bird. While Grandad had rolled his eyes at it, Grandma whispered to Emily and me that it was the only thing she chose for herself when they got married and that she was determined to keep it. In the end it outlasted her, and it was the place that we found Grandad the most after she died.

And now he was gone too.

The morning after the news, I lay in bed for as long as I could. I remember a strange taste at the back of my tongue, like I'd been facing the wind with my mouth open. Grandad's face floated before me, grey fuzz hovering around his head like a halo. The little crescent glasses. The little crooked smile. I could tell that already he was becoming a fiction. I wondered whether my brain had done that as soon as it'd registered Dad's words, turning Grandad into something flat that could be slipped into a drawer. Filed away. His rusty smell, the pressure from his hands holding me on his knee. I was sinking, and the only person I'd have called to save me couldn't come. I pulled the duvet over my head. I couldn't think about it. I wouldn't think about it.

That Saturday morning, no one came to shake me from my bed. Lying there, I began to imagine melting into the mattress, the springs wrapping around my arms and legs like weeds. All I wanted to do was to sleep, to be entirely covered by green and to see no more light. I willed and willed it to be that way, but still the sun glowed through my eyelids, and still I could hear Dad's low grumble through the wall as he talked on the phone. As I listened to his slow and steady words, I started to experience this pulling in my chest, like elastic about to snap. I clasped at my chest but it made no difference. I needed someone to help. I wanted someone to touch me, to hold me steady.

Panting, I scrambled from the bed and burst onto the landing. I only caught a glimpse of Dad before he heaved himself from his bed, its surface scattered with papers. Some looked like letters, some looked like lists written in Dad's overly large handwriting. But next to those, spread over the pillows, were maps. At least two of them. The one closest to the door had been marked with around nine red circles. Three of those had a big black cross through them. The landscapes were mountains, hills, rivers, valleys.

"Get out!" Dad yelled, pointing at the landing. His face was twisted oddly, like he was in pain. He slammed the door between us, and my body shook from the force. I'd never heard him so loud.

"David? What are you doing?" Mum's voice called from the kitchen. I found her standing by the sink, her hair all frizzed up on one side. I stood next to her, one hand on my heart, my tongue ready to click.

Her fingers grazed my elbow. "David, your arm, it's freezing. Go in the living room. Give me some space to think." She led me to the sofa and switched the TV onto a children's channel, stuff meant for younger kids than me. Though my eyes stung, the garish cartoon colours seemed to numb the ache in the back of my chest, the thumping in my ears. Soon Emily joined me, dressed in a white dressing gown, her face as pink and puffy as a birthday balloon. She reached out and put her arm around my shoulders. "Don't worry," she whispered, "I've got you." Without even thinking about it I leaned in. She smelled of coconuts and sugar, and for some reason this made me want to cry.

Neither Mum nor Dad said anything more about what had happened. It was as if each of us were living in our own little bubbles and bouncing off each other if we got too close. I pressed myself into Emily, my eyes closed against the feeling in the house, and aware of every thud of my heart. Dad shut himself off in their bedroom with his papers and Mum rattled around the house, moving random objects and piles of clothing from room to room.

That afternoon, the callers came.

It started at midday. The first time, Mum went straight to answer it, but after peering through the peephole released the handle and crept back into the living room. "Don't answer it, Emily," she whispered, her finger pressed to her lips. "Scavengers. They'll leave a flyer; they always do." After that, when the knocks came Mum peeked through the net curtain until whoever it was had disappeared again, blocking my view of the street. It wasn't until evening when they dropped something through the letterbox that Mum leapt towards the door to retrieve it. Still wrapped in Emily's dressing gown, I took the opportunity to leap from her arms and press my face to the window. "David, don't!" Emily stepped behind me and pulled me back by my shoulder, but not before I caught sight of two men, dressed in pale blue fleeces, climbing into a car together. One of them had a phone pressed to his cheek and was rubbing the back of his neck. Mum came back into the room with whatever they'd posted torn into tiny pieces. "Vultures. Can't believe they're here already," she muttered. "Grief-feeders. Don't they have any shame?"

After that, more callers came to the house, but Mum didn't hide from those. They were the sort I'd seen before, men and women who eyed the curbside mounds fearfully, their faces pale and strained, as they held up photos and repeated, "Please, please, have you seen my son?" Or, "This is my sister, she was last sighted around here – have you seen her?" Mum always returned to the living room with her faced flushed and a strangely pinched mouth as if trying to hold something in. She'd often take a copy of the missing person's photograph and look at it for hours, her lips pursed as if the face teetered on the edge of her memory, but it never came to anything, and all the photographs ended up in the recycling.

That day, I could hear her telling the door-steppers about Grandad, about how we'd lost someone too, and how dreadful it was. At one point Dad stumped down the stairs and the door-stepper reached out to grasp his wrist. His eyes opened wide as he listened to the small woman with the thin mouth, a photograph of a young man thrust in his face.

Now.

Slipping behind Dad, I scurried up the stairs on all fours

and pushed open the door to Mum and Dad's bedroom. "No," I whispered. The bed was clear. Where were the maps? The letters? Desperately I flung open Dad's clothes drawers, sticking my arm right to the back, before throwing myself on the carpet and stretching under the bed. Nothing – just dust and shoes.

Dad would be back in a minute. I only had a few seconds. I needed to know where Grandad had gone. What'd happened. How it'd all gone wrong.

His bedside cabinet.

I crawled up to it and opened the door with a creak. There. The top shelf was stacked with large paper envelopes. Many of them were stuffed to capacity, their aged corners frayed and disintegrating. I grabbed a handful from the top. All were labelled with Grandad's swirling script. Most words had smudged and I couldn't make them out, until one small envelope slipped from the pile. Unlike the others, this one was clean, crisp, and had only one word written on its face: 'David.'

"David!" Dad loomed above me, his eyes hidden beneath his brows. A broad hand extended towards me, palm up. It was dirty, its lines scored with soil. "Give that to me, now." His arm shook.

"It's got my name on it. It's mine, Dad."

He took a step closer to me so his knee was against my shoulder. "It's not for you," his voice was softer now. "It's not for you." And just like that, the envelope was in his hands, and in his pocket.

I didn't see Dad again until Sunday morning. I didn't ask Mum about the envelope from Grandad. When I remembered what'd happened with Dad, my face would grow hot. There were no words for what I was feeling. I didn't know what it meant. What had Grandad wanted to tell me? Why had he left an envelope for me at all? And what else had he left behind?

Lying in bed, I heard Dad through the bedroom door.

"...Shouldn't be long, just grabbing a few things."

"They wouldn't start sorting through his things now, surely?" Mum whispered.

"I don't know. They have a key, don't they?"

"They wouldn't dare."

"I'll only be a couple of hours."

As if yanked by elastic, I ran to my bedroom door and opened it just enough to see the back of Dad's head as he descended the stairs. "Take me, Dad."

He turned around. His beard, normally reddish brown, was threaded with grey like a dying bush. His eyes were wide. "No. Stay with Mum. I won't be long."

"I want to go." I opened the door fully and stood at the top of the stairs. For a moment, I felt so light that I considered leaping to him from the top step. In that brief second, I was weightless, and Dad must've seen it too because he took a step towards me, his arms held up as if to catch me.

"David, what–"

"Please." Even my voice was thin, insubstantial. I gripped the banister.

Dad looked at Mum, who was staring at me, her chest heaving. Her brow seemed to have as many creases in it as tree bark. "Maybe take him, William."

Dad's arms were still aloft when he replied, his voice soft. "OK, David, it's all right. Keep your PJs on, just choose some trainers and let's go."

***

Dad ushered me to the car and locked the door gently behind us. Across the street, a woman with curly grey hair was standing on her lawn with a silver watering can. Mum talked to her sometimes, always loudly, always laughing *too much*. All her flowers were at the very front edge of her garden, which meant that she had to stand in the middle of the street to tend them. Sometimes they became partially buried under abandoned bouquets, so she'd gently nudge them into the road with a toe, eyeing up the neighbours to see if they were watching. But that morning, as I watched her through the car window, I thought that if she'd lived with someone, they might have pointed out that her watering can was empty and she wasn't helping the flowers at all – no matter how many times she tipped it.

"We're just going for a few things." Dad didn't look at me when he spoke. It was as if he was speaking to someone outside the car, through the driver's window. I knew the trees and farms we passed like the cracks in my bedroom wall. Left here. Around the big fir trees. Along the sloping road that arches up at the shepherd's gate. On towards the higgledy-piggledy sheds. Past the allotments, wild and untended.

About half an hour later, Dad pulled up outside the house in silence. A tall, three-story terraced house, old, grey, flaking white. A bright blue front door, chipped. Number 63. The backs of photo frames rested against the window. I could almost see Grandad's face hovering above them through the net curtain, where it should have been. It looked different. Cold. Dead.

"We're just going in for ten minutes," Dad said. "The

house is empty now. I need some paperwork from his office. If it's too much for you to be inside, you can wait in the car. Does that sound OK?"

"It's fine." I nodded and unbuckled my seatbelt.

Dad's eyes were piercing beneath his reddish eyebrows. I turned away. "David, you do understand what's happened, don't you? He's gone. He's not coming back this time."

His face was inches from mine. And just as I noticed that the dark hollows below his eyes were just like Grandad's had been, something broke, and I fell into myself, cascading downwards into darkness. I couldn't speak. I couldn't think.

But I could move.

I nodded and kept my eyes on the gearstick. Dad released one long stream of air through his lips before pressing his hands over his face. One, two, three deep breaths. I felt myself piece back together. *Was he hiding from me behind his palms?* He held them there for so long that I got out of the car and waited at the front door, my hand reaching up to hold the brass knocker. Dad followed a few seconds later, a large and jangling set of keys clutched in his fist. The key between his trembling fingers was small and shiny silver, as if new.

The front door opened onto a long purple hallway, from which three doorways led to the living room, dining room, and kitchen. But all the doors were closed, and all the lights were switched off. I'd never seen the place so dark and still, even in the weeks after Grandma died. That had only been a year ago. I couldn't remember much of her last days, only snapshots sticking out of ordinary days like shards of glass. Grandma in the hospital bed, reaching out for my hand. The strange, astringent scent of her skin that reminded me of the bottle of green in our bathroom. And Grandad's face as he sat on the only chair in the hospital room, bewildered, as if he couldn't understand what was happening.

In the months that followed her funeral, we didn't see Grandad much. Dad moved in with him for a while. When I asked Mum where Dad had gone, she chewed the inside of her cheek and said, "He's gone to keep your Grandad on his feet." I didn't understand what she meant, but something in her tone made me not want to ask again. One Sunday a few weeks later, after an afternoon of banging and swearing in the kitchen, she drove us to Grandad's house and let herself in with the extra key on her fob. "William," she called down the hallway, "I can't do it anymore, I need a break." Dad led her through to the kitchen while Emily and I hovered in the doorway to the living room. Grandad was sitting in Grandma's chair, the yellow flowery one next to the sideboard crammed with photos and sculptures of shepherdesses and little boys in wide-brimmed hats. Grandad's hands were palm-up on the arms of the chair and he stared blankly ahead at the switched-off TV. There were no lamps on, and the late afternoon light through the net curtains turned everything blue.

Emily hung back, swinging on her heels behind the door and peering out with saucer eyes. She gripped a handful of my t-shirt as if holding back a dog, but whatever she thought she sensed, I didn't pick it up, so I strode in – right up to Grandad's side. He didn't turn to look at me, but his lips squeezed together, so he knew I was there. Grandad had an old, fading map spread across his lap, so I carefully set it onto the floor before climbing onto his knee and wrapping an arm around his neck. His radio sat on the sideboard next to the chair, so I flicked it on, and the low murmur of an orchestra poured from its speakers. Something about

Grandad's stillness and the cold of his flesh frightened me a little, so I leaned into his chest and closed my eyes, just so I could pretend everything was normal. A few seconds later, his arms were around me and squeezing me so hard that it hurt. I let out a little cry and gasped for a breath but he still didn't stop. I turned my head as much as I could to see if Emily could help. By now, she was sitting on a footstool by Grandad's feet, tilting a gold compass this way and that. She wasn't looking.

Grandad stifled a sob, and whispered into my ear, "You never know when it's time to say goodbye, Bumblebee. No one tells you. But you know that I love you, don't you, my special one?" I nodded and he relaxed his arms enough for me to breathe normally again. I burrowed my face into his jumper and took in that strange, rusty scent that was entirely his.

But now, a year later, now that he too was gone, I'd never do that again. Everything that brought the place to life was a memory.

As I followed Dad into the house, the air transformed from the crisp December bite to a strange bitter smell. It was like walking into cobwebs. It didn't even feel like Grandad's house at all. It was as if an alien squatted there now, a man made of dust, and rot, and damp. I took a step back. Dad's hand met my shoulder blades and I looked into his face to find a half-smile. He gave me a little push. "Why don't you collect some photos from Grandad's bedroom? On the chest of drawers. You know the ones. He'd want you to."

From that ominous corridor, the landing above seemed illuminated. Without a word, I bent over and ascended the stairs like a spider, planting my hands and feet silently into the carpet. A green vase of flowers with plush, white petals

sat on the windowsill – too blooming, too new. One broke off between my fingers, and I laid it against the window reverently so the sun shone through the plastic. It didn't feel right to be here. Every footstep disturbed a fine layer of dust, marking it forever. Even sound could trouble the dust. The *memory*.

Resting my hands on the bedroom door, I pushed it gently to the dragging sound of wood on carpet. The darkness oozed out, and a rush of damp washed over me in a wave.

I'd been in that room hundreds of times. Hundreds. Grandma rolling me up in the king-size duvet. Grandma showing me through her bottom drawer, where she kept her knick-knacks – jewellery boxes with women dancing inside them, little pieces of bone china with gold inscriptions, drawings of constellations that Grandad had done for her, gold chains in velvet boxes. And sometimes, while everyone else talked in the living room downstairs, I'd come up on my own and fiddle through the drawers of the oak writing bureau, flipping up the lid as high as I could and dabbing the thick black fountain pens on the brown and crinkly paper.

But now, I didn't even want to turn on the light.

I didn't know what I'd see. I knew the room was empty, that neither Grandad nor Grandma would be there. But something hung in the air, thick and wet, and I didn't want it to touch me.

But I knew I had to. *I had something I needed to find.*

Behind me, I heard the *thump thump thump* of Dad coming up the stairs, so I quickly reached up the wall and flicked on the light. The duvet was askew, the pillows standing flat against the headboard. A blanket lay draped over the foot of the bed and across the floor. The curtains were closed. Everything looked darker, as if viewed through a grey lens.

Five bluebottles crawled across the empty white sheet. The window looked all fogged up, like the bathroom window if you didn't open it after a shower. Everything was so very still, like debris sunken to the bottom of a tank of water. It was hard to breathe.

The floorboards behind me creaked as Dad made his way to Grandad's study, and I lurched forwards. *The book. The Key Verbatinea.*

As quietly as I could, I slid open the top drawer of Grandad's bedside cabinet. The place where "All the most special things are kept, so you dream about them," he used to say. But the book wasn't there. My hand fumbled against paperbacks and lotion bottles and dusty glasses cases. It was gone. Our special book was gone. That tightening in my chest returning, I stood up and started to search through the chest of drawers, but it wasn't there either. Why wasn't it here? The room began to spin. I needed that book. Our book of words. The book that joined us.

Through the wall, in Grandad's office, something slammed.

My nails dug deeply into the skin on my arms. It helped to steady me. To remind me that I was still here. I still existed. That this was real. Could Grandad have taken the book with him, on his research trip?

"Nearly done, David?" Dad's voice rumbled through the wall.

Pushing the book from my mind, I looked up. The chest of drawers was crammed with silver photo-frames. Some were faces I knew: Jordie, the border collie whose smooth back had helped me stand for the first time; a slim Dad and Mum sitting on a wall at the beach; one of us all together at a restaurant in Scarborough. One was on my birthday almost a year before, where I was leaning over a cake with nine candles. It was the last time we were all together before Grandma fell and went to live in hospital. But the rest of the photos contained people I didn't know at all, and it troubled me that I hadn't noticed before that Grandad and Grandma's bedroom – the most private place I could imagine – was home to the faces of strangers. Strangers who'd watched me go through the secret bottom drawer with Grandma, and scratch my name in the underside of the writing bureau where I thought no one would find it.

I could only just about reach the frames at the back. I picked one up with Grandad standing in the centre of a row of men who all looked very much like him. Grey hair. Little glasses. White coats. They stood at the front of some sort of theatre, with a big white illuminated square behind them. It had writing on it, but it was all blurry. Grandad's hair looked fuzzier than I remembered, and stood up in tufts like mine. His smile was wide, his lips pressed shut.

I put that one back. Dad hadn't said what pictures he'd wanted me to get, but I didn't think that one was right. One with Grandma? Using the tips of my fingers, I edged one of the photos at the back towards the front. Grandma and Grandad together, with Emily squeezed between them. Emily must've only been two or three, and her chubby round face stared at the camera, her cheeks red and flushed. Grandma was laughing at something happening off-camera, a short glass of something dark in her hand. That one. Next to it was a small, framed photo of Grandad clad in waterproofs and standing in front of a tall, bald mountain. On either side of the lilac slope were the sort of trees that reminded me of Christmas. His mouth was a thin firm line, his eyes squinting against a low sun. I touched his face with a fingertip, and my eyes started to sting.

As I pulled them both down from the chest of drawers, something dark caught my eye. A winged thing was fluttering against the wall above the wardrobe, brown and black, like the bark of a tree. It must have been at least a couple of inches across, and bumbled across the pink wallpaper like it expected to find a way out. I watched its clumsy looping warily, ready to dodge if it suddenly flew in my direction, until something in my stomach squeezed. On top of the wardrobe was a hollow that shouldn't be there.

Usually, the space was plugged with Grandad's yellow backpack, the one I'd last seen half-packed in his university office. It was always here when he wasn't travelling. He said it helped him to "keep an eye on the sky."

But now the bag was gone.

The book. The bag. What else was missing? I took three deep breaths and held my hands over my face. *I needed to know. I needed to see.*

As silent as I could, I made my way over to the wardrobe and teased the doors open to reveal a rainbow of fabric. Most of the dresses and flowing skirts were crushed to the left, with the more sober colours and straight lines hanging to the right. I stuck my arms in as far as they'd go to the right-hand side, feeling for a familiar knit, that rough bristle. The warmth of a round belly.

Nothing.

I stepped back and covered my mouth again. Grandad's favourite jumper was gone. He wore that orange jumper all the time. Grandma used to laugh at him in it, and called him the Honey Monster. He told me once that it made him feel big and strong. Not long before she'd died, she sewed a shiny brass button onto the collar. It felt heavy and cold, and I liked to play with it between my fingers. He'd shake his head at it, his mouth twisted in confusion, muttering, "I have no idea why she did that. I'll cut it off later." But then she died, and he never did.

And now the jumper was gone. As was his bag. And our book. Why would they still be gone, if Grandad had come back?

Dad said he was dead. But maybe he wasn't. My skin tingled. The heavy load in my head was crumbling away like rocks in an avalanche. Maybe Grandad was like the others. The ones the door-steppers look for. Maybe he was just … gone.

But why would Dad lie?

Next door, Dad slammed another drawer in Grandad's study. At first I thought he was on the phone, but no, he was muttering to himself, as if reciting a list, and searching. The metal of a filing cabinet. The slap of paper on a table.

Slipping the small framed photo of Grandad into my pocket and hugging the other photo to my chest, I stumbled on numb legs to Grandad's study. I'd never seen it with the bright big light on. The dark green paint that made it look like the inside of a glass bottle was streaky, and in some places I could even see the white beneath it. The room, usually meticulous, was in disarray. There was paperwork strewn across the floor, and drawers in filing cabinets hung open, the insides all mixed into a jumble. The shelves, usually filled with strange metal instruments, were bare, and the rows of heavy textbooks had been pulled down. At my feet lay a copy of the red book he'd been making notes in when I'd last seen him: *Hidden Worlds*. I picked it up and ran my fingers along the author's name, Dr Francis Porter. I'd always been in awe of Grandad, having his name on a book that looked so important. I flicked through the pages. Mostly incomprehensible words like 'string theory' and 'existentialist.' But every so often there'd be a diagram that looked like one of the constellations he'd shown me through the telescope or a black and white photograph of some wooded and wild location. I turned to the back pages where I knew the photos would be and stopped dead. There, the first five photos were of the same strange purple mountain as the one in the frame in my pocket. In each photo Grandad stood or knelt with some piece of equipment I didn't understand. One looked like a telescope. One looked like silver struts, supporting a huge sheet of glass. Or maybe it was a mirror.

The air in the study tasted very thin. I was just about to speak when I was interrupted by three loud 'clicks' from over my shoulder. Quick and quiet, like nails on a pane of glass. I turned so quickly that a pain shot through my neck.

"Grandad?" I whispered. But the landing behind me was empty. The only sounds were coming from Dad now. He leaned on the desk, his breath coming in large gasps. With his head tilted down like that, I couldn't tell if he even knew I was there. He definitely hadn't heard the clicks. I hugged the picture-frame and *Hidden Worlds* to my chest and approached him with a smile I couldn't soften. I handed the book to him. "Can I keep this?" I said, "I want to read it."

Dad stared at it as if recognising an old friend, before hurling it against the wall. "No. Never." He leaned forwards, sobbing into his hands.

He wasn't letting me keep anything. He's taken my letter. Now the book. I had to be strong.

"Dad," I whispered, "Grandad would want me to have it. Like my letter." He looked up at me then, sharp and small-eyed, and stuck out his arm as if to slap me. I stepped back against the wall and the picture-frame tumbled from my arms. Dad's hand was still held high when he twisted up his face and covered his mouth with his fingers. I turned away, my palms and face pressed against the pink.

Before we left, Dad sent me to the car while he collected a few of Grandad's things. He carried them from the house in a small black bin bag tied with a red cord and flung them into the boot. We drove home in silence. I didn't know what I'd done to upset him, but when I thought back to what had happened in the study my stomach felt hot and bloated. I kept my eyes on the world through the window and watched as the grey bricks and tall silver lamp posts bowed out to hills and hedges. I wiped my nose on my sleeve and realised that the smell of the house had seeped into my clothes. I carried it with me now.

After pulling up to the house, Dad held the handbrake for a couple of minutes, gripping the knob this way and that, as if his fingers wouldn't settle. My hand was only a few inches from his, ready to release the seat belt. I waited, holding my breath, but he got out of the car without a word. I followed him into the house, keeping my head down as I passed a huddle of grey-haired, cardigan-ed women standing in the middle of next door's lawn, clucking like chickens and flapping their arms like fat little wings. It didn't even sound like English.

I raced up to my bedroom and tore open the pages of the little black notebook for the meaning of the three quick clicks but nothing matched. Chewing on a fingertip, I squeezed my eyes shut and *wished, wished,* that I had the Key Verbatinea. But then if I had it, Grandad wouldn't, and perhaps he needed it more where he was, wherever that was. Could he still be out there, on his research trip? But why would Dad say he was dead, if he wasn't? Grandad was *his* dad, after all. None of it made sense.

I clutched the book to my chest and repeated the moment of the three clicks in my mind. It felt like him. It did. But Dad didn't hear it. And he hadn't let me take the book. It was probably still resting where it'd landed, against the wall, pages askew, already being forgotten.

Mum and Emily never asked about our trip, but then if Emily had known where we'd been she'd have demanded to come too. Later that night, I found Grandad's name in the open pages of a newspaper on the dining table, crushed between the missing persons adverts and death notices. The only page with little headlines in an otherwise stormy sea of bad news.

FRANCIS DAVID PORTER
Passed away unexpectedly on 15th December,
2015, aged 73 years. Beloved husband, father, and
grandfather, who will be greatly missed by all who
knew him. In lieu of a service, Francis requested
donations to be sent to the Blue Pilgrims, care of M
J Hart Memorial Services, Cornerstone, Yorkshire.
Telephone 01945 387457.

On the following Monday morning, Mum insisted Emily and I return to school like nothing had happened. We dropped Emily off at the high school first, and as she stepped through the gates it was as if she had cast off a dark and weighty shroud. She ran into a cluster of girls in the centre of the yard and screamed before squeezing each one in turn. After completing the ritual, they stood in a close circle, each standing on one leg, then the other, like pale flamingos in the rain.

But when Mum dropped me off at my school next door, I stood by the fence between my sister and I, waiting for the bell to ring, my eyes on my shoes and the shadow where Emily's shroud had fallen. Every face in the schoolyard reminded me of one person. One person I had been told I wouldn't see again, and whose end I couldn't understand.

4.

I needed to talk to Emily about it all. The letter. Grandad's missing travelling stuff. But it was impossible – she flitted from thing to thing like a butterfly, difficult to pin down. At home, she twisted from my questions and at the school gate she was a stranger. I looked for her through the fence during break times, but she was either nowhere to be found or at the centre of a gang of teenagers, all shrieking and linking their arms. Behind me, three girls from my class were flapping their hands and slapping them on each other's wrists in a pattern they seemed to understand but made no sense to me. As their palms touched, they sang:

Where did he go? Where did she go?
Listen to the black crow – he knows!
Woman on a mountain with white hair.
Boy in a cupboard, under the stair.
Man in the mud, coiled like a snake.
Girl in a white dress under the lake.

I shivered. The only quiet place was in the corner by the entrance. No one looked up when I passed their groups. I rested my head on the huge padlock strung between the gates. The chain – as thick as my arm – was new, the silver

shining almost white. It was cold and stung a little, like a
burn. I couldn't tell whether the lock was there to keep us
in or keep something out. I'd heard a girl telling Emily that
both schools had the same double locks now, since that older
boy had disappeared during afternoon break the previous
year. Most kids kept their distance from the gates, as if they
might be dragged through the railings when they weren't
looking. But I didn't mind. I liked to stand with my back to
the metal, waiting.

That day by the gate, I pinched my wrist and pretended
all the voices in the yard were ghosts.

A few weeks after we returned to school, my teacher sat
us all down and pressed her finger to her lips for quiet.
We'd all been given a blank sheet of paper and a box of
crayons, pens, and pencils to share on our tables. Some of
the pens were still in their packets. The classroom had been
overheated and faced the sun, so all the windows were wide
open, letting in the crisp January air. My fingers stung.

Miss Reynolm was studying a piece of paper, her lips
pursed. "Right. Today, we're doing something a bit different.
An experiment." A ripple of movement passed across the
classroom. "All classes are doing it this afternoon, all across
the country. So it's very special." A few whispers from the
table behind me. Miss Reynolm didn't notice, all of her
attention focussed on the page in her hands. "What I want
you to do," she said, her voice like butter, "is draw me a
picture of how you're feeling." She leaned over my table as
she spoke. Miss Reynolm had these bright green eyes that
stuck out of her head, and she always wore her hair in black
knots, clipped to the sides of her head like an extra pair
of ears. If she brushed by me, my skin tingled. Sometimes,

when we were busy filling in our activity books, I'd watch her from beneath my fringe. It seemed like she wanted us to think she was there for us, but most of the time she was lost in her own little world; rubbing her cheek, spinning the ring on her finger, or fiddling with the blue flowery pin on her dress. During those moments, I knew that even if I'd stood up and waved my arms around, she wouldn't have noticed.

Miss Reynolm continued, her eyes scanning the paper in her hand. "You might be happy, or sad, or hungry, or worried. Pick a colour, or lots of colours, and have a go at drawing it." No one moved. She pressed her fingers together in a pyramid and pouted towards the ceiling. "You could draw yourself, doing something you'd like to do today. You could draw your face. You could draw something completely different – it doesn't have to be you."

Slowly, a few of my classmates tentatively reached towards their boxes. Some took the first colour they touched, and the rest stuck their hand deep in the box and held it there. Miss Reynolm started to weave around the tables. "Ten minutes and then we'll share what we've done with our neighbour, and tell them what our picture means. That's the most important part. Ready everyone?"

Some of my classmates already had their heads down, a thick pen clutched in their fist, but most of us still had our hands on our knees. I didn't know the boy beside me; he'd joined the class only a few weeks before. His gingery hair was so long that it almost reached his shoulders. He'd picked up a blue pencil and had already drawn a big blue box. I looked back at my own piece of paper and thought about what to do. I didn't know how I felt, or what colour I was meant to be. Either everything seemed flat and lifeless, or the moment I thought about Grandad an angry flash would tear through my head. Was I grey? Red? The longer I sat there with my hands beneath the table the more lost I felt. It was as if I was falling out of my own body – so I did what Dad had always told me to do when I needed something to hold onto. I thought of Emily. Perhaps I'd draw something for her?

Miss Reynolm's soft voice beside my ear. "What's that, Tom? Who's that?"

The boy beside me had drawn a woman's face inside the box. I knew it was a woman, because the lips were red and he'd given her long eyelashes. Underneath the woman, he'd written 'MISSING.' Miss Reynolm's forehead had gone all wrinkly. "Who is it?"

"My Auntie Polly. Polly Watts."

Miss Reynolm let out one long breath. "How long has she been gone, Tom?"

Tom sucked in his lips and bit down on them for a moment before answering. "Since summer holidays."

Miss Reynolm closed her eyes, her lips tight. She looked back at the sheet of paper in her hand. "How... do you feel about that?"

Tom shrugged. "Dunno. My Mum cries a lot."

Miss Reynolm's eyes were ready to pop out of her head. I glanced down at the page in her hands:

DEPARTMENT FOR EDUCATION
CHILD COMMUNICATION EXERCISE

She shifted position and turned to my blank sheet of paper. "David, do you need some help with your picture?"

I shook my head, and I meant it. I knew what to draw now. As I reached for a black pen, Miss Reynolm squeezed

Tom's shoulder and left to help another table. Tom dropped the blue pencil and laid his head on the paper. Under his breath he whispered, "Woman on a mountain with white hair."

I didn't spend long on my drawing, and when I'd finished, I poked Tom's shoulder for him to look. Leaning into his ear, I whispered, "Man in the mud, coiled like a snake."

Tom stared at it for a few seconds. "Who's that?"

"It's my Grandad. He's gone too."

Tom slid my picture so it was side-to-side with his. It made it obvious that I'd copied his drawing but added a beard and a pair of round glasses, but he didn't seem to mind.

"When did he disappear?"

"A month ago."

"Does your Mum cry about it, too?"

"I think my Dad does." I shuffled in my seat, and felt my face grow hot. "But I don't see him do it."

Tom spread his hands flat on his poster. "Mum says that Polly must be dead and frozen somewhere now. Because she didn't come home for Christmas. But it's sunny now, isn't it?" He pointed at the clear sky. "So I think she's OK."

"Does your Mum know where she went?"

Tom shook his head and started to pick at the corner of his paper. I paused before saying the next bit. "Dad said Grandad is dead, too. He told us he died in hospital."

Tom wrinkled his face. "In hospital? So he didn't disappear?"

I stayed quiet. Tom slid his poster away from mine. "That's not the same. He's just dead." Then he turned away to look at the girl beside him who was drawing something that could've been a cat. I wanted to ask Tom more questions but I could tell that he wasn't going to share anything else, so I slumped low in my chair and ignored the girl beside me who was trying to show me her picture. What I couldn't shake was the feeling that though the two disappearances seemed different, they weren't that different at all.

That lesson didn't seem to be much of a success, as Miss Reynolm never asked us to draw like that again. At the end of the day, her fringe stuck to her forehead and her lips chewed, I caught her balling up the page of instructions, muttering under her breath, "Waste of time. If they're going to go, they're going to go."

When I next saw Emily, it was in the community hall after school. Mum didn't finish at church until after 6:00 pm, and now that I couldn't go to Grandad's, that left me with Emily's theatre club. I hadn't wanted to go, but Mum just brushed my hair with her fingers and muttered, "Just copy Emily. It'll be fine."

But it was chaos. Over thirty kids, jostling for their place like bees in a hive. Some kids squealed to see each other, flapping their arms theatrically like sparrows, whereas others clung to the walls, watching the clock. A group of kids even younger than me were dragging a plastic table across the stage. They all held their eyes wide, as if they needed to see the world at all angles, all of the time. It looked exhausting. Everyone seemed to be walking in circles or dropping things and picking them up. I couldn't understand where they were going or what they were doing. Nothing ever settled in its place, things moved around with no meaning. Occasionally Emily would glance up from her script and give me a little half-smile, but she didn't come over, as if whatever I had was catching.

One kid, a boy with ginger hair who looked to me to be

about five or six, fiddled with the lock on the door handle as if trying to tease it open. The heavy chain and silver padlock were the same as the one on the school gate. Just above them hung a wrinkled handmade poster, painted with:

WHEN THEY DISAPPEAR, YOU COME HERE

At first, Emily had seemed annoyed that I'd be joining her. She left me on my own by the costume rails, only occasionally glancing in my direction as she huddled over a script with the rest of the cast. I watched as they repeated their lines in a round. I couldn't take my eyes off her. In the blink of an eye, she could transform from my sister to an angel to a coiling snake and back again. With poetry in her mouth, she wasn't Emily, she was something else which was both magical and terrible at the same time. She was becoming something new. I wanted to have Emily back, but I also didn't want her to stop transforming. It was like a trick where a magician is about to slice you in two. You want it to happen, but then again, you don't.

Behind Emily stood a boy clutching a tambourine and two girls blowing clumsily into tin whistles. Emily didn't even seem to notice them, but the shrill notes stung deep inside my head. *It hurt.* But Grandad had always said music was special. "Do you know why we love music, Bumblebee?" he'd sing, holding my hand and spinning me on my toes. "It wakes up all the brainy bits that're sleeping. Like when you eat something tasty. It's physics." In the memory, Grandad lowered himself to his knees so we were eye to eye. "Music helps us transcend," he whispered. "It opens up whole new worlds – in here." Grandad tapped the side of my head with a finger before grasping my arms and swinging them wildly in the air.

Back in the community hall, I quickly wiped the tears from my eyes when I felt Mrs Meyer grasping my shoulder. Her blunt white fringe covered much of her face and she looked down at me like I was a puzzle she was too tired to solve. She kneeled by my side, her face puffy. "David," she said, "what do *you* want to do?"

Me? I wanted to go home. No, not home. Somewhere else. *I didn't want this at all.*

Mrs Meyer squeezed her cheeks like bellows and strode away into the wings, leaving me alone centre stage. By my feet was a big tub of sand. I stuck my finger in it and started to trace a spiral, small in the centre but by the end sweeping widely to the edge of the bucket. When Mrs Meyer came back, she handed me my purple zip-up top and squeezed my shoulder. "I've got something for you to do."

She led me to a secret part of the set, behind the stage itself. A tunnel, stretching from wing to wing, only a few feet wide. It was lit by a bright strip light above but still seemed dark. It was somehow colder here than in the open hall, and so I zipped up my jacket. Along the tunnel were huge wooden boards propped up against the wall. They were about twice as high as me and were covered in thick black painted lines, but from that angle it was impossible to see what the lines actually were.

Mrs Meyer pointed to the boards. "These are going across the back of the stage. We need someone arty to paint them. Can you do that? Look," she traced one of the black lines with her finger, "They already have the landscapes on them, all you have to do is follow the colour code." She pointed to the numbers on the empty stretches of pine and then down to a stack of paint tins. "Here you are." She reached around the back of a board and I heard a sound like pebbles in a glass. I opened my hand to take a paintbrush. It was wide and had white paint crusted into the roots of the bristles. The handle wasn't clean.

"Get started. The tins are already open. I'll see how you're getting on later."

She walked off down the tunnel unsteadily, one hand skimming the wall. I was alone. I turned to face the wooden panels. Some of the numbered spaces were smaller than the end of the brush she'd given me to use, so I chose a long, wide panel near the bottom, labelled '3.' There were around ten tins of paint and '3' was near the back, so I dragged it out with both hands before popping off the already half-open lid. I plunged the brush into blue and started to swirl it round so that flakes from the edges of the tin broke off and were mixed in. Only some remained on the surface, cracked and dead.

Through the wall, the rest of the group were still shouting, screaming, laughing. A couple of girls squealed as a boy I didn't recognise growled, "It was the woman on the news, the one found in that tree, all hollowed out like a bone." I wondered if he knew the woman he was talking about, or whether it was just another news report, like all the others that Mum didn't know I watched. I imagined my fingers that held the paintbrush turning dry and white, like sticks of chalk. "They found her in a bird's nest," the boy muttered. "Her arms stretched out like she was trying to fly."

The paint went on thick and gelatinous. I tried to sweep it across the space to finish the job quicker, but the brush would run dry and I'd have to dip again. I shivered and zipped my purple jacket right up the neck. Grandma had dabbled in painting, towards the end. After she fell the first time, she developed a slower way of walking, a way of watching everything with her head tilted. Her long grey hair was always a bit stragglier, her skin paler. One time, I sat on her knee while she was painting on an A4 piece of cardboard. She sucked her lips in when she concentrated. I tucked her hair behind an ear. I could see her scalp, white and icy, in patches through the roots. Inches of skin around her ears were bald. Her fingers shook, dotted blue and grey and green. Hills and cliffs, I think. A lake. It was just like the photo of Grandad in the mountains in his book. Just like the brutal, wintery landscape in the photo I took from their house, stashed under my bed. At the funeral, that one was propped up against the flowers on her coffin. Grandad stood next to it in his bristly orange jumper, his eyes fixed on its horizon.

I could smell him, there in the corridor. Like rust. Like the metallic, bitter smell of his old coffee cups. Like wax and soap and wool. I turned on the spot, desperate to find the source but terrified to move in case I lost the trail. My chest hadn't felt so full since I'd last been with Grandad in his office. *Where was it coming from?*

"Grandad." I whispered it into the dim light, and almost as soon as I'd said it, the scent was gone.

I dropped the paintbrush in one of the jars and prised open '5,' a bright marmalade. I let the wet brush drip water in the paint before stirring it, watching how the water disappeared into the mix. I thought back again to the yellow backpack, the one that Grandad took on his research trips and holidays. The orange jumper. The Verbatinea. Grandad's most precious things. Dad didn't have them – he'd only carried a small bag of Grandad's things when we'd got back to the house. That could only mean one thing: Grandad had them with him. He must still have them with him.

Maybe whatever he was looking for on those research trips, *he found it.*

My hands shaking, I scooped as much paint on the brush as I could and swept it across the board like a sunrise. A boy I didn't know stuck his head around the edge of the passageway and watched me for a few seconds before disappearing. When he returned, he'd brought two other boys along with him. They were taller than me, maybe Emily's age. Their eyes and smiles were wide and shining, like clowns.

When Mrs Meyer came back a little while later, I'd covered most of the board in orange, obscuring the crude black outlines almost completely. She stood there, not saying a word, her mouth hanging open in a perfect 'O.' The boys had stopped laughing and now looked between Mrs Meyer and me, as I began to sketch a small bird in the corner with a permanent marker from the shelf.

Her hand gripped my upper arm but I didn't stop and fought against her. *Why was she pulling me back?*

"Stop, David. Stop!" She prised the brush from my fingers, stiff and sore. "What have you done?" She kneeled and held her face so close to mine that I could feel her fringe on my nose. I rubbed my hand across my face, and it felt wet.

"What happened, David?"

The boys behind her skulked away. When they were around the corner, I heard them laughing. Mrs Meyer stood up and pulled me by the shoulder towards the end of the backstage tunnel and towards the light.

AFTER

~

I struggle against the weight of my own body, but tapes – stringy like black hair – drag me deeper into the gloom. There's a sweet smell, like rotting wood, rushing up through my nose. I'm blind, and kick and pull at slippery reeds and wriggling things that drift away when I reach out and drift towards me when I give up.

I'm drowning.

I stretch, flailing my arms to the left and right as my chest fills with fire. *A branch.* I wrap one hand around it and pull, reaching out with my other hand for something else to grab. A handful of something soft and my face breaks the surface. I retch and a flood of brown chugs back into the pool with a wet slap.

Around me, the mud is eating mud, the world turns, and solid ground no longer exists. I can't see which direction is which – I'm walled in by tall straw-like reeds, topped with flossy heads. I tip back my head and let myself bob there as I wait for my heart to stop racing. Here, I can't even hear the stream trickling anymore. If I don't move, the bog is as still as soil.

Using the grass stems as support, I try wading back a few feet, but the bank is nowhere to be seen. I try each

direction, one after the other, but it's as if I'm miles away
from dry earth. Above, the sky is a deep slate, and deep
inside I shudder. A few black clouds break up the sky but are
as still as watercolours.

Every second I'm here I'm sucked down a little more, so
I use fistfuls of the long grass to cut through the bog like
a knife slicing cake. My heart pounds inside my chest and
my hands are stiff and sore. Every breath is another tear
in my throat but I need to find an edge before my mouth
goes under. Around me, strange white bulbs occasionally
rise and bob out of the water. One floats close to my face
and I see it extends beneath the surface by about the length
of my forearm, and the submerged end dangles with thin
white tickles, like roots.

Finally, my shoes touch something wide and flat, and
I gulp and gasp as I walk my toes forwards and drag my
sodden body from the bog with a deep, wet suck. I lie on
the grassy bank on my side, shaking with relief or cold, I
can't tell.

I have no idea where I am.

I'm so heavy, now. Soaked through, my bones shake and
I'm aching inside and out. No amount of research could've
prepared me for this. The last rays of the low winter sun are
kisses on my skin. I spread my hands on the ground and
grip. Ahead of me is another stretch of trees, but this time
the trunks are thick and brown like oaks or elms, and the
leaves overhead mesh together into a golden canopy. How
are there still leaves here, in the dead of winter?

I drag myself to my feet and look back out over the marsh.
If I hadn't just pulled myself from it, I would never have
thought it was anything other than a field of wild grass.
It stretches on as far as I can see, and is ringed by a circle

of trees, plugged deep into the water. *But where's the stone? How could it have disappeared?* The strange stone that split the river is out of sight. Without it I have no idea where I've come from or where I'm going. *Think. Think.* Was there anything like this on the map? I curse Michael for only allowing me ten-minute stints with it, but all I manage is a low growl before I clutch my throat again. If only I had a mirror, I could see what was happening to my neck.

At least, lost as I am, the shadows must be far behind. I've bought some time. From here, there's no sight of them, and the woods are so silent that they *hum*. Yet beyond that, I can almost hear the 'tick tick tick' of their timers. *Why won't they leave me alone?*

I hobble as best as I can through the first copse of trees, my limbs weak and waving like grass. Itchy wet knit and sodden trousers cling to my skin, dragging me down. Here, the ground is topsy-turvy and makes my hip joints jolt and ache with the strain of staying upright. All the while I listen behind me for footfalls, but the only sounds are my shoes in the undergrowth and the slow sigh of a breeze.

Soon it's too dark to keep going. There's no shelter anywhere around, only the foliage above, through which the sky has turned a deep burgundy. I find a tree where its base has broken the earth apart and slip between the roots. I remove the unfamiliar brown brogues and tip out the mush that's caught inside. Like everything else, my socks are sodden, but I don't want to see what's beneath. Not yet.

I lever myself between the roots and nestle into the bowl of dirt. There's no controlling the shaking now, and my teeth clamp tight around my tongue. But the earth is warm and soft, like a heated blanket, so I strip off the orange jumper and trousers down to my underwear. I'm this freezing,

stone-like thing in a childhood sick bed, but the soil is a
hug. I let the gentle quietness of it tumble onto my body,
encouraging it by prising away the dirt from under the tree
trunk with a finger.

I'm still cocooned in the balmy soil when the night
comes. I press my hands over my heart to conserve as much
heat as I can. *Why did I leave in winter?* My head is heavy,
and my eyes are closing against my will when there's a
flurry of wings and a high whistling above the roots. It's
as if the atmosphere is thinner than it was, or that the air
is just passing through, so every breath I take is shallow
and snatched from the wind. Above my head, the whistling
grows and transforms into something that sounds like skin-
on-skin. At first, I think it's the wind blowing leaf litter
across the forest floor, but soon the shapes are tumbling in
all directions and latching onto the tree above. The dense
canopy blocks out the buttery moon, so it's impossible to tell
in the absolute black what the shapes are. I close my eyes
and imagine wrapping myself in goose-feathers.

It's just a storm. The rain is a voice, soft and white, like
milk. *"Thunder can't hurt you,"* she coos.

The ground is moving too. There's something beneath
me in the mud – it rumbles and quakes in an attempt to
emerge, but I'm trapped in the roots like they're ropes tying
me in a knot. I cover my face and feel whatever the flitting,
flapping things are brush against the backs of my hands like
whispers.

"Can you hear me?"

And a fine mewling, high, almost a drone, and it's
as familiar as my heart beating but I can't place it. It's
like equipment, something metal, or made of sinew. I've
heard that sound so many times, but what is it? I feel it,

sonorous and warm against my cheek, but it's alien, too.

"Don't run."

I'm torn between screaming back at the murmurs or protecting my throat from more harm. They know nothing. Why can't they leave me alone? I'm shaking, yet trying to be invisible, and as the night comes alive and says everything I don't want it to, I fight back the ghosts until I, exhausted, sink deliciously into their arms.

Everything hurts, but it is light. Crisp grey light flashes through the canopy and bleaches out the night. Everything is still and spotless, like a photograph. Not a wing or feather fallen. The forest is innocent. My legs are so caked with mud and root-twisted that I can hardly tell which parts are mine. How is it possible to ache, yet feel so numb?

I hardly know what to do first, but one thing is certain: I'm not yet dead. I'm still alone, there's no sign of the hunters. Had I lost them? My right leg is bent towards me, so I clench my jaw and pull down my sock. The joint is swollen and inflamed, and there's an odd bony bump sticking out the back. I worry about getting the brogues back on, but thankfully the fact that they're too big means the edge doesn't dig in too much. I daren't even think about my toes. They'd been in such a state the last time I'd looked.

I tilt my head to the left and right to loosen up my neck before digging my way out from the roots. Awkwardly, I drag the trousers and jumper back onto my body. The jumper feels strange on my back, as if it's not quite sitting right. I pull the collar down from my throat, which helps a bit. Looking at it, it's a mess of holes. Loose orange wool dangles from the sleeves and the hem, and it seems to have shrunk in length. The sparrow button on the collar still shines, though. I touch it for good luck.

Now that it's light, I can see there's a trail leading through the trees. It's only lightly worn, but worn trails mean travelling feet. Around its borders are thick clusters of leaves that fill the air with garlic. It takes me back to summers as a child, tearing off leaves and laying them on my tongue. But why is it flowering now? What is happening? I bend and pull up a handful. As I chew, I close my eyes and pretend it's a roast dinner – chicken breast, potatoes, stuffing, all the trimmings – but then I can't help but think of a certain grey house, a floral chair, a face that creased up like a cabbage when it smiled, and my stomach groans all the worse for having eaten anything.

Further away from the path and into the woods are patches of low shrubs, a bit like strawberry plants, with white little berries dangling from the branches like mistletoe. Each one is topped by a wrinkled 'X' where the flesh folds in on itself. They're oddly familiar, their bitterness already knifing my tongue.

Putting as much weight on my right foot as I can, I follow the path as it winds through the trees and up to a little ridge where there's a little wooden cabin, about the size of a garden shed. The wood is raw with a greenish tinge, as if it's covered in a fine layer of mossy frost.

My heart leaps at some shelter, but I'm cautious – how can I know that my pursuers aren't inside already? Logically, I realise that they couldn't have made it here without following me through the swamp, and there's been no sign of them since. But still, whatever's behind that closed door is unknown, and the unknown hasn't always been kind to me.

Nevertheless, I need to look. There might be something in there to help me. Everything I had with me is gone. My waterproofs. My notes. My firelighters. But I have to be silent. Michael was adamant that the only way through Mothtown was to be *imperceptible*. "Practice," he'd said, leaning towards me as if I needed to feel the word on my skin. His pointed chin practically jutted into my own. "Go back to your room and practice nothing. Be nothing and whenever you have a thought – cancel it out. Melt everything down to a great white blank. Eat anything that oozes out. No one knows how it all goes in Mothtown, and no one ever comes back to tell us. So, all you can do is practice being nothing and then hope that when you get there, you disappear."

I had practiced, religiously, in the room with no windows. In that room there was little else to do other than blend into the wallpaper. None of the furniture was mine. I had nothing to pull me outside of my own body. I never spoke to anyone else, other than Michael. Never saw any other candidates. I spent the long nights reciting Michael's rules and counting the items in the yellow backpack, *one, two, three, four, five.* Over and over. He said this was essential to my disconnecting from the world. But it's another thing entirely to be in pain and trying to not exist. And Michael hadn't known that I'd be followed here. That they'd try to stop me finding the door.

It was my fault. I waited too long, and then only ran when their hands were reaching out to grab me. I've never had a clear view of their faces, but I can just about see them in my mind's eye, even now – broad-shouldered, shaved heads, both dressed in featureless white, their shadowy forms slinking from tree to tree. I've dreamed of their breath, thick with chemicals and the rotting aftertaste of meat gone rank.

I've felt their hands grab my shoulders, and the full force of them dragging me south with fingers sharp as syringes.

I won't let that happen. One of us will die first, and find out first-hand if there really are other routes to salvation. Even if it's me.

So slowly I approach the cabin. Up close it's even more ramshackle than I thought. It looks to be held together with small nails hammered in at strange angles, often bending and jutting out from the wood an inch or so from where they went in. The front door is closed with an old-fashioned copper knocker, and the front step is a stone slab with a small tangle of ratty clothes on it.

Each step I take is delicate, treading only on the softest grass. As I reach the stone slab, I prod the strange heap of fabric with a toe before leaping back.

It's skin.

Not human, but piled as neatly as if someone had unzipped themselves and stepped out of it. The surface is mottled brown like a wasp's nest, but with hints of silver that catch the light. And inside the translucent folds are a mess of fine bones, each only a couple of inches long, either broken from their brothers or still connected and dangling from tiny joints. Like small arms without hands, ending in a knot like the pointed bud of a flower. At least thirty of them, flung into the heap like rubbish. Could it be an animal has left this here? That it's just the remnants of a last meal?

I step over the slop and push the door to the cabin ajar. It's not as dark as I thought it'd be. The windows, as grim and dirty as slate from the outside actually do let the light in. The cool blue dawn shines through a high pane of glass about the size of an A4 sheet of paper at the far end of the cabin. Beneath it is a comfortless straw bed. To the side of this is a large cupboard with a single door, and then opposite is a small desk but no chair. On the desk is a box of matches and three candle stumps, only an inch long with burnt black wicks.

I close the door behind me and realise there are no locks, no bolts to barricade myself in. I push that from my mind and turn away to stroke a finger down the wall. It was painted once, maybe white. But now it had flaked away, leaving the wooden panelling with only a few vertical scores of magnolia scratch-marks. The air catches in my nostrils, as if it's already been used too many times and now carries a burden.

I step towards the desk and check the matchbox. Three. The window above the desk is foggy as if a fire has burnt beneath it, so I wipe it clean with my sleeve.

There. I know where I am.

Through the window I can see it: the mountain. The one from the map, the one with the two crags on either side. On its face are craggy eyes, hollows for cheeks, and – my heart leaps – an opening, about halfway up. A mouth. Dark and round and lipless. And teeth. It's not even that far. Just through those trees, then down towards the violet heather, and then a little climb.

If only they could see me now. *All of them.* I push their faces from my sight. Why should I remember? They'd likely already forgotten me. Some people already had.

The sun is only now high in the sky, but the moon is up too – bloated and spongy. I hold up my fingers to pinch it from the blue but it's slippery and smooth, like the surface of water. I roll a finger around the edge and imagine it ringing, forgetting the nature of things here. A Tibetan prayer bowl. A brass bell. A glass of lemonade. I lean on the table and chuckle before parting my lips to whisper one last name to the mountain. But nothing comes out. Only a gust of air, as if I'm being squeezed around the ribs. I grab my neck and try again. Nothing, not even a breath this time. But as I strain, something grates and I retch onto the floor. I'm on my knees then, my hands splayed on the blood-splattered wood. I retch again, and out drops a thick red clot, which splits on the wooden planks like an egg.

BEFORE

5.

I need to breathe. All this talking. My voice breaks. Just one moment, please. My dust still hovers on the air. *My mist.* See it dance? It hasn't even settled yet.

But perhaps it won't, until I'm done. Until I tell it true.

I'll go on.

Mrs Meyer told me to sit on a plastic chair at the foot of the stage, where the band fiddled awkwardly with their instruments and made terrible noise together. No one seemed to be listening to anyone else. When Mum burst into the hall, I had my hands flat over my ears. She didn't say anything, just picked up my school bag, grabbed me by the coat, and dragged me out into the cold. Her face was all red and strange.

"Mum, what about Emily?"

She pushed me into the car. "Emily's staying there until six."

She started the engine and pulled away, only for the car to stop suddenly.

"Fuck." Mum beat her hands on the steering wheel and then turned the key again before setting off. "David. What were you doing? Your teacher that you've vandalised the stage?"

I sat there, dumbfounded. I had done no such thing.

Mum shook her head. "I don't know what to do with you, David." We stopped at a traffic light. It was starting to rain, and the water on the windscreen broke the red light into little particles that moved about. Mum's jaw stuck out at the side like a cow chewing grass.

"You're going to have to sit in the pews while I finish. Margaret will watch you."

I imagined old Margaret with her curly grey hairdo and soft grey apron, sweeping the pews, chattering to me about school, about theatre club, about why I was there. I didn't want to talk to Margaret. I didn't want to talk to anyone.

I wiped the condensation from my window and trained my eyes on the big blue house looming ahead of us on the left. I'd never seen one in real life before, but I recognised the violet shutters, the faint iris bricks from TV. The sign said: 'Blue House of Melton Wark.' I pointed and whispered, "Mum. What's in there?" The green traffic light sparkled through the rain on the windshield and Mum barely even glanced at the house as we drove past. "It's a place for sad people," she muttered. "That's all."

A few minutes later we pulled up outside the church, St Anthony of Padua's. A small stonewash building attached to a newer, white extension. A small doorway, mostly glass, was almost covered in handmade posters. Narrow stained-glass windows at either side were lit with yellow bulbs.

"Can I go in there?" I pointed to the extension. Margaret wouldn't talk to me in there.

"No, David. Come on." She nudged me towards the church but I resisted and pointed up at the light through the front door.

"The library's still open. I can do homework."

Mum sucked in her lips. "David–"

"She can watch me."

A woman with blue-rimmed glasses stuck her arm out of the door to take down one of the notices pasted there. Mum's eyes flicked between the church and the library. I knew I had her.

"Excuse me… my son's just going to do some homework in here for half an hour. Would you keep an eye on him, please? Can't be too careful."

The woman frowned. "We're not child-minders. We can't take responsibility. I'm sorry." With that, she disappeared back into the library.

"I won't leave, I promise. I won't disappear."

Mum looked down at me then, her mouth wide and her eyes popping from her head. "What?"

"I'll just sit at a table and do my homework."

Her face didn't relax but something softened in her grip. She nodded, and as she scuttled back to the church, she muttered under her breath, "…It's only twenty minutes. What can happen in twenty minutes…"

I was alone. Out in the world. My skin prickled. I don't think I'd actually believed that Mum would let me wait in there, away from watching eyes. But now that she had… I wasn't even sure if I liked it. Clutching my bag to my chest, I scanned the posters sellotaped to the glass door. Club notices, and 'For Sale' cards advertising cars, bikes, and a kid's garden slide. Squeezed in between the notices were several small passport photos of people I didn't know. Men and women, gazing blankly into the lens. Each one had a date handwritten in the bottom corner. A few were from a year or two earlier, but one was only a few weeks ago. A man with a heart-shaped face and blonde hair tied up in a knot on the top of his head. Of all the people in the photos, he was the only one that was smiling at me, laughing as if we were at a party and I'd told a really funny joke.

I pushed the door open and the three women behind the reception peered down at me from over the desk. They could have been sisters. All three were the same height, and had the same shoulder-length brown bob. All wore pale blue shirts, and a long purple cord around their necks with an ID card hanging from it. At the back of the group, the woman with the blue-rimmed glasses was halfway through blowing her nose into a long piece of toilet paper. The woman closest to me looked a little older than the others, and she loomed over me, her lips pursed. I clutched my bag tighter to my chest and scurried past into the central atrium. I just needed a corner, a quiet place to think.

The library was surprisingly big, about the size that the community centre had been. Around the walls, long shelving units jutted out, and in the centre were eight round tables painted bright blue. Only one was empty.

"We close at six," a crackling voice said behind me. "You don't have long."

I nodded over my shoulder at the librarian and headed towards the free table. Just as I began to pull out a chair, I spotted the noticeboard on the wall opposite and my heart began to thud. It was covered with dozens of posters with faces, like the ones Mum pulled me away from on the street. They all wore smiles and shining eyes. Some had 'REWARD' printed across the top. Many had 'PLEASE' scrawled over them in black marker. But none of them had been crossed off or corrected to say 'FOUND.' Young and old, they all watched me as I watched them. I could've stood there forever, scanning all the faces for the one I loved best. Why did Mum not want me to see these?

There was an odd sound behind me, like a cut-off gasp. The woman with the blue glasses had the toilet paper pressed tightly to her mouth and the older woman was rubbing the tops of her arms. I tried to listen, but their voices were lowered and I could only hear snippets.

"Nine days…"

"Have they helped at all? The police?"

"They've taken a statement… Some of his things… I can't believe this is happening. *To us*."

"Did he not say anything? Did you have no idea?"

"It's just like you see on the news. On telly. What's happening to the world?"

"He'd been spending more time in his room, online. Forums. Endless scrolling. Mumbling about people we don't know that he must've been talking to."

"It's surreal."

"Mum found a printed-out map in his bedroom. It's too faded to make out. She's catatonic. I needed to get out of the house."

There were lots of 'tutting' sounds, before the shuffle of papers.

"Sit down, chick. I'll get you some tea."

I sat down just as the older woman drifted past and slid the book that was already open on the table towards me. *Bugs, Great and Small.* In the centre of the table was a computer screen, and a laminated sheet of instructions.

How to use the library catalogue:
Type what you're looking for in the search bar
Write down the shelf colour and book number on a
slip of paper

Our handy floor arrows will help you find the book
you need

Around me on the floor were colourful painted arrows
pointing off in every direction. Baking, children's books,
crafts, large print, history... I clicked the mouse. The screen
jumped to life and asked me what I was looking for. I typed
slowly, deliberately: 'Francis David Porter. Hidden Worlds.'
    Search.
    A few seconds later, a long list of books came up with
titles and author's names. I recognised the red cover at the
top of the list straight away. It was *Hidden Worlds*, and had
'Unavailable' printed across the image. Beneath that was a
long black line, and 'Other things you might be interested
in.' These other books had titles like *Parallel Paths: Walking
the Invisible Road*, and *String Theory for Dummies*. Further
down the list was a book cover that didn't seem to fit the
line-up: *Transfigurations in Nature*. The cover was a dark
brown colour, and in the centre a photograph of something
long and dangling, like a dried-up sausage.
    I scribbled a few numbers onto a scrap of paper and
followed the green arrow to the science section. The rustle
of my coat and bag was electric in the silence. When I found
the book, I returned to my corner table and sat beneath the
noticeboard. Why was this book connected to Grandad's
Hidden Worlds? I traced the outline of the strange, bulbous
growth on *Transfigurations in Nature*. Was it an egg? It
reminded me of something I'd seen in Grandad's office at
the university, squeezed between rows of thick hardbacks
on one of his shelves. A small transparent case, about the
size of my hand, half-stuffed with cotton wool. Nestled in
that bed was something that looked like an old cigar. He

caught me looking at it once, as I balanced on the arm of the sofa. I had a finger pressed to the glass, and had already left a greasy smear across its crystal. Grandad lifted it from the shelf and placed it on my knee. "We need to keep it upright, David. Because this," he pressed his finger on top of mine, so we both pointed to the strange thing, "is a new beginning. And new beginnings must be treated gently." Snuggled into the cotton wool, the thing *pulsed*. Just once. I flinched, leaning back into Grandad, who was as still and strong as ever.

"Is it alive?"

Grandad smiled. "Yes, it's alive. It's the in-between. Once it was larvae, and one day it'll be a moth. Right now, it's both. Before and after its transformation – it *always* exists. It's only afterwards when it really lives, opens its wings, and fulfils its purpose. And first… there's a crack like lightning. You just wait."

Grandad looked at the case in a way I'd never seen him do before. It was different to how he handled the instruments and tools in his office. His hands moved gently, the way he stroked my hair if I grazed my knee. "But why is it here?"

"Moths symbolise change, David. They're ticking clocks to metamorphosis. And throughout their lives, they always seek the light. That's what we do, don't we?"

He leaned towards the glass and smiled. It was then that I realised what his expression reminded me of. It was the way he used to look at Grandma, before she died. But I couldn't tell you what the look meant.

Grandad never saw the cocoon split, as it was still intact the last time I saw him. I do wonder now how long it'd been in that case, and whether it ever would've hatched at all. Maybe it had always been a relic. I don't even know what happened to the case after Grandad never returned from his research trip. Perhaps someone else owned it now, or perhaps it'd been smashed like so many other dreams.

This is what you want to hear, right? About the things that existed – before and after. Things that I wish I'd noticed earlier on. Scenes that I should've held close.

I'll continue.

Anyway, back in the library, until that moment, I hadn't paid much attention to the people at the other tables, but I did then. All of them were men, wearing coats the colour of mud, bark, and things that fluttered in the dark, the creases hanging around their shoulders like folded wings. They looked wet, but weren't, and I began to notice that the room smelled funny, like an old shed or the inside of a garden bin. Their hair was long and tangled, or in the case of one man, shaved close to his head – his scalp was a maze of faded blue tattoos. This man was younger than the others, and wore an oversized black duffle coat with a broken zip. Unlike the other two, he didn't have a beard, and his full lips were cracked and bloody. He, like the others, stared blankly down at an open book on the table in front of him, his hands trembling. I watched the clock as the final minutes ticked away towards closing time, keeping an eye on the men sitting at the tables. They looked very much like mudmen, but as I'd never seen them up close, I couldn't be sure. But I didn't like them. No-one moved or hardly even turned a page, enraptured by whatever they were staring at. I looked down at *Transfigurations* and then at the librarians behind the desk. They already had their coats on and were looking at the men and then at the door, as if giving a signal. As carefully as I could, I slid the book under the table and into my backpack. Weaving through the tables, I noticed that one of the men was holding up a book in front of him like a shield. It was called *Worlds Under Mountains*.

As I got closer to the glass doors, I could see Mum on the other side, staring mindlessly at the stuck-up notices with a blank expression on her face. I strode past the reception desk and pulled open the door. A loud beeping sound went off somewhere, but I leapt out anyway and grabbed Mum's arm. "See," I said. "I'm still here."

Mum's mouth twisted as she slid into the driver's seat and buckled her belt. I quickly leapt into the back seat beside Emily and closed the door, the alarm still ringing in my ears.

Emily leaned towards me in the back seat of the car. Her mouth twisted, and she wrapped her hair around her finger like black liquorice. "Why did you do that?"

Mum hadn't mentioned what I'd done since getting in the car, so stupidly I thought I'd escaped an interrogation. My face flushed hot, so I turned away to the window.

"Davey," she whispered. "*You have to try.*" She grabbed me by the wrist, and though she was quite forceful with it I didn't mind. It pulled me down to earth. I retrieved the library book from my bag and pointed at the long, dangling thing on the cover. "What's this?"

Emily continued to stare. "Aren't you listening? Mum's upset as it is. Can't you just try to fit in, just once?"

In her glittering black stare, Grandad looked back at me. Suddenly, my eyes filled with tears. I turned my face to the book and bit my lip.

"Oh, Davey." Emily leaned over and wrapped an arm around my shoulders. Her wrist looked broken as she tried to pull me in. Her mouth twisted. "You're such a strange fit." Though her embrace felt awkward, the warmth of her against my side made all my muscles relax. I fell back into it, the warm and the soft, like sinking into a hot bath. Even when I was furious at her, she was my anchor. I sobbed.

"I know it's hard. Grandad wouldn't want you to be sad. You were his best little friend, you know."

I looked up at her then, through the tears. "But what if," I whispered, "he's still here?"

"What?"

"What if he's not dead?"

"Why?" To my alarm, she wasn't keeping her voice down. "Why would you think that?"

"He never brought his things back from his last trip. Maybe he's like those people on the news—"

Emily looked horror-stricken then, and I felt sorry for saying it out loud. I dug my fingers into my palm. This wasn't going to plan. Why didn't she see what I saw?

She sighed and squeezed my arm. "He's gone. He died. But it might not be the end. I think it might be balls but Mum said he's gone to a better place."

"Where?" I blurted.

She leaned back, her brow furrowed. "Where do you think? Where the rest of the God-botherers think. Paradise."

Emily and I didn't speak again in the car. If Mum had heard what we'd said she didn't admit it. As soon as we arrived home, I took the library book upstairs to my room. The door to Mum and Dad's bedroom was slightly ajar, and the light from their TV danced on the wall. I paused on the landing, listening to Dad's slow and rhythmic breathing. My face to the crack, I waited while my eye adjusted to the semi-darkness. Dad was sprawled on the bed, asleep, his face resting on a huge map. The picture on the TV was paused, and the graininess and strange brown tones told me it was one of Dad's old video cassettes. And as I pushed the door open an inch to make out the details on the screen, my heart began to race.

It couldn't be.

It was Grandad, standing on a white platform, the night sky behind him. He was wearing a white lab coat, and looked younger than I'd ever seen him with thick, black-rimmed glasses and a moustache. His cheeks were flushed as he pointed to the horizon. The white subtitles were stuck on:

prospect of doorways. But then it becomes
a philosophical question, whether our bodily

I crept as close as I dared and inspected Dad's face for a clue to why he was lying to me, but all I saw were the dark circles beneath his eyes and thin papery skin that I'd seen on Grandad's face before he packed his rucksack and left me behind.

6.

I sometimes feel like I'm locked in a circle. What's that creature, the worm that swallows its own tail? The ouroboros. Which bit is the beginning, and which is the end? And when they meet so seamlessly, what difference does it make?

Dad was disappearing. In the evenings after school, Emily would ask Mum, "Where's Dad?" Only for Mum to mumble that he was in bed or still at work.

But it wasn't true. His shoes would be gone from the front door, his long green coat also missing. Whenever I next saw him, usually early in the morning – staring out of the window with a cup of coffee – he seemed greyer, as if the light around him was dimmed. A reverse spotlight. He spoke quietly, in a measured way that seemed unnatural even to him. He stuttered over words and would pause halfway through sentences only to start again, saying something else. Most of this I noticed at a distance. I didn't know what to say to him. The sight of him made something twist low down in my stomach. But then he didn't try to speak to me either. We passed across each other in the hallways like shadows, never touching.

Emily, though, she was chameleonic. If I caught her and

Dad close together in the kitchen, she'd be mumbling too, Dad's grey light enveloping her like a fog. But as soon as she moved closer to me she'd be herself again, all luminous. She'd seek me out, kneeling on the bedroom floor beside me in the lamplight, whispering, "Are you all right, Davey?" and, "Come downstairs, let's watch a film". She lit up the room, and made my skin prickle. One night, she reached out and held my fingers in her own, and it was only then that I noticed how cold mine were. All bone.

One Saturday morning, when Grandad had been missing for three months, I was lying in bed with the duvet over my head. Beside me lay my copy of the Verbatinea. Through the cotton, the light was purple like a bruise. This I what I did when I could feel the world turning, and far too fast. Something about curling up gave me hope that the clock would stop ticking, but it never did.

It was Mum who peeled the duvet from my face, and the cold March air stung my cheeks. Her arms were full of clean weekend clothes, and she clutched them roughly to her chest. A red and white sock dangled precariously from her wrist, ready to fall. Her face was a question mark.

"Have you not been up yet?"

As I shimmied deeper down the bed, she flipped the duvet onto the floor, leaving me exposed on the mattress like a frog on a dissecting table. I tried to pull my dressing gown over my face but it wouldn't stretch. Mum dropped the clothes in a pile on the end of the bed and yanked open the curtains.

"It's eleven already, David. We need to go." She flung her hand in the direction of the pile on the bed. "Find something in there and brush your teeth. I have to be at Church by lunch for the Easter festival." She pushed open the window wide on its hinges like a door. I didn't even know it opened that far. Outside, everything was crisp blue light.

Mum rummaged in the pocket of her dress and pulled out an oat bar. She pressed it into my palm and clasped her hands around my fist. "Have some breakfast." She grinned and kissed me on the cheek. Her lips were hot, and when she pulled away, her blue eyes flicked left and right across my face as if she was searching for something. I stared back, keeping my eyes wide so she'd find whatever it was and leave me alone. After a few seconds she cocked her head and sighed, before leaving the room with the bedroom door wide open. I reached across without getting off the bed and pushed the door closed.

Silence.

I didn't want to see anyone. One minute, my insides were alive, twisting and tickling against other inside bits, but the next they were still and dead. I found myself talking to Grandad in my head, all clicks and tuts. Asking him why he left me. Why he didn't tell me that this would be it. Why he didn't care that I was alone. My tongue rolled in my mouth as I made the sounds.

A cough, from the back garden. I sat up and craned my head to see what was happening without having to actually get up.

It was Dad.

He was sitting on the low back wall, facing out into the sheep fields behind the house. His fists were clenched and his wide back heaved like a whale breaching the sea. Every so often he'd lift a hand and wipe his face, but then go back to the same hunched-over position, staring at nothing but green. I don't know how long I watched him for, but as the minutes passed my hand inched towards an empty mug on the windowsill, and I had to fight the urge to throw. I looked down at the Verbatinea on the mattress and then squinted at Dad again. I couldn't reach him. I couldn't explain. I didn't have the words.

A moment later, Mum joined him in the yard and placed her hand on his shoulder. Leaning over, she whispered something in his ear and he turned to her, the trance broken. I felt like I shouldn't be watching so I went back to the bed and retrieved trousers, underpants, and a polo shirt from the crumpled pile of clothes. I couldn't find a complete pair of socks, so I went with one green sock and one blue sock, which were the closest match I could find. I left the oat bar on my pillow.

Downstairs, Emily laughed.

I slid down the stairs slowly on my heels, landing on each step with a thump. As I passed the living room, I saw Emily and a girl I didn't know kneeling on the rug. Around them on the carpet were shiny tubes and little square boxes spilling from zip-up pouches. Some of them were open, and inside were squares of colour and mirrors that caught the light.

They didn't know I was there, so I watched through the bannisters. I could only see the back of the mystery girl's head, but Emily was facing the open door. She'd wrapped her hair in two dark knots on either side of her head, like cat ears, and her arms were wrapped in black net. *But her face.* Her face was a warped, nightmarish version of her face. It was white like the whites of her eyes, and dark red streaks were painted under her cheekbones and across her temples. It turned her soft, round face into something terrible. Her lips were dark blue, and her eyebrows were thick and dark across her brow.

She looked up at me then and called me down. "Davey! I'll do you too!" The girl with the ponytail turned around and her face looked just as dead as Emily's but her lips were as red as a post box. She laughed, unaware that her teeth were smeared with red too. It looked like blood.

Mum came and stood between us in the hallway. "Get your coats on, time to go."

"Oh, Mum, can't I just stay with Kitty?"

Mum took a good look at Emily. "What have you done to your face?"

Emily smirked and wrapped a piece of black silk around her neck. "Experimenting."

Mum covered her face with her hands. "Doom and gloom. Come on, then. Kitty, your dad's on the drive."

Kitty sighed and started picking up the tubes and cases. Mum watched her for a few seconds before pressing her face to the glass panel in the front door. Emily and Kitty met her there, their faces even more ominous in the dim light. Mum waited for Kitty to lift her leather coat off the hook and slip her boots on before opening the front door, wiggling her fingers to the man in the car, and then closing it again after her.

"Come on. Time to go out."

Emily met herself in the hallway mirror, pouting her lips and sucking in her cheeks so she looked even more skull-like that she did before. "Is Dad coming?" she asked. Mum pressed her face to the glass panel in the front door again and didn't answer.

We pulled up at a huge supermarket. Emily slumped low in her seat, picking at her nail varnish. When she saw where we were, she rolled her eyes and slumped down further.

"For fuck's sake," she whispered. "What's so important about this?"

Mum had a tendency to take Emily and I places without telling us where we were going. The truth of what she'd do next was something secret and sealed, something she sat on like an egg. This bothered Emily more than it did me, but even I thought it strange that Mum kept a check on everything we did, yet her thought patterns remained such a mystery. Even then, at ten, I had so many memories of being traipsed from place to place. In the years before the 'missing' posters and the door-steppers and the photographs posted through our doors, Mum hadn't clutched us so close. She'd smiled more and looked up at the sky freely – not so afraid to take her eyes from the crowns of our heads. Sometimes, passers-by on the street would knock Emily and I against Mum's knees until she'd look down in surprise to see us clinging to her skirts and shake us off as if we were spiders scaling the fabric. But since the disappearances, she clung to us like we might evaporate.

At the supermarket, after we got out of the car, Mum pointed to a plastic shelter in a distant corner of the carpark and told me to go and grab a trolley. The sun was blindingly bright, and cackling gangs of people were crossing the roads between us and there without any sense of a pattern. Everywhere I turned there were people blocking my view, and I couldn't understand where the cars were all coming from. The place was chaos.

"David. Get a trolley."

Emily was looking at me quizzically, and I knew my cheeks were flushing. I hated this feeling, so I had no choice; I scuttled across the tarmac, ducking and diving between families to reach the shelter. But once I grabbed a trolley,

I couldn't see Mum or Emily. All I could see were other families holding onto their children's hands. Kids tethered to parents with leashes. Trolleys with toddlers or piles of shopping bags loaded into them, taller than me. Everything was *loud*, rattling and chattering and roaring like some sort of mechanical jungle. I thought about screaming for Mum, but I knew she wouldn't hear me, so I closed my eyes and ran – hoping to reach where I'd started from.

When the trolley stopped, I opened my eyes to see Mum had hold of its side. "What were you doing, running like a juggernaut?" She pulled the handle from my grasp. "You could have hit the side of the car." She frowned, tutted, and strode off towards the supermarket entrance. I kept my head down and my eyes on the backs of Mum's heels as I tried to imitate Mum's footsteps exactly – left, right, left, right, click-clack. She hummed as she marched, and I hummed the same tune under my breath. It didn't help.

As we approached the doorway, a horde of shoppers poured out, all talking over the top of one another and gesticulating wildly – their faces red and arms straining with the weight of their bags. A few of them were wearing big blue flowers made of paper, pinned to their jackets. The roar in my ears was as violent as an earthquake, so I ducked to the side to avoid them while Mum and Emily glided through the group like swans on a lake. I leaned back on a rack of newspapers, the headlines smearing bold and black across my palms: 'Economy slumps again', 'Search and rescue overwhelmed', and 'The Modern Problem – what does it really mean?' As I rubbed them on my jeans, I watched the back of the group that had knocked me into the stand.

And I shouted. *Loud.*

It was Grandad.

There he was, walking at the back of the group. That was the back of his head – the curly grey hair that flicked out to the sides in wisps. That square frame. The slight dip in his step. He was wearing black trousers and a brown jacket that I didn't recognise, but dangling from the coat's hem was an unmistakable flash of orange.

The orange jumper missing from his wardrobe.

For a second he turned as if he heard me, and I saw that he was carrying a stack of newspapers in his arms. He glanced side to side in the throng and carried on walking. I didn't get a good look at his face because of the crowd, so he couldn't have seen me either.

I didn't know what to do. I wanted to shout for Mum and Emily, but they were already pushing off past the checkouts and into the magazine aisle. Mum was edging away from a man dressed in a blue polo shirt, who was shaking a bucket with 'Blue Pilgrims' and a tray of blue flowers. Mum always told us to stay away from them, to "keep our heads down," especially since they'd started visiting Grandad after Grandma died. She answered their questions with one-note answers and grinned like the Cheshire Cat in Alice and Wonderland, all teeth and tongue. But the man in blue didn't look dangerous. He smiled at everyone, but hardly anyone smiled back. It was a soft smile, like the smile a teacher gave you if you fell over and hurt your knee. When he turned, I saw that the back of his top had 'Talk to me' stitched on the back, and it occurred to me that if anyone saw that and actually wanted to, they'd be met with the back of his head. It didn't sound like there were many coins in his bucket. I turned back to Grandad and watched as he split from the group and made his way along the front of the supermarket, his arms straining under the newspapers.

Grandad.

Why was he here? I couldn't let him go. Not again.

Another group of shoppers passed through the entrance and blocked my view. I pressed against the wall, waiting for a gap, until I saw my chance to squeeze through the stragglers at the back. I bolted into the car park, looking left and right and jumping on the spot to see over the tops of cars coming and going. An old couple, their arms linked and wearing almost identical grey coats, stepped back from me as if I was an animal. I felt like I was running along a cliff-edge. *What am I doing? I shouldn't be here. None of this is right.* But I needed to follow him, to find out why he'd left me here alone. Why he'd abandoned us. Whether or not I could make him come home.

And then I spotted him – at the far left of the car park, not far from where Mum had parked. In a few seconds he'd be around the side of a row of white skips overflowing with cardboard and out of sight. He was so far away already, and my stomach was flipping, flipping, flipping. For a moment I thought I might be sick. I'd been so close but he was faster than me and almost gone again, and I'd never be able to grasp his hairy, horrible jumper in my fist and hear him whisper in my ear, "It's going to be OK, David. Be quiet. Be still, Bumblebee."

"Grandaaaaaaaad!"

I screamed it across the car park so violently that the families near me stopped in their tracks. My throat felt like it was torn to ribbons. One blonde-haired woman had her hand over her mouth as if I'd been struck by a car. Another woman wearing a long green coat looked around her, as if she'd find him for me without even knowing what he looked like. As if it were that easy to bring something back from the dead.

I yelled again; my eyes screwed shut only long enough to scream before I forced them open again in case he disappeared behind the white skip. But it didn't make any difference; he was nowhere to be seen.

And then a dark feeling started to grow, like when you know something bad is going to happen and there's nothing you can do to stop it. Black oil bubbled low in my body. Everything went a little bit grey and fuzzy, like the bit when an old video cuts out. I could hear radio static, and it thundered louder and louder.

"Are you all right, kiddo?"

Through the haze, a woman's face floated next to mine. Her hair and face were colourless and she was all eyes and nose. Her fringe was stuck to her forehead, though it wasn't raining.

"Who are you shouting for, son? I can help. Have they left you?"

I leaned away from her nose. All she was doing was blocking me from reaching Grandad, so I pushed her back with both hands deep in her belly. Her eyes widened, and she raised her hands to either side of her face, before looking up at someone I couldn't see. "Did you see? I didn't touch him. I didn't do anything." Her voice was as faint as someone calling from the far end of a tunnel.

A crowd was forming around us and buzzing like a nest of hornets in a tree. It was in my ears, my mouth, my heart.

I ran, the soles of my shoes slipping on black ice.

Horns now, like ships at sea, and screeching like owls over the fields at night. A man shouted, "Watch it!" But I could hardly see – the car park was all grey and far away. *This is a dream, it has to be a dream.* Suddenly, I slammed against a hard surface and my head made a 'thunk' sound.

I was under a car. I was going to be squashed. I was going to die.

But nothing happened. Seconds passed and I realised that though I was lying on my side on the tarmac, it was a lot quieter than before. The air was still. I opened my eyes slowly to bright blue. Serene and cloudless. My head was pounding. The car I'd ran into was parked, and there was no one kneeling over me anymore. And there, just beside the car, was a block of white. Dark smudges. Scratched initials.

I'd made it.

I scrambled to my feet. The supermarket was small and far away. Somehow, I'd made it all the way to the far left of the car park, to the skips. Here there were no people, no cars moving. Just a few lonely parked cars and lots of empty spaces. No one had followed me.

But I wasn't alone.

Clicks and tuts. Muffled taps and low knocks. At first it sounded like the Morse code they'd shown us at school. But then I realised it felt more familiar than that. It sounded like our language.

The Verbatinea.

I was afraid to move. I'm not sure why. Afraid of seeing Grandad. Of facing his betrayal, I suppose. Above my head, a pair of crows were perched on the skip, picking apart the shreds hanging over the edge and hopping side-to-side as if egging each other on. The smaller one launched off his perch to where I needed to be behind the skip and fluttered out of sight.

"Grandad?"

My voice croaked and didn't sound like me. The clicking stopped, but there was no reply. I had to look, I had to know. I had to hold his hand and pull him back. I could do it. Maybe that's why he was here. Maybe he'd come back just for me.

I edged around the skip, the fingertips of my left hand glancing across the surface. Every time I turned a corner I felt a bit sicker, until I found that I was at the front of the skip.

He was gone.

I went to the back of the skip again and pressed my head against the brick wall behind it. It burned hot against my ear, and over the wall I heard the metallic taps of metal on metal. Had he gone through the wall? I took a long hard look at the brick for a doorway but there was nothing – not a seam, not a join. In the midday sun the surface glittered like broken glass.

I needed to get to the other side.

I ran along the wall until I left the car park and stood on the street, cars roaring along the road. No one walking on the pavement noticed me. In fact, everyone had their heads down, headphones in, or eyes on their phones. Everyone seemed to be lost in their own little world.

Taking advantage of a gap, I skirted the wall until it turned in again under an archway and I found the source of those metal clangs. A digger, old and jerky, was digging a grave just next to the wall, and beyond it stretched hundreds of gravestones shining black. Even just standing there felt wrong. Like trespassing. But I had to see if he was here. If somehow Grandad had passed through the wall and had led me here.

"Grandad," I whispered, too quietly for anyone to hear. With little baby steps, I made my way down the gravel with my head low. The stones and flowers were sprayed with frost. In a moment of fearlessness, I reached out towards one particularly tall headstone to brush my fingers against the gold lettering and shining black that reflected me back. So many names that I didn't know. People who no longer existed.

As I crept along the path beneath the strangled trees, I scanned the horizon for Grandad. Perched on a headstone a few feet ahead was the crow from over the wall – or at least, a crow that looked just like it. It was so starkly black that it looked like it wasn't there at all. The shape of a bird cut out from the sky. It opened its beak and shouted. It wasn't a caw, yet it wasn't human. It was an in-between sound, desperate and stifled. It looked at me with one glittering eye before hopping a stone closer and then swooping off to a grassy area further down the cemetery where there were no stones at all. There, thousands of tiny blue flowers poked through the grass, and in some spots, bouquets and elaborate centrepieces made with the same blue flowers were laid on the ground. They looked just like the bouquets people left on our street and that I'd seen on other streets on the news.

I followed the track to the edge of the grassy stretch. Some of the offerings had cards and photographs attached, and I leaned across to read the closest one. 'My darling Grace,' it read. 'I wish we could have said goodbye. I wish that you'd never left us. I wish that I could say to you everything that I didn't say.' The sign on the wall behind said:

GARDEN OF EXODUS
For those we have lost and cannot find
and hope one day will return

The crow pecked amongst the flowers of a wreath before

hopping onto a nearby headstone and wiping his beak on its sharp edge. It didn't seem to care that I watched as it ran its mouth down the long shafts of his wings. It was completely free. And even though the bird was only a bird, my chest tightened with the limitations of my own body. I felt heavy and sick, and imagined myself plucking the bird, feather by feather, and sticking them into my own skin. Would I then be as unrestricted as the bird? Would I fly too?

This part of the cemetery felt different, smelled different. Fake and floral, like Grandma's bowls of potpourri. And even though it hadn't rained in weeks, the air was heavy and damp, tinged with ruin and wet stone. It smelled like the heaviest books I used to open in Grandad's office, or the box of old letters in Grandma's glass cabinet – of things that I knew I shouldn't be looking at. Further along the Garden of Exodus, not too far away, two women dressed in black rested their hands on each other's shoulders. The taller one was wiping the face of the shorter one, or brushing hair from her eyes. When they turned to look at each other, I realised that though they weren't speaking, they were making each other smile little sad smiles. I watched them as they smoothed each other, held each other, and supported each other towards the exit. I was left alone.

Next to where they'd stood were two stone towers, around twenty feet high, mounted to the cemetery wall. Between them was a black iron gate, and what lay beyond was mostly in shadow, but I could just about make out a pale stone bench inside, and a plaque inscribed with rows of finely engraved words. It looked like more than a list of names. A huge bluebottle, as big as my thumbnail bumbled through the air. As I got closer to the railings, a cloud of winged things consumed me, bouncing off my face and coat as if drunk and apologetic. Flies, hornets, moths… Some wriggled into the folds of my scarf and I tried to bat them away, but couldn't tell through my thick gloves if I was succeeding or just squashing them. I squeezed through a gap where the railings were bent and leapt into a shadowy corner. A little voice in the back of my head said that the flies wouldn't follow me there, because flies liked the light, but though I couldn't see them they hummed everywhere – in my ears, on my ankles, down my throat. I moaned and dropped to the stone, wrapping my arms around my body and any foreign and unwanted things that had already burrowed their way in. They were *inside my head. Was I made up of flies? Would I break apart when they decided to leave me?*

With my hands clamped over my ears, I crawled out of the shadow to beneath the frieze with the curly script. The edges of the words had eroded, softening to the extent that I couldn't make any of it out. Below the words was carved a wide flower that jutted out, or perhaps it was a spiral. In its centre was a blank space on which my eyes couldn't settle. The air between the wall and I shimmered like steam above a boiling kettle. As I watched, the shape twisted and transformed into a wide-open mouth with thick stone lips. Where the throat would be, there was a deep hollow, and the slight shine of water. A tongue. A creature, sleeping but poised to gulp and swallow.

"Grandaaaad!" I closed my eyes and pretended that I wasn't there. Where was he? Couldn't he hear me? *Why was he doing this to me?* But when I opened my eyes, I was still alone, the flies had gone, and the little yard was almost entirely in shadow. Only a sliver of light licked my boot.

As I scrambled towards the railings, I took one last look over my shoulder at the mouth. Something hung down from the top lip, almost as long as my palm. Dark and soft, it absorbed the light and dangled from a thin twist of cord. I stopped and stared at this thing, this thing that was both life and death. It was just like the thing on the book cover and in the case in Grandad's office. The thing bristled with white noise. Was it where the flies came from? It was a cocoon, and I wanted to touch it, squeeze it gently to see what treasure slept inside. But what if more bad things broke out? I felt that if I could see what was hidden beneath the layers, I would understand it better than anyone. But I couldn't touch it, despite my longing to. What if what was inside was dark and horrible?

I turned away, and ahead of me the cemetery was all lilac and smoke. I kicked up stones and swung my arms as I ran from the mouth, the thing I didn't understand. I ran from death.

I was almost at the entrance when I happened to glance at the side of the cemetery I hadn't yet explored. Dad was there, kneeling at a headstone. Part of me wanted to run to him, to push against his wide chest and breathe in the smell of home. To tell him what I'd just seen, to take him to the wall with the noise and the cocoon – but he was a stranger. I knew he wouldn't come. He'd hold my hand and keep me there and tell me that everything I'd seen wasn't true. Even the back of his head reminded me of the lies he told to stop me following Grandad. To make me stay where I didn't belong.

I watched as he staggered to his feet and then stumped off towards the entrance, walking like a man who didn't want to reach his goal. His lips were sucked in, his forehead full of wrinkles. I waited a few minutes before heading over to the stone he'd been looking at, my heart thumping with every step. Here, the path was littered with stones, petals, and small white pebbles that looked like knuckles. The low leaves of the hanging tree brushed the top of my head when I was finally close enough to read the name there, and as I did, my throat tightened.

In loving memory of
MAUD PORTER
18th July 1940 – 23rd March 2014
Beloved wife, mother, and grandmother
Passed away peacefully in her sleep

I don't know what I'd expected to find, but the relief that trickled down my back was replaced with a cold, strained feeling that I couldn't name. *She was actually in there.* Lovely Grandma with her wrists as soft as silk. Not far below. But how far? Tufts of yellow grass sprouted from the grave, and I thought about the time Mum dropped an open bottle of bleach on the landing and turned the green carpet skin-pink. This was like that, but almost a solid rectangle, like a door fallen flat on the floor. I read the names on the stones beside her: Harold Johnson and Rita Johnson. Mabel Gorman and Anne Gorman. Eileen Kennedy and Jarvis Kennedy. David Mendez, Domnhall Mendez, and Brendan Mendez. Hers seemed to be the only one with only one name on it. All the others had at least two names, sometimes three or four. Husbands and wives. Parents and children. But here, Grandma was alone. I hoped she wasn't cold. Heat kindled my belly. Grandad hadn't only abandoned me, he'd abandoned Grandma too.

I pushed my fists into my eye sockets and took three deep

breaths, just like they'd shown us at school. By the third, I'd stopped shaking. I stood there for a long time before weaving my way back towards the supermarket. This time, I skimmed the sides of parked cars with my eyes wide open.

When I reached the entrance, Mum was sitting on a green plastic garden bench encircled by men and women wearing red fleeces and name tags. The man in blue knelt by her side. They were holding hands. Emily sat on the other side of her, her skin ashen beneath the face paint, and her fingers fiddling with the tassels on a cushion she had across her knees.

When Mum saw me, she screamed and pointed as though my face terrified her. The men and women in red all looked up and started to talk into their black radios. Mum didn't get up but waved me to her with her hands as if drawing in a smell. I walked up to her hesitantly, and she crushed me to her chest before immediately pushing me away and slapping me across the face.

"What were you doing? Why did you do that to me? I thought you'd gone!" She shook me with every word, before taking a few deep, jagged breaths. "Don't you care? Don't you know what my nerves are like? Haven't I told you about my nerves?"

All the faces in the air were looking at me. I understood some expressions as relief, while others were biting their lips or jutting their jaws. Had they really thought I'd disappeared as easy as that? Had they even looked for me? Mum turned to the blue man beside her. His name tag read 'Here to listen. I'm Fred.' She sobbed. "He's going to be one of them, isn't he? He's a little torturer." She grabbed my hair and I winced as a clump was caught in her stack of gold rings. Beside us, Emily's face paint had smeared so that the black on her eyelids was now beneath her eyes. She was gasping for breath, and gave me a desperate look before pressing her face into the tasselled cushion, so all I could see were flowers.

It took Mum a long time to calm down after that. Her hands were the thing I noticed the most. They gripped her handbag so hard that I could see all the bones in the back of her hands fanning, like a bird's wing. The staff gave her two cups of tea and lots of pats on the arms and shoulders while Emily sat with her head in her hands, her eyes fixed on me through her fingers.

Once Mum's voice had returned to normal, she rushed us from the supermarket and back to the car, her heels only occasionally slipping on black ice. Her back was so straight, her head unusually high, as if looking up at the sky. No one spoke in the car, but Emily kept staring. It made me feel small, and anything I thought to say sounded stupid. I wanted to tell her about Grandad, about the thing I'd seen in the cemetery. But I couldn't. I didn't have the words.

You know what I've just remembered? That though what I'd done seemed like the worst thing in the world, no one asked me where I'd gone. No one. Not even Dad. It was as if when I wasn't there, I'd ceased to exist. The truth is on the air, in this room, with you. It swims in the air like meat in soup. I can smell it through my fingers. Pick apart the elements. Is this the way I am now, or is this your doing?

What is happening to me?

AFTER

~

I lie folded on the floor for some time, watching the clot seep into the planks and transform into a black knot – half wood, half blood. It continues to shine as if it hasn't dried, but I don't reach out to touch it. The floor is a nest of splinters. I press a thumb to one and it sticks itself in me uninvited. My throat burns. Every breath is a gargle underwater. I daren't unclamp my lips in case something else erupts from my throat.

Something gnaws at my stomach, from the inside-out. Is time passing? Tensing my jaw, I close my eyes and count one Mississippi, two Mississippi, three Mississippi, but I'm distracted by the strange, prickly feel of my skin and I lose count, start again at one. Lose count. Is it my beard? Can I feel it growing? Lose count.

I'm failing.

I think of him, his face wrinkled and pink, a smile that warmed my belly. His little round glasses. The smell of his hairy jumpers and the strength in his arms as he lifted me to the window and showed me the stars. I think of him, he who made this same journey nineteen years ago and left not a trace. Made it to Mothtown without being tracked. All on his own, without anyone's help, not even Michael. Did he find this cabin, take a candle? Did he think about me as he trekked up the mountain, or when he stepped through the door? And what would he think if he saw me now, curled on the floor like a whimpering dog?

This time, I rise on the hot steam of shame. I need to move before the sun sets again. If I can reach the door up the mountain by the time the day is over, I'll be on schedule.

Michael comes back to me again. "Take what you can scavenge. You'll need it."

I stick the matches and one of the candles into my back pocket and set out into the woods once more.

During one of Michael's final lessons, he'd talked me through the last of his many faded handouts. This one had been filled with black and white sketches of fleshy fruits, berries, and roots like rat tails. The words were as faint as the drawings, and felt much like a copy of a copy, or a rumour of a rumour. Towards the bottom of the page, the plants and their descriptions faded away to the most abstract of ghosts.

His lips squeezed together, fighting something back. "The longer you're there, the longer you'll have to manage. If all goes smoothly, you'll be up and through the door before you need to forage. Food won't be a problem when you're through the door." I could still taste the breakfast I'd scraped together that morning: a slice of white bread and a small, slightly green satsuma.

As Michael spoke, I glared out of the window, sure that I wouldn't need to know this. The journey through Mothtown was a journey I was born to take. It was in my blood. Surely Michael knew this by now? There he sat behind his desk, lesson after lesson, dressed all in Godly white. Behind him on the shelves floated a collection of golden photo frames as if they were disciples – Michael in his kurta with his arm around a young woman, then another where he's clasping hands with an Indian man in a business-suit. In the next he was hugging a woman, middle aged and wearing bright yellow, and in another his arm was around a man who looked just like me but rounder and softer in the face. In this one, Michael was beaming and crushing the slender man to his side and waving a piece of paper in his other hand. All of the pictures had the same background, a plain cream office wall with a wall clock displaying the time and date. I wonder if all that will be left of me one day will be a photograph, fated to forever watch the back of Michael's head and the tired, miserable faces of the people listening to him, desperate to begin their journeys.

I'm distracted and a stone slips beneath my bad foot. As I find my feet again, I choke back a dislodged lump in my throat. Here, the trees thin out into a short stretch where the ground is dry and dusty like chalk. Little bushes of lilac heather have broken through where the earth has split. About thirty or so feet ahead are the feet of the crags, reaching up to join the mountain. High above, the peak is as jagged as an arrowhead, and the face is grizzled with cracks and tufts of dead grass. If I crane my head a bit, I can see the opening overhead, a hole in the rock just shorter than me. It's not too far, perhaps as high as a double-decker bus, though there's no trail, as such – just a rough ladder of stone.

I take one last look over my shoulder and listen for movement in the trees. I haven't heard anything all day – which worries me almost as much as if I had. Before, even if I couldn't see the hunters, I could hear them snapping twigs or whispering. They are ghosts. And yet… something about them is so familiar, that I know they're just as real as I am. They're here to drag me back, to take me somewhere cold, empty, blue. I know that in my heart. The thought of it stings. And they're strong, they won't stop following me. So not seeing or hearing them at all since falling into the marsh seems wrong. Up there on the mountain face I'd be laid on bare rock – with nowhere to hide.

Still, the sky is already getting dark. If I go now, I could be up there and through the door by nightfall.

On all fours, I'll crawl.

I start the ascent, putting as much weight on my hands as I can. Up, up, up, and down come a tumble of stones. I wedge the pointed toe of the brogues into crevices to stop me slipping. My trousers, still wet, are stiff with mud and feel almost impossible to bend.

My back…

Something inside my head flips and my eyes squeeze shut. If I can only just grip the rock. My stomach shoots fire up my throat. A blow from behind knocks my shoulder blades out of place. I'm slipping, my arms are numb. Deep breaths, deep breaths. Within seconds, the scream of pain subsides and is replaced by a deep throbbing. The air tastes tinny, as if I can smell the red iron hidden in the stone. Looking up, the opening is almost within reach – but suddenly it's an open mouth, crying across the valleys and hills, overlooked by stone eyes that watch me scramble up like a spider towards my prize.

It's so close.

Focusing on the darkness of the mouth, the setting sun is too bright for my eyes and I squint against the violet sky. This is it. I've almost done it. I clamber up the last few stones and face an opening reaching up to my waist and only just wide enough to squeeze through. Inside is so completely black that it looks like cloth, and for the first time since I started on this path, I wonder what's on the other side of the door. I'd been so focussed on finding it, on escaping this world, that I've never thought to imagine what waits for me on the other side. And what will happen when I walk through it? Will I pass straight through and out again into light? Or will I have to carry on, crawling through the absolute dark? Will it hurt?

Michael's voice comes back to me in the low, conspiratorial timbre he used when I grew angry. "Follow everything I say, do whatever I tell you to do, and you'll find a way out of this awful world forever."

Inside the opening, the darkness shifts as if little creatures on the walls are crawling deeper into the mountain. A trick? The longer I stare, the more frantic the movements get, until they settle into a single figure standing in the centre of the cave. Too small to be one of the men following me. No, it's a woman, small, but strangely proportioned. Something is wrong with her middle; it swells outwards and she clasps at it desperately. A rain of dark hair falls around her round face like running water.

I reach into my back pocket for the matches and light the candle stub. There's hardly enough of it left to grasp it well, but it's all I have. So I hold it out in front of me like a beacon and stagger into the shadows.

BEFORE

7.

No one spoke to me until later that night when Emily stormed into my bedroom. I was sitting on the bed with *Transfigurations in Nature*, my finger trailing the picture of the moth cocoon that matched the hanging egg in the cemetery. Mum had resumed sticking her head into my room every half an hour, and in-between the visits I could hear Mum shrieking about what'd happened. "He was nowhere," "he needs to be kept on a leash," "he's wild," and "it was just like what happened to Nicola's boy, you know Nicola?" But this seemed to me to be massively unfair. It was Emily who was the unpredictable one, meeting friends in the evenings, and not coming back until dark – but there was never any mention of tethering *her* to the house. Often she'd skulk in, slipping through the front door like a shadow, smelling of smoke, her eyes smeared with black kohl. She'd lift a finger to her lips conspiratorially, as if she was letting me in on some big secret. But she wasn't, really. It was a lie. Everyone knew when she was out, and everyone knew when she came back, because that's when the lights came on.

But now, Emily's light was red. "What the hell were you doing, you idiot?" She stood over me, her hands gripping the edge of her sleeves. "What makes you think it's all right to wander off? Do you know how close they were to calling the police?"

I shook my head.

"Look at me, David."

I looked up but I couldn't meet her eye. It burned.

Emily let out a long, exasperated sigh. "You CAN'T do stuff like this. Can't you just stay in the lines? You're going to break Mum. And Dad's already considering keeping you in a cage. This is serious." She fell to a crouch and ran her fingers through my fringe. "We don't want you to be bones on a mountain. That's all."

Long after she had left, I was still shivering. I propped the library book open where my bed met the wall, wrapped my arms around my chest and imagined I was in the cocoon, where it was warm, dark, and silent. Where I was growing, ready to burst.

As I pulled on my red school uniform that next Monday morning, there was a knock on the door. Gentle and reluctant. I could tell by the sound of it that it was Dad.

"Can I come in?" His voice vibrated the wood. I opened the door for him so that we stood inches from each other, though my face still only reached up to the middle of his chest. "We're doing something different this morning," he murmured. "Keep your uniform on, but you're taking the morning off." He grasped my shoulder and shook me gently, before heading off slowly downstairs.

In the living room, Mum was perched on the arm of the chair, dressed in her brown fur coat. Emily was slouched back into the chair beside her, dressed in her black secondary school uniform and a huge blue scarf the colour of bubble-gum. As I walked in, Mum grimaced and clapped her hands. "Come on then!" she croaked. "All of us ready?"

The ground outside was frozen, and my black school shoes slipped with every step. Rain fell from the sky in sheets of straight sleet. I whispered in Emily's ear, "Are you coming too?"

She didn't turn, but muttered, "I suppose I am."

Emily and I squeezed into the back seat, our wet coats pressing against each other. She picked at her fingernails, her mouth opening and closing as if she was trying to say something. I'd never seen Emily like that; she never struggled. So I just sat there, watching her like an exhibit at a museum for a good ten minutes or so before she finally leaned over and spoke to me. "You've done it now, Davey. Be careful."

"What have I done?"

But her eyes were set on the fields, tinted blue. The stark trees, only starting to bud. Her right hand wouldn't stop twitching and picked at the knee of her tights where a hole had been stitched up. I started to feel sick.

We drove through country lanes for a long time, bouncing around in the back seat before we hit the smoother motorway. After an hour or so, the world became less grassy, trees were traded for huge grey warehouses, and farmers' fields turned into tarmac. It was difficult to spot anything that had grown naturally. Everything was made for a purpose. Next came the tightly-packed red-bricked houses that reminded me a bit of Grandad's house, nestled comfortably between its neighbours. Here, clothes lines with fluttering t-shirts and skirts blew over yard walls into next door, and electric cables hung low over back alleys. It gave the impression that everyone encroached on everyone else's space. But again, I could see no people. Only dark windows, curtains closed.

"Nearly there," Mum chirped over her shoulder.

Very quickly, houses transformed into windows, the first ones run down and old-fashioned but soon they grew bigger, fancier, with more lights and words sprawled across them. A few more corners and we rolled up a ramp into a multi-storey car park. From there, we walked out onto a busy street swarming with pedestrians in suits and fancy coats. Dad strode out ahead of us, parting the crowd like the prow of a ship. Around us hardly anyone was speaking, unless it was into their phone. Ears were plugged with headphones and noses were pressed to tablets, yet no one bumped into one another. It was like everyone had this sixth sense, an ability to establish a wide berth when people moved as erratically as ants pouring from their hill. And amongst the crowd, standing by a wall, was another person dressed in blue. This time it was a woman, rattling a blue bucket and holding a strip of blue paper flowers. As she got close to someone, she'd hold up a blue pin and say, "Raising funds to support survivors of the Modern Problem."

Most would blank her and skim past, but the girl's stretched-out smile never faded and she never stopped trying, ricocheting from person to person like a pinball. She approached Dad but he waved her away with a hand. The road roared with engines. I pressed my hands over my ears.

As we waited at a crossing, I looked down at a huge puddle that'd formed where the drain had blocked. Its surface rippled in the wind and reflected the lampposts and the billowy knees of Dad's trousers. But no matter how much I looked, I couldn't see me at all.

Mum pulled me across the road and we continued along

a row of shop windows set up like living rooms, too perfect to be real. Without anyone sitting in them, they looked dead. Across the street was a squat grey building with a long queue pouring from the door. Many of the men and women looked uncannily like the people I'd sat with in the library. A few looked like the mudmen who migrated up our street with their sleeping rolls and their maps. I pulled at Mum's sleeve and pointed at it, thinking whatever was inside must be popular. "That's where people find a job, David," she said. None of the people queuing looked like they wanted to be there.

In the distance, a woman's voice rose above the crowd's murmur. The voice was jagged, desperate. Car horns blared. First one or two, then more in a terrible chorus. Dad reached out and grasped Emily's hand. Emily peered around passers-by to see what was happening, but no one else turned. No one stopped walking. It wasn't long before there was a break in the crowd and I could see her: a woman with long wavy hair, wearing black trousers and a white shirt. She stood in the middle of the road with her hands clasped to the sides of her head. She turned in a circle, glaring at the cars with their noses almost touching her legs. Her hands pulled her face back and stretched out her lips. Dad pulled Emily quicker through the crowd and turned his head to check if I was coming too. Beside me, Mum's eyes were straight ahead, her lips moving as she mumbled softly to herself as if in a dream.

"Look at me!" The woman screamed in every direction. "Can you see me?"

The car horns were dying down.

"I'm here! I'm here!"

The crowds swarmed along the street as if she wasn't

there. The cars were still, and through the window I could see one man leaning back in the driver's seat, looking in the rear-view mirror. His car was the one pressed to the back of the woman's legs.

I trotted forwards to keep up with Dad and Emily, but kept turning to see what happened next. Soon there were too many people in their black coats rushing between us and I couldn't see anymore. Eventually her cries faded into the murmur of cars and muffled voices.

As the crowd dispersed, I saw Dad pointing to a white building at the end of the street. A white sign plugged into the grass read 'Wheatsheaf Medical Group.' A man with a fuzzy black beard sat on a bench beside the front door. His pale yellow t-shirt hung from his chest, and a small piece of paper in his hand rustled in the breeze. His cheeks shone, flushing purple like polished plums.

Why were we here? Dad spoke to the receptionist while we sat down in the waiting area. There were only four other people waiting there with us. Two of them were old and on their own, and leaning into opposite corner walls. Both were still as dead wood, and stared at the empty chairs ahead of them. Their faces were a pallid yellow-grey, puckered like old apples. One of them wiped under his eye, where a tear had broken free.

The other two were a couple. Younger than Mum or Dad, they were dressed in co-ordinated bright colours. Even their hair was the same shade of reddish-brown. The man was squeezing the woman's hand tightly, pinning it between his knees. The woman had a leaflet on her lap, and though I couldn't read it upside down, I recognised the blue house on the cover. It was surrounded by fields of yellow flowers and looked like somewhere you'd go on holiday. She occasionally pinched and squeezed the paper, picking the corner so it had started to curl. Her ashen eyes reminded me of a fish. Round and quivering, they didn't focus on anything in particular, and darted around as if looking for a place to rest. They stopped on my face when I was looking at her and I turned away, my face burning. My hands twisted in my lap. From the corner of my eye, I saw the man she was with rubbing her leg, making her green dress move up her thigh.

A man appeared in the corridor next to the receptionist's desk and scanned the room.

He held a brown folder in his hand. He looked young, even to me, almost like one of the boys I'd see Emily with in the park. But his shirt was pressed, and his tie was straight. He looked between his folder and me and smiled, "David Porter?"

I looked at Dad. He stood up and beckoned me forwards.

We followed the young man along a dark corridor and stepped through a white painted door with '7' written on it in peeling black paint. He directed us to a pair of chairs beside his desk. The room was small and square, all the magnolia walls covered in posters filled with information, but from my chair I couldn't make out any of the words. There was a bed in the far corner, half-obscured by a green curtain. That wall only had one poster on it, dull blue and calm. 'TALK TO US' in huge letters, followed by a phone number. All the walls at that side were covered in posters about worry and the familiar sea-silver branding of the Blue Pilgrims helpline. The air smelled like turpentine and rubber. Dad's breath rattled in his throat.

The doctor sat down and smiled at me with all of his teeth. "Hello, David. I'm Edward." He looked up at Dad. "How can I help you today?" I was distracted by a large plastic duck on his computer stand. It seemed wrong for something so frivolous to be in here.

Dad coughed into his fist. "David's been having some trouble… with things."

"OK?" Edward smiled at me.

"He's pulling away. I've seen this before; I know the signs. I know he's young, but it's happening. And he doesn't talk. Well, he does when he needs to, but the rest of the time he's silent." Dad nudged my arm. "Right, David?" It was the first time Dad had touched me in a long time and I pulled my arm away.

"See? His teachers say that he sits on his own at break times, too."

"Hmmm." Edward turned to his computer and started to type. "I see he was born in…"

"He's ten. Nearly eleven," Dad replied.

"And when did this start?"

"Oh… well, I don't know." Dad rubbed his face. "He's always been that way. I don't remember a time before."

Edward scrolled through reams of information on his screen. His jaw jutted as his eyes moved left and right across the page.

"I do speak," I whispered. "Just not to him."

But Edward kept scrolling as if he hadn't heard. Dad's eyes were on the words flicking up the screen, too quick to read.

"Let's take a look in those ears." Edward picked up what looked like a pointy little hammer and forced it into my ear. It was cold, but strangely soothing. He did it to one ear, then the other, and then asked to look down my throat. Afterwards, he went back to looking at his computer.

"I'm sorry, there's no guidance for treatment this young. It's just not done."

"His mother is petrified. Seeing the numbers on the news every day and fewer and fewer people being found. He walked off last weekend, no one had any idea where he'd gone. We can't keep him under lock and key…"

"What you're concerned about is practically unknown for a child, Mr Porter. The Modern Problem isn't a concern here. Or is there something you're particularly worried about that you haven't shared?"

I locked eyes with Dad for the first time in months. He looked so very, very tired. Inside, I dared him to say it. To admit it. That Grandad disappeared, like those people on the news who transformed into things that were no longer human. The bodies that were found dried out like logs. Or that lay in the grass, twisted with the roots of trees.

"Mr Porter? Is there more to this?"

Dad's eyes fell to his knees and he whispered. "Family history. You should have it in the notes."

Had he just… *admitted it?* I tried to keep listening, but Dad and Edward's voices faded into a distant hum and my head seemed to float from my shoulders. I was there, but not there, and could only take little light breaths as I struggled to stay in the room.

Couldn't they see me falling? Why weren't they looking?

After what felt like a few minutes, I opened my mouth to speak but became aware of Edward turning away to his computer. "Please, take these." He handed Dad a folder of leaflets. "If you're still worried in six months, then come back and we'll talk again, OK?"

Edward started typing at his computer as Dad stared blankly at the brochures. As we left the room and re-joined Mum and Emily, both of whom were looking at Dad quizzically as if asking something with their eyes, I realised that though the appointment was about me, no one had asked me a single question. As we exited the surgery, I couldn't help but quietly click with my tongue.

After we piled into the car, Dad sat in the front seat for a few minutes, his hands wrapped around the steering wheel. Mum didn't say anything either and rummaged blindly in her handbag before tilting the rear-view mirror to face her. A few seconds later, she'd stretched her mouth like a letterbox and was painting it with a violent pink lipstick. My head was still spinning, and the colour made my eyes sore.

"Dad?" Emily's voice was quiet as she combed her hand through her hair. "Are we going to school now?"

Dad didn't turn. "David. Why didn't you speak?"

The car was silent. My head was all in a jumble. Dad had admitted it, right there. He thought I was going to disappear, like someone else in the family. Both Mum and Dad thought it.

"David. Answer me."

I clicked an answer with my tongue and Dad immediately turned in his seat, his hand raised. Mum covered her pink mouth with her hand. "William!"

"Don't you dare answer me like that. Speak, you fucking idiot. What the hell are you?"

"I did speak." I said, quietly. "I did."

Mum pulled Dad back into his seat and he turned to stare out of the car window. We all sat like that for what felt like ages, but maybe it was only a minute. I can't remember that. But what I do remember was that Emily held my hand and it was warm and soft. She was the one to break the silence. "Dad," she said, gingerly. "Maybe we should go now?"

The back of his head nodded and he started the engine. Emily leaned over. "Mum said that they think something's really wrong with you. Is there?" Her eyes squinted and I felt myself shrink.

"No. The doctor said I was fine."

"Did you talk to him?"

"Yeah."

"And?" Emily closed her eyes and tipped back her head. "If you don't want to tell me that's fine. But I can't help you if you don't tell me."

My throat contracted. "No," I whispered. "I'm not hiding anything. Honestly."

Emily shook her head. "For fuck's sake, David," she whispered before letting go of my hand and turning her head to the window. As she committed to watching the world roll by, she rubbed the hand that'd held mine on her trouser leg, as if it was dirty.

After school the next day, as Emily and I headed towards the house from the bus stop, we passed a woman squatting by a pile of dead flowers. Dressed in a long grey coat, she fingered a label on one of the fresher bouquets, a crush of pale pink roses. As she turned to look at us, she sobbed, her face streaked with black. Beneath it, her skin was like white marble, all the veins visible. She looked like a monster. Emily held my hand and pulled me past, but the woman grabbed my coat by the shoulder and thrust a photograph in front of my face. The girl in it looked quite like Emily, but wearing a lot more colours than I'd ever seen Emily in. And there was something about the face that reminded me of a bird, like one of those great grey owls that lock you with a stare. The woman has the same round face, but I could hardly see her eyes beneath all the black pooled there. "Please, please," she said, her voice cracking like ice. "Have you seen Jemima? She was here, walking down this road. I have the report," she held up a crumpled piece of yellow paper. "But it doesn't say where she went."

"He's only ten," Emily spat. "You're scaring him."

"Please, I need to know where to look."

"Sorry." Emily yanked me free of the woman's grip and dragged me down the road. I thought she might follow us, but she didn't. In fact, when I turned to look, she was totally focussed on the browning bouquet again, as if she'd forgotten that we were even there.

"Emily, what are all the flowers for?"

"Gifts, I suppose."

"But they're on more streets aren't they, not just ours?"

"A few. Here and there."

"Why?"

Emily sighed softly. "I think they want their disappeared people to feel that they still love them. Shame they didn't just tell them that before they disappeared."

I turned to look at the woman one last time, as she lay down amongst the flowers, her stained face hidden behind her hands.

8.

I still have this recurring dream. It started around then, when I was ten, after Dad thought a doctor would sort me out. It's always the same. Emily and I are sitting on the rug in Grandad's old living room. The room is dark, other than Grandma's floral armchair. Spread beneath us is one of Grandad's old maps. Emily is trying to tell me something but when she opens her mouth all I hear is white noise. Her face is chalky, and her hair shines, swirling down the front of her like a dripping black candle. I'm flapping my arms, becoming more and more desperate to understand, but she just carries on, regardless. I'm about to grab her fully around the shoulders when I spot Grandad in the floral armchair. He's watching us together, making notes in a brown notebook. He's thin and grey, just how he was when I last saw him, and the hand holding the pen trembles. I leap up and grab his cold wrists but his arms retract and fold across his chest like an insect. He clicks his tongue furiously, but I don't have the Verbatinea, and I can't keep up. Tears in my eyes, I turn back to Emily, who behind me is sprouting black feathers down her back.

The first time I had that dream, I woke up sweating. My pyjamas were on the floor and I shivered in the April air. My arms and legs felt long and awkward, as if each had more joints than they should. Through the window it was still dark, with only the slightest hint of lilac on the horizon. I'd never seen the village this early in the morning. The street looked almost blue, still as stone. But after watching for only a few minutes, I spotted a solitary figure, stooped and heavy, stumbling down our street towards the cow fields. Once or twice he turned his head to look at the rotting offerings in the curb, but he never paused. He walked like his feet hurt him. He walked like everything hurt him.

I took a deep breath and grabbed some clothes from the pile at the bottom of the bed. Still pulling on the jumper, I made my way down the stairs, thinking light thoughts to not set off any creaking.

My heart was racing, but I had to do this. I just had to.

I stepped out onto the street, still in my slippers. The air felt damp on my face, and a thin mist hovered just over the grass. It was so silent that my breath *echoed*, or at least it seemed so to me. The man was at least halfway down the street now, lurching with every step. Keeping my distance, I mirrored his slow trudge, desperately trying to work out what I'd say if he turned around. What had Grandad said to one of them, that time a year or so before when he'd approached one of the mudmen late at night? No one had known I was watching from my bedroom window, that I'd seen Grandad limp across the road to grab him by the shoulder. The man had stopped for a second to look at the map Grandad was flailing, then had given Grandad a strange look that I couldn't understand. It struck me as a look of surprise, but he was biting his lips shut, as if he had to fight to keep silent. Grandad pointed towards the cow fields and then back at the map. Grandad was talking furiously, but the mudman's face didn't shift. He just waited until Grandad stopped talking, then continued walking. Grandad followed him and grasped his shoulder again, but the man shook him off with a huge, bear-like paw. Grandad was left in the middle of the street, watching as the man disappeared through the gap in the fence.

I wouldn't make the same mistake.

By the time the man reached the end of our street, the sky was beginning to break into light blue. How could it take one person so long to reach the end of the street? Everything about him drifted, like he wasn't driving himself at all but instead was moved by the wind. As he reached the broken fence, I braced myself to follow him through the gap, but instead he turned to the left and dragged himself towards the empty pink house on the corner.

Hot breath and a whisper behind my ear. "What are you doing?"

I fell from crouching onto my knees and gripped my chest. It was Emily, wrapped in Mum's brown fluffy coat. Her eyebrows were scrunched up and she looked at me like I was a stranger.

"Go home," I whispered, as forcefully as I could manage.

Emily just shook her head and grabbed my sleeve. "Only if you're coming."

Yanking my arm free, I turned back to track the mudman but he was nowhere. He'd disappeared. "No," I whispered. "No no no no no." I stood up tall and scanned everything for a trace of him. I had only turned away from him for a minute. How had he vanished, just like that?

"Emily, that man. Down there. Where did he go?"

She pouted. "Who?"

"You were looking that way, you must have seen!"

She gave a little shrug. "I didn't see anyone. Who was it?"

I pushed my fists hard into my eye sockets. *This had been my chance, and I'd blown it.*

"Come on." Emily stood beside me. "We'll talk about it at home, all right? Come back before Mum and Dad know you've gone."

Something red hot shot up from my belly. "Why did you follow me? You've spoiled this."

"I saw you from my window," she said, her voice soft. "Creeping along the gardens like a weird little beetle. I waited for you to make your way back but you didn't. So I came to get you."

We were inches from each other when she reached over and pulled me into her chest. One arm around my shoulder and another on my hair. It was warm, and smelled like vanilla. It was like being petted. For a moment I could almost sense the next words she'd say before she shaped them and I recoiled. Emily held out a hand. "Come on. Let's talk to Dad."

I stepped back again. "Why?"

She opened her mouth and closed it again, but nothing came out. Her cheeks were starting to flush. I saw her in a new light then, Emily. She was all colour. Amazing, angry, and blinding, whereas my eyes longed for the earthy shape of the mudman. I couldn't let him go. I needed to know.

And then I turned from my sister and I ran down the centre of the street, not even caring if anyone saw me, because the truth is, I knew no one would be able to. It wasn't that I was invisible, it was more that I didn't matter. When I reached the pink house, I scrambled over the wall and ran up to the black front door to hurl my entire body against it again, and again, and again. But it didn't budge.

"Stop, stop!" Emily was behind me again and pulled me away from the door, "You'll break your shoulder."

"Get OFF me." Everything trembled, like I was made of electricity. My skin tingled where the breeze licked it, and where the dew caught on my ankles. It flashed across my mind that *this must be how an insect feels* – something small enough to feel the world as this huge living thing.

Emily yanked me by my arm and I looked up at the bedroom window, the place I always avoided looking. And in the darkness I saw *her face*, her peach hair trailing down her back. I remember her staring out from the top window, a small bear clutched in her hands, the skin on her arms bone-white, dotted with freckles. I remember the last time I saw her kind face, around two years earlier, following Emily and I with her eyes as we made our way to the bus stop. They were wide and grey, *just like mine*.

"Do you remember her, Emily?" I shouted. "The woman who lived here. She was nice."

"You said you didn't," she whispered.

"What happened to her?"

Emily leaned back but didn't let go of my sleeve. "She just… left."

"But WHERE? Where do they go? Where do any of them go? What's happening?"

"She was sad. They took her to a blue house. She might still be there."

"No… She left. She left like all the people on the posters. She went somewhere."

"She did," Emily's voice slowed right down. "She went to a blue house."

"NO."

"She did. That's what everyone says, anyway. Someone died, and she needed looking after. It's not a mystery."

"She was different. Just like me. Just like Grandad."

"OK."

"They did something…" I was running out of breath, out of momentum. "Something."

"Come on," her soft, vanilla voice in my ear. "Come home now. I won't tell Mum or Dad, if you come now."

"Is Grandad," my voice faded to a crackle, "in a blue house? He was sad too, from Grandma."

Emily gasped and pulled me close, squeezing what little air I had left out through my mouth. "Is that what you think? Oh, Davey, no." I closed my eyes and sank onto her, clinging to the masses of Mum's fluffy coat. "He's dead."

"He isn't. I've seen him," I pulled away and gasped for air. "At the supermarket. I followed him. He disappeared."

"He's dead," Emily rubbed her hand across her lips. "How can you think this? You need to talk to Dad."

"Dad lies. Dad lies." Though we were both still, Emily was becoming smaller and smaller. No longer did her skin warm my skin. She seemed to change shape, into someone bigger and alien. Emily wasn't my Emily. Not now.

"Dad never lies. Dad's still grieving." She reached out her hand. "I saw him crying again last night," whispered Emily, "on the wall outside. You're making everything worse for him."

"I'm not doing anything."

Emily shook her head slowly. "David…" She clasped her face in her hands. "I don't understand you."

And in that split second, I remembered being in Grandad's office, a year or so before, and Emily and I were standing between those wall-mounted mirrors. As I looked left and right, hundreds of Davids spilling out into the distance, my breath caught in my chest. Grandad sat in his chair in front of us, those beetle-black eyes glittering with excitement, saying, "See them? See them? Worlds upon worlds of you, separated by light. Imagine that? And though they look the same, they're not at all."

My chest tightened, though I didn't know what he meant. And beside me, Emily just shrugged and swept her hair back from her face. "But they're all just me, Grandad. They're all just me."

She would never see. Perhaps she couldn't. Emily was exactly where she needed to be, but me... Grandad knew that I was something different. Just like him. Searching for our own kind. We stood out. And perhaps the rest couldn't see that. *We weren't all the same.*

And then it all snapped. What had been soft and safe between Emily and I became a void. She couldn't help me. She wasn't looking for more.

"Please, please come home."

I nodded my head once. "All right. I'll come." Our fingers met, and her hands were cold. Just before we headed across the lawn, I took one hard look through the window next to the front door. On the floor was a dirty red bed roll, and beside it, a scatter of what looked like newspapers. Something brushed against my bare left wrist and I flinched, scratching at the contact spot. It was close to impossible to see in the dim light, but it didn't look bitten. As I kept rubbing it, a burning sensation flushed up towards my elbow like hot running wax, and then just like that, the sensation was gone.

In the corner of the room, something *glittered*. How could

I have known then what I was looking at? Around a foot from the floor, about the size of a football. Something silver, and moving. Turning in a circle. Years later, I described it as like tin foil, being quickly flattened and moulded by hands as dark as the wall behind them. Folding in on itself again, and again, and again.

The house sold not long after that, maybe just a couple of weeks. The buyers knocked most of it down and rebuilt it so it was no longer pink. It sat, grey and square, just like the others on the street, but the windows filled with light. Another grey-haired couple, curtains open, looking out onto the street beyond their TV. Our street was the place where eyes watched, but no one spoke. And by the time winter rolled around and Grandad had been missing for a full year, I still stepped up to the garden wall, peering inside to find that silver slice of air. But the house was alive again, and whatever I'd witnessed had gone.

I was at a dead end. Trapped in a lie. Starting to realise that Grandad hadn't wanted me to know the truth. He'd left me, just like he'd left everyone else. I wasn't special.

Emily was spending more and more time at her theatre group, and I still had nowhere else to go after school, so a couple of nights a week Mum drove me to church with her while she helped Father Patrick. Most of the time, I was happy to hide where no one would talk to me. All I wanted to do was watch, clinging to the walls like moss. And from what I could tell, St Anthony of Padua's volunteers mostly consisted of a bunch of old women who flapped around the priest like chickens. Mum was the youngest of the group, and while there, she always seemed to be dressed in clothes I hadn't seen her in before. She always took her coat off, even when the church was cold enough to make your breath puff out in plumes, to reveal floral dresses that swished at the ankle, and tops with frills around the neck. She normally told me to wait in a pew, so I'd sit in the back corner where it felt dark and damp, running my hands along the cold wood. When Father Patrick walked in with his fluffy black quiff, Mum's eyes became wider and she'd touch her hair over and over. As Christmas approached, Father Patrick often held evening services, so I sat at the back even longer those nights. As the priest spoke, the volunteers all stood in the wings and nodded constantly, like they were in on a secret.

"Hope has power," he bellowed, as if calling to someone at the end of a tunnel. The small group in front of him barely twitched. "How can we use the teachings to rise above our weight? The Modern Problem." He chuckled to himself. "There, I said it. The epidemic. The disappearing. The eloping. The exodus. It touches us all, directly or indirectly. We might have loved ones who've made a difficult decision to cut away from their community, turn away from God. Or we ourselves might have felt the loss of our own selves, or that… dislocation… of heart. The lust to break away from God's path." The congregation shuffled in their seats. He continued, "We might even know someone who is in-between, in a blue house." Someone sniffed towards the back. "But I'm not here to judge sin. Today, we consider the power of optimism through the writings of the Apostle Peter, since he himself is known as the 'Apostle of Hope.'" When he raised his arms, his white cassock rose up a little and revealed his black shoes and black trousers. Underneath, he was just as dark as the rest of us. "Because, family, we all share our garden. Our world. A place of contemplation and nourishment. It is what we make it." Father Douglas cleared his throat. "We all know someone who has made a problematic choice. Those who live in God's light and grace can't know what makes our friends choose the dark path, but dark times could be ahead of us all, if we give way to temptation."

Above Father Patrick's head, a streetlamp illuminated the stained glass. A white dove carrying a twig. Flying from fire. The congregation hummed like wasps. A few pews ahead of me, a woman in a blue coat bounced a toddler on her knee. He was already asleep, but she kept jiggling him mercilessly, causing his head to loll about. *How couldn't she see?*

The priest's words and the volunteers' mindless nodding was making me sick, so I stood up, grabbed my bag, and crept from the pew out into the night. The thick layer of white that'd made everything clean was starting to drip from the roof, and the path in front of the church was now slushy and muddy with footprints. I shivered and breathed in as deeply as I could, savouring the metallic sting of the evening air in my nostrils. It smelled far better than the damp inside the church. Everything there felt like Father Patrick.

Slinging my bag across my back, I strode towards the light of the library. The front door was a mosaic of faces now, competing for space. They looked younger than the last time I'd seen them. I flung open the door and strode past the blue-spectacled woman at reception, who muttered, "We close at six," without even looking up.

Like last time, there were mudmen sitting one to a table, each of them intent on an open book or a faded print-out. Some traced lines of text with their eyes and fingers. But this time there were far fewer than before, only four of them. But still, at the sight of those four, warmth rushed through my arms, right down to my fingertips. When I reached the nearest occupied table, I tapped the man seated there on the shoulder. His hair was long and matted, the ends twisting past his shoulders. His beard and moustache were so dense that I could hardly see the face beneath, but what skin I did see looked red and ruddy. Every inch of him, skin and cloth, looked smeared with a layer of dirt. He breathed loud through his nose, quicker and quicker, as if building up to something. In his hand he clasped a book, and I could just about make out a drawing of a bird with a long tail that curled around its tapered body in a circle.

The man froze. He didn't even appear to be breathing. But I was satisfied of one thing at least: he was flesh and bone. Warm and alive.

"Please," I whispered. "Please."

The man's broad hands spread over the diagram in front of him. His fingernails were chewed down to stubs. A groan erupted from his throat and a rotten smell plumed up towards my face.

"Where are you going? Tell me," I pleaded.

The man squeezed his eyes shut and then – *and I swear I'm remembering this right* – he growled. Low and rumbling, like a dog ready to attack. I took a couple of steps back, and as I did so I whispered, "Please, please." But the man didn't turn, just rattled and groaned like a ship at sea. I fought the urge to grab his hair, to shake him, to show him how much I needed the truth. My teeth clenched as tears flooded my eyes. I stood there, shaking, choking, finding it harder and harder to take a breath. Inside, I screamed, 'Someone, help me.'

"Home, boy. We're going home."

A tap on my forearm, and I turned to look right into the eyes of another of the mudmen. This one had a shaved head, painted with tattoos. His skin was so thin that it looked blue, and his eyes were as black as ink. Almost without realising, I was counting the blue veins running from his temples down to his throat. He looked at me like he knew me.

"We're going home."

That night, I watched out of my bedroom window for Dad leaving the house. As I waited, a strange noise, like static, rose slowly in my ears and the same itching sensation I'd felt in the pink house tickled my left wrist. This time, there was enough light from my bedside lamp to see what was happening. I peeled back my sleeve, expecting to see a red rash or white bump from an insect's sting. But my wrist looked entirely normal. I was rubbing it when – at a little after nine o'clock – Dad stumbled down our path and onto the street, heading in the direction of the cow fields. His hands were shoved deep into the pockets of his black jacket, a tight grey hat pulled low over his ears.

Already in my coat and shoes, I crept out after him, clinging to our neighbours' dark walls. When he reached the broken fence posts at the end of the street he paused for a moment, gripping the splintered wood in his gloved hands. I held my breath, willing him to take a step – pushing him to. But after a minute or so, he turned to the left and staggered around the newly grey house and down the lamplit street. I kept my distance, thinking like a cat. But suddenly the pavement jolted. Or was it me that did? Keeping up with Dad seemed to take all my concentration as I staggered side to side. My knee and ankle joints were too soft, and buckled beneath me with each step. What was going on? I dragged my palm along a fence for stability as I kept going. After a minute or so, the sensation passed and I was strong enough to stand on my own again. A few deep breaths and I carried on.

I must have followed him for almost an hour as he slowly meandered through the village, his face turned to the ground. Occasionally he paused at a corner to lean on a wall or a lamppost. I kept to the fences and the bushes, ready to hold on if my legs were to go again.

Eventually, he turned a corner again and I realised that he had effectively been walking home all along, but he'd taken the most ridiculously long route. When we reached our front gate, he closed it behind him before I got there. Not caring anymore, I forced it back open again with a loud and angry creak. Dad turned on the doorstep, his eyes small and dark.

"Oh, you," he said. "Why were you following me?"

I didn't say anything. What could I have said? Sheer desperation?

"What do you want, David? I'm just getting some air. If you wanted to come with me, you just had to ask. Why are you creeping? Why are you like this?"

I clung to the bushes. There was nothing to say. He hadn't been going anywhere, after all. I was wrong.

"God, David. How are you going to get anywhere in the world," he muttered, "or be anyone, if you don't fucking speak? What are you? Crawling around with your books on beetles and dark things that live under stones. Why can't you just be normal, for once?" He stared at me for a long minute before unlocking the door. Finally, he snarled, "I give up. I suppose you should come in, then."

He turned and walked into the house, and without thinking I followed him into the darkness.

Once inside, there was only one thing I wanted to do. I was shaking, and my fingers – too long, and too wrong – fumbled with the black book. Right in front of me, my hands became these huge white spiders, grasping at the cover. I closed my eyes and sobbed. *I wasn't right. I wasn't supposed to be here.* Dad had silenced Grandad's last words to me by taking that letter he'd left for me. And now it was my turn to do the same.

I took the Verbatinea, *our dead language*, and plunged it deep into the kitchen bin with the rest of the rubbish.

That look. Why won't you catch my eye? Is it my honesty that makes your skin crawl or is it what you see when you look at me? *I dare you.*

Look at me.

AFTER

~

The air in the mountain slicks down my throat like soup. Despite the candle, I can't see a thing. Its flickers don't even touch the sides.

After entering the cave, I'd been squeezed through the narrow passage almost by peristalsis. Too narrow to turn around, the sheer need to breathe draws me forwards. After a few minutes of bent-double staggering, the tunnel opens up so that I can stretch my arms above my head. When I cough, it echoes four times. I try to speak again, this time a whispered, "I'm here," in case anyone can hear me. But nothing comes out but a croak, and there is no reply.

Perhaps the woman was a trick of the darkness? Like a child seeing creatures in the night? And even though I'd wanted it to be *him* so much, it hadn't looked anything like him. No. It must have just been a trick. Michael did say to be on guard.

Hunching over hasn't helped my back much, because trying to straighten up is agonising. I try rolling my shoulders up and back, but something crunches deep inside. Being in a wider cave space also means that I don't quite know where I should be going. Unless I hold the candle down by my knees I can't even see where to put my feet. For all I know I could be walking straight into an empty void.

I think back to Michael. Did he ever say anything about what the doorway would look like? You know, I don't think he had, really. He told me what he told all the delegates: look for a space that looks normal, but shimmers. But when it's dark, how can I see what might shine under the light?

I sense a draught on the nape of my neck, and I whip my head around and hold up the candle.

Nothing.

I release the breath I was holding and lower the flame. I'd know if I'd been followed in here. I'd feel it.

I move forwards a few paces. My right foot feels odd in my shoe, as if it's turning slightly inwards. Between each of my steps, there's a strange shuffling sound like something heavy being dragged across a carpet, but as soon as I move it goes silent again.

I hate this world.

The wind picks up and the candle flickers and goes out. Fuck. I pull out the two remaining matches and strike the second. The flame is brought back to life and illuminates a wall of stone crawling with beetles only a few feet ahead of me. Their shells are all mottled with different patterns: some as black as oil, and others light as peaches, their backs marked with outlines of disordered faces, eyes slitted, mouths agape. Each beetle could easily be the size of my palm, and as I hold up the light they swim away and into the cracks. I stumble backwards and there's a crunch beneath my left heel. The ground is reeling with beetles running in all directions in a panic. I circle myself, brandishing the candle like a sword, and in a few seconds, they're gone and I'm alone again.

No.

The wall. It's not a wall at all. It's a pile of boulders, as if there's been an avalanche. I don't know what I expect to happen, but I push at one of the smaller stones with my free hand. Unsurprisingly, it doesn't budge.

This can't be happening.

I wedge the candle in a gap and try to prise the wall apart, piece by piece. Some of the smaller stones fall away, but whenever one does, a beetle wriggles from the hole and I have to fight the urge to leap back. It's not that I'm scared, as such; it's just that there's no way of telling which world these creatures are from. If the door is behind here, how do I know that these are even earth-born? What if they're poisonous? Beneath the crumbling outer stones is a wall of rock, so dense and unmoving that it could be a painting of itself. There are no signs of bigger gaps here, and I can't for the life of me work out where the beetles are even coming from.

There isn't much left of the candle now, just a tiny wick floating in a puddle. I won't be able to do anything when I can't see my hand in front of my face. I press my hands over my ears and think. Is this the wrong tunnel? Could there have been another? No… I'd assessed the mountain high and low. There was only one way in and I'd followed the path, as straight as I could. Perhaps the avalanche happened when one of the previous delegates passed through the doorway? Maybe there was a burst of energy, and it caused the walls to crumble. I rest my hands flat on the rock. What if there's a body here with me, crushed beneath all this earth?

Why, why didn't I bring the three candles? Why did I bring just one?

In desperation, I pull at a stone about the size of a breadbin, and to my surprise it comes loose and tumbles to the ground. But this time from the hole something pink and naked squirms as if desperate to escape. I stumble back, and as my ankle buckles under my weight, I go down, soon followed by the twitching, jerking, tumbling thing that flaps its limbs and lands with a soft thump by my shoe. It gasps and gurgles before flipping itself over in an attempt to find its feet.

What... is it?

I can't place it. There's a white beak and little flaps on either side of its body that might've been wings if they'd had feathers. Its head ducks and weaves as if it can't see, its eyes glinting like little beads of jet, swaying drunkenly. Even when it uprights itself, its spindly, twisted legs can't support its bulbous body and it flops face down again and again. But the worst thing – something I only understand when it stretches up its head to find the light – is the knot tied in its long and stringy neck.

I press my fist to my mouth to stifle my cry. I don't want to look at it, but I can't even blink. How is it even alive? It subverts nature. What's happened to it? If there's no one else here... did it do that to itself? Was it born tied? Did it twist as it grew? Or did something happen to it to choke it?

It's only inches from my foot now. Too weak to move, it raises its small flaps, looks up to the ceiling and calls out with a sound that's rasping and despairing. The cry doesn't echo; it just lifts up into the ether and disappears. I'm now sure it's a bird, but plucked of anything that would make it recognisable. Its head flips from side to side, dragging its beak across the floor, and every second that goes by it desperately tries to draw in breath through that cruel pulsing knot.

Without thinking, I kick out my foot and crush the creature to the rock, before staggering back towards the tunnel and the light.

***

What the fuck is happening?

I don't know how long it took to reach the cabin from the mountain; I'd descended the rocks more by falling than climbing, and despite the failing light I managed to navigate the trail back to where I'd started, dragging my right leg behind me like dead wood. By the time I close the cabin door, the sky is a deep mahogany and the forest canopy is singing in the rising gale of black fluttering things. Once inside, I push the desk against the door and collapse back onto the bed. I press my face into the straw mattress and the scent of woodsmoke floods my lungs.

Had I killed it? Is it dead?

I want it to be dead. My hands are shaking, so I grip each opposite elbow. Buy why? Was it only because it was suffering? No. Something else. Where had the urge come from? I had lashed out without thinking of anything other than how the thing disgusted me. My head swims and I can't think. I don't want to.

What if it isn't dead, and I've only made it worse?

Just then, the constant throb in my shoulder blades bursts into white hot pain that shoots through my back. I grind my teeth and wait it out but it doesn't fade; it just grows and grows until even my bones are shaking, *breaking*. I want to scream but even gasping makes me gag, and my heart beats so forcefully that it could burst from my chest.

What have I done?

I yank my jumper over my head and turn to see what's happening to me but the pain in my neck means I can't turn to look, and my arms are too stiff to even inspect the damage. I don't know what to do. I'm terrified to lie back on what could be an open wound, but I'm so, so tired. I inspect the back of the orange jumper for blood or holes but there's nothing to explain the pain, though the knit is stretched oddly out of shape and the weave is so strained that you can see through the knots.

I wait until the pain recedes to a constant throb. *What am I going to do?* Was the door definitely behind the wall? Was I even in the right place? *Is this Mothtown?* It matched the map Michael showed me – the mountain with the two side peaks. The valley with the stream. But Michael has said explicitly that the mountain was where I needed to go. "Up there," he'd said, one hand pinching his pointed chin. "I don't know what it looks like, but look for a space that shimmers. Silver-like. To some it's like tin foil, but translucent. Things will feel... different. Fundamental forces don't work quite the same in that spot. And no one that's ever gone to Mothtown," – he gives me a side-look – "even the particular gentleman that you're interested in, has ever come back. So these directions are true."

But the way is blocked. It couldn't have just happened; the stones looked like they'd been piled that way for years. The dust had settled. Was there anything else? I once asked Michael if there was a chance that I might not find the door at all, but he'd just replied with, "If you've got this far, you've got this far by listening. Whatever happens to you out there will depend on how much you've learned and how much you've listened." His fingers met in front of his face in a temple shape. "Now, can you tell me what you've learned?"

Hot fury twists in the centre of me. Talk, talk, that's all he ever wanted to do. Why didn't he ever *do* anything? He raised more questions than answers, and what good has that done me? The more I trawl back through everything he did and said, the more I get confused about even the basic things.

Hopelessly, I cry. There's no sound now, but my mouth is wide as if I'm screaming. The windows rattle with the sounds of night, and as I look up, I finally see what the darkness is truly made of.

Moths.

Pressed flat against the windows like two palms unfolded, mottled with light and dark symbols like runes. Their bodies are the size of cigars and coated in a thick, bristly fur, and their long flicking appendages tongue the glass. They pound the glass with dull thumps, and soon they're layering on top of each other, all blending into a wall of woody bark blotting out the stars. They quiver and shake as they're crushed, and just before everything goes dark, I catch a glimpse of their faces – almost human, with glaring eyes and mouths open wide and round in terror.

Is this a tree? Am I in a tree?

I only have two candles left on the desk; but should I use one when I can't see any other option but to try the mountain again? And there's only one match left, anyway. As I rise, I catch a new sound – dry, like paper on paper. Slithering on the floor is an enormous snake, sluggishly dragging its weight towards me. I swing my legs onto the bed as it approaches, my hands grasping at the straw. A beam of light from the window catches it and I see it's not actually a snake at all, but a bulbous worm without eyes or mouth. Its body ridged and sickly purple like a fading bruise and flailing at each pulsing end like a fish out of water.

I have nothing to use to force it back if it comes closer, and just as I'm pulling up straw in a pathetic attempt to fight it off, it turns, its head-end jabbing the air like a tentative paw, and twists its body towards the cupboard door and squeezes beneath it.

SLAM.

Above and behind me, the window cracks. A slender white hand is pressed to the glass, and further back, a still white face floats like a moon, obscured almost completely by the swarm.

BEFORE

9.

Are you still there? Are you still listening to me? I can't tell, you're so quiet.

Are you sure you want me to keep talking? Is there any benefit to this? I'm not sure I'm seeing what you're seeing. On the surface, things look different, but the roots are the same – just deeper and more tangled. It's only when something bad happens we remember to hold ourselves tightly, to count our fingers, our toes. To regard the machine that gets us from A to B. To finally make the call to break the machine.

But the rest of the time, it's easier to close our eyes and keep quiet.

One thing Grandad never told me, despite his specialisms, was that keeping quiet and routine speeds up time. Routine became my friend. When every day becomes a dance of repetition, soon you're switching on autopilot more than you're not. You're barely there, until one day the light switches on and you wonder how the hell you got to where you are.

I remember that happening one morning not all that long ago. This is years after I had followed Dad into the dark. I was behind the counter at Flynn's, waiting for Paul to release me for lunch. My back ached from leaning over the desk. Too low. Always too low. The world felt too low. Even Paul was too low, the top of his head polished like a pool ball, looking up at me with beady eyes behind thick, black-rimmed glasses. He moved around the shop like a prairie dog, snuffling, his arms and hands pinned close to his body. Paul used me to reach the instruments on the highest shelves, the sheet music from the back of the racks. If a keyboard or clarinet needed bringing down from the shelves in the stockroom, that was my job. I'm not a giant, barely six-foot-six, but you'd have thought that I was an alien creature sent to Paul to help him through his daily challenges. When I stood behind the desk, he'd habitually loiter a few feet behind me by the entrance to the stockroom, shaking his head and muttering under his breath. Often, he flustered over words as if searching for something in the back of his head. "Was it Rose? Or Rosemary? Myrtle... Petal..." So often, it was flowers, but sometimes it was other things. "A green cardigan... Yes. Yellow cardigan? Loose threads. And clementines. Citrus-y. Yes. No. Cedarwood."

He never seemed to want a reply, so I never gave him one, and that was the way we worked together. It worked because I accepted that Paul made no sense. It worked because when the customers walked up to the desk and stood there in silence, their mouths opening and closing like guppies in a tank, he knew where to direct them. Sometimes it was percussion. Sometimes it was woodwind. They'd follow him blindly, their arms wrapped around their middles like they were anchoring themselves to the ground. I'd often see them touching Paul on the arm, or side, just for a second, checking that they and he were both there. Like a little prod. Either Paul didn't notice or he didn't mind, because he never said anything. A few minutes of pointing at various easy-to-play instruments and the customers would leave as silently as they'd entered, all of them clutching a paper bag to their chests like a replacement organ.

I'd worked at Paul Flynn's Fine Instruments for eight years, ever since leaving school at eighteen. Emily had moved to London years before, and Mum and Dad's house was dead. I needed out, and I needed something to do, and compared to the bright and unnatural light I faced out there in the world, Flynn's seemed safe and dark. It reminded me of one of those saloons with a swing door in an old Western. Set into a corner of the fading shopping arcade in Melton Wark, hardly anyone went in or out. So specialised, the shop seemed, that it was one of those places that you felt might be a front for something else. And that made me strangely comfortable, the fact that the face was so obviously distinct from its innards – and its smell. It reminded me of the library next to St Anthony's: musty and warm, a nest of pages and old things passed through many hands.

I think Paul kept me because I didn't complain, and because I followed every rule to the letter. I liked to write things down, from how to work the till to how to roll the stockroom racks. I used my little black book that I kept with me all the time. The look on his face when I wrote something down told me that he liked me doing it. So I kept doing it, and despite my total inability to learn anything about music, he kept me on. And so, I'd fallen into quiet and routine, and the years passed like one long day. Rare as they were, I liked watching the customers, particularly the ones who knew what they were doing. You could tell that they did, because they would never ask anything; they'd just pick up an instrument and start tuning. Of course, if they were actual musicians and asked anything I'd have to go and retrieve Paul from the back office to help them. They spoke in code, and then when I'd stare back blankly they would just repeat the same thing over and over, completely unable to translate it for me. But Paul spoke their language, and only sometimes would I catch him looking over his shoulder at me with a look that said, "Why are you here?"

I couldn't blame him, really. He was one of the few people I'd ever met who didn't seem at all concerned about disappearing. You'd never see him gripping the walls, pulling his ears, or turning to me and saying the words you often heard on the street: "You can see me? You can see me?" The shop was an extension of his body.

Of course there were other types of customers too, ones who were just as solid as Paul. They'd usually come in to Flynn's on their own, heading directly for their area of interest, be it spare keys and strings, vintage music scores, or anything else. They were on a mission. But my favourite thing to do there was to watch the musicians who came in in pairs or small groups. They'd gather around the sheet music or instrument and chirp together like little birds. Sometimes they'd choose a couple of the store instruments to test something out. It seemed like magic, how they could listen and play at the same time. I couldn't work it out. Customers who shimmered like drizzle on glass would darken and settle as they harmonised. Paul didn't seem to notice this, and he would usually look annoyed as they played, occasionally tutting and muttering, "Too loud, too loud." When the shop was empty, I'd sometimes leaf through the racks of sheet music, old and new, to see if I could understand that magic. But as always, none of it made sense, and it left me cold.

That morning, Paul's voice called from the back office, "Half an hour, David."

I straightened my back from leaning over the desk and pulled my sleeve down over that old familiar itch irritating my wrist. I left the shop with just a blue carrier bag in my hand. I had a routine, a route, a ritual. I'd kept to it all year. But first, I'd see if Agatha was there. The shopping arcade was mostly empty other than a small queue outside a pastry shop. I headed that way and then stood by the bins, craning my head this way and that to see if Agatha was hiding behind a stand of sketchbooks or paints. Usually her purple hair was visible from here, no matter where she stood. But not today. The man behind the desk, a wide, red-headed man with no neck caught my eye and started towards me, but I wasn't in the mood to talk to anyone other than Agatha. I imagined her fingertips grazing my arm, just below the wrist. Her squeezing my leg and moving her hand up there. And when she opened her mouth, she sounded like a violin, low and purring.

Agatha.

She was just like music, you know. From the first time we met, we harmonised. It'd been about a year and a half before. I was waiting for my bus home from work, watching a street performer who'd set up a little folding stool quite close to me. He sat on it, staring into the road, and every time a car went past he'd raise his left arm and let out a cry. His face was dusted pure white and his hair was slicked back with black paste. His arms were bare and painted electric blue. I clutched my bag across my chest, and every time he yelled my heart squeezed. Agatha was heading towards us from the arcade. Her hair was liquid black in those days, and she wore an ankle-length leather coat. For a second I thought it was Emily, from when we were young and she wore a curtain of black every day. Her eyes were fixed on the performer until she looked at me and my head exploded. She gave me this perfect little smile, all eyes and full cheeks. And you know what? I smiled back. It just happened, I didn't even need to think about it. It was that right.

As she got close to me, she whispered, "I hope he doesn't jump out on the road. I won't look."

Answering her came as naturally as the smile. "He won't. He's here every week."

Her cheeks squeezed, and a rush of air gushed from her lips. I'd made her happy, I think.

"He looks like a magpie," she whispered. And she was right. I'd never thought about it before, but he did look like a magpie. How hadn't I seen it? How?

The important thing was that she'd noticed.

"I actually like his hair," she smirked. "I love birds." As she passed me, the back of her hand, the one clutching her bag strap, brushed against my arm. For a moment we stuck together, skin to skin. It stung when she pulled away. "Oh, sorry," she laughed as she rubbed her knuckles.

I tried to laugh back, but I must have done something wrong because she gave me an odd look and then kept on walking down the street.

Hair like black liquorice.

Immediately after that, I went home to Mum and Dad's and locked my bedroom door. My bed, shelves, books, and experiments... They all looked alien now. Smaller. Pathetic. Childish. Importance had transformed into impotence. That tiny conversation with Agatha had changed the world. She was real, something none of this stuff had ever been. How long had I wasted here, holed up in a childhood bedroom, reading books and dreaming?

A rush of red clouded the room and I was tearing through it, shoving books into my waste paper bin, sweeping up spidery sketches of bones and wings and cross-sections of pregnant eggs and throwing them into a plastic bag. Finally, I opened the wooden box hidden in my wardrobe. Inside lay a silk cigar, just like the one Grandad had kept in a case in his office. I'd found it on the ground outside the house, as if it'd fallen from the sky. I'd read a lot about chrysalises by this point, so at first it seemed the right thing to do to find a shady tree and hang it back up. But I couldn't bring myself to do it, so I'd stored it in my room, thinking that it was most likely dead, and I could study it. But the day I met Agatha, I opened the box and the egg was broken, split, torn in two. It rolled around in the box, lost. When I looked back up, there it was: a ringlet butterfly, soft and gentle black on dust, edged with electric white. Its wings lay flat against the wall, and it stared at me with ten glaring eyes across its spread. They were Grandad's eyes, all of them. I covered my face with my hands. It was all dreams and escapism, all of it... but not this. It was a sign that it was time for me to make a change. Time for me to use what I'd learned. All this time, I'd thought the thing in the box to be dead, but it had just been waiting to be freed.

Back at the music shop, I walked out of the shopping arcade into heavy November rain, the kind that falls straight like ball bearings. Despite the fact that it was barely midday, it was almost dark, and the street was already a little river. I was only wearing a t-shirt and jeans, but that was OK.

The cold meant something great was approaching, and the icy whip of wind thrilled me.

I strode down the street, left at the corner by the doctor's surgery, and around to the cemetery entrance not even feeling the rain at all. My legs bent at odd angles, and it jarred to walk. The few people walking along the street were all alone, dark hoods pulled low over their eyes, only their chins illuminated above the glare of their phones. And as ever, there was someone standing in front of one of the derelict shops, speaking to the empty street. That day there was just one, but sometimes there were three or four, all of them projecting over each other. They weren't doing it for the money, no cap or case lay in front of them. Some clutched a whistle or cornet as if it was the first time they'd held it, chugging out a few basic notes over and over, their faces red and strained with the effort of playing. Some looked like they'd walked straight out of an office after a stressful day, with their shirt untucked and tie askew. Some still wore aprons with restaurant logos on them. Once or twice I'd seen one of Paul's silent customers playing their instruments on a street corner or park bench. Always tuneless. Always desperate. Ever-frustrated with their inability to create something beautiful. Lately, their acts had been getting even more diverse. Some hummed a monotone or muttered childish nursery rhymes, their eyes focussed on something only they could see. Some read tonelessly from poetry books, or even, on one occasion, a *Woman's Weekly* magazine. And then on days like that day, they were just... talking. Sometimes crying, "Can you hear me? Are you listening? Show me you're listening."

The woman stood beside two wheelie bins, which were parked in front of the papered-over shop window like black teeth. She was wearing a pink dressing gown which reached the top of a pair of slippers shaped like white rabbits, their fur soaked by street water. Behind her was a huge poster showing two old people sitting side-by-side on a sofa, leaning into each other and laughing. Each clasped a cup of tea as if it was the funniest thing in the world. Above their heads in white lettering: 'Solve the Modern Problem with an old-fashioned remedy.' This struck me as something clever, but I was confused about what they actually meant. An old-fashioned remedy? What was that meant to be? Tea?

The woman had her hands hidden deep in her sleeves and swayed a little to a steady rhythm. I avoided looking at her directly as I passed by, but I did notice she had her eyes squeezed shut, so I took the opportunity to watch her lips as she spoke. As they moved, I pretended she was speaking to me, and it made me smile. "…Do you know? Do you know? She held my hand and that was it. My hand. My hand. It felt like hot oil. My hand." The woman cupped her hands up in the air, as if catching rain. "They're wet and cold now, wet and cold. Twigs. Twigs. Tw-igs."

Her voice faded into the rush of the rain behind me. The high street smelled of sweat and petrol, but I was used to this now. The smell burned my nostrils, but it meant freedom. Walking meant I wasn't tethered. That with every step I might encounter a new thing. A change.

From the high street, I glanced up and over the wall to the top of the shopping centre, listening intently, but only for a minute before doing a round of the cemetery itself. Even though it'd been sixteen years, it hadn't changed all that much since I was ten. The trees still bloomed with their cherry blossom for a week in spring, the willows still hung low like hair, draping across the stones. The Garden of Exodus was a blue river now, running along the perimeter wall, but the blue was marbled by golden rot. Like Mum and Dad's street, there were fewer and fewer new offerings these days, and if there were any, they got lost on the piles of decaying bouquets never removed from the grass. The forget-me-nots that had sprouted from the earth were now buried beneath mountains of plastic, peeling photographs, and mud.

I didn't spend long there; I only had half an hour to do my circuit, after all. Above my head, the branches were shedding their leaves like dead butterflies. I watched as a man in an ugly hi-vis jacket swept these browning wings up into rotting piles like things forgotten, things to be brushed away. These were the mounds I would scavenge for skins, bones, and tissues. But not right now. Not until I was alone with them.

I kept walking.

The crypt, where I'd seen the chrysalis and been swarmed by flies, was now inaccessible, bolted closed behind a chained gate. It didn't matter. I could now see it for what it was, and it was nothing more than old stone. Like everything else in the cemetery, it was dead. Every few feet, I'd pause and scoop a few handfuls of rotting leaves and place them carefully in my carrier bag. It was getting harder now to find the right type, but even winter wasn't going to stop me.

Grandma's grave was the final stop on that walk. The plot, which had been beautifully dug out and planted with pansies and heather, was now covered by a stretch of grass like all the others in the row. The grate at the headstone was empty again today. I marked that in my little black notebook and then left the cemetery through the little back entrance, which took me back to the shopping arcade. As I dropped the notebook back into my bag, I spotted a soft mound pressed into the corner where the cemetery wall met the gate. The man in the yellow jacket was nowhere to be seen. At first, I thought that the lump was just moss, but when I leaned closer I noticed the tail, like a long grey worm missing the tip. Using an old tissue, I picked up the lump of mouse and dropped it in the carrier bag.

And there was that sensation again in my legs: butter soft joints, weak like walking on daisy stalks. I reached for the wall to steady myself and leaned against it with both hands. It had been happening more and more, that loosening. It'd begun that night I'd followed Dad as a child, and it had come and gone randomly ever since. It wasn't consistent enough to ever do anything about it, so I'd just clench my jaw and wait for it to pass. It didn't exactly hurt, but for a minute or two I was entirely fluid inside my skin, only holding myself up by my fingers. Claws in the mortar.

Finally, it passed, and I could stand independently again. Just as I set off, my phone vibrated in my pocket. As 'Mum' flashed across the screen I debated whether or not to answer it, to pretend that my lunch break was already over. But then I could see in the top corner that she'd already called me several times that day, and there was probably a limit to how long I could avoid her.

"David, David, have you heard from Emily?" Mum's voice was dry, desperate.

"When?"

"Today. Today. She hasn't called. She was meant to call and she hasn't. Please. Please. Have you heard from her?"

"No, Mum."

"Call her for me. Call her. I need to keep the line free in case she calls. She's three hours late, she's never late like this. What if, what if…" Her voice crackled and she began to breathe heavily into the handset. It sounded like her medication wasn't working this time.

"She'll be fine, Mum. She does this every time. Is Dad there?"

"No, no, he's away on one of his walks with the ramblers. He's miles away. I can't take it, David. I can't take it. I've already tried to ring Jed." Now, that made me pause. Emily was late for her scheduled check-ins with Mum a lot, usually blaming work or the London Tube, so Mum wouldn't usually go as far as calling Jed. But then again, Dad was usually there. He accepted Emily's lateness and Mum's collapsing outwards as a part of life. I'd been at the house when Mum spiralled before, and Dad would just sit her down and hold her, wrapping her tight in his silence. She'd twist and push away at first, but he held her there with all his physicality until she softened, sobbing into his shoulder. And then, usually a few minutes later, the phone would ring. And it'd be Emily, like magic.

Down the phone, Mum wailed. A hollow sound like a whale in the deep of the ocean. Or a wild dog, howling down a long tunnel. Even there, a town away from her I could feel it pulsing through the ground. I turned my face to the exterior brick wall of the shopping arcade, moving one hand to my mouth so I could continue to chew the nail of my index finger down as far as it'd go. In my head, as I'd done for years, I began *the clicks*. Around me, rain battered the pavement like white noise. Looking down, it looked like it was hitting the ground through my trainers.

"Noooo, David, stop, please. That noise. Are you listening? Are you listening to me?"

At first, I had no idea what she meant by that. But then, of course… How could I not?

"Ring her, ring her please, David. Find her." This was followed by a yelp, and sobs. I could just about make out Mum mumbling, "Bosey hurt me, William. He hurt me." It was as if she was hoping he could hear her, out in the fields. And as for Bosey, I didn't know what else she expected. She had taken Bosey in a few years earlier – a thin ginger tom she'd coaxed in from the back yard and hadn't let go. His forehead was split down the centre by a bald scar, and he only had three whiskers on one side of his face. He didn't like to be touched, and would slowly roam the corridors and landings like a prison warden on duty. Doorframes were scored with scratches from hip-height down, and Bosey's fur coated the carpets, turning the deep navy blue in the living room to a dull grey. Wooden litter lay permanently strewn across the kitchen floor where he'd kicked it from the tray and Mum hadn't cleaned it up. Downstairs started to smell different, like talcum powder. Every room began to make mine and Dad's noses itch and our throats sore, but Mum kept trying to lure Bosey up onto the sofas and beds, her smile more desperate as the years passed.

I put the phone back in my pocket and leaned on the lamppost beside me. My chest felt... odd. Like it was being squeezed, or like my ribs were too small for what they contained. I trained my eyes on the lamppost as I breathed in and out, in and out. Slowly, the faces pasted all over it became clear again – as clear as they could be, anyway. Though the lamppost was almost entirely covered in 'missing' posters, none were new. All had yellowed, peeled, faded.

Could she really be missing this time?

No. No. Not Emily. That truth didn't suit her. That wasn't something she would do. No. Where would she go? Besides, it didn't happen so much these days. You only ever heard about the mass disappearances on the news. Suddenly, Emily's face seized my mind, her eyes wide and her mouth twisted as she looked down at me, kneeling on the green carpet in Dad's office. I groaned and shook her from me like dust. *No. No. I didn't want to remember that. Not now.*

As I stood with the lamppost in my grip, one of the pasted-up posters caught my eye, and my teeth clenched. It was an old one, a very old one. I leaned in closer to inspect the wan and wrinkly face. The text on the poster was indistinguishable, the ink having run and run and run. And the photograph, crudely printed, was hardly more than a ghost, but still…

The light went on.

It looked like *him*. I traced the outline with my fingertips. I hadn't thought about him for so long. It still hurt. It still made my stomach twist. I held my face so close to his that our noses almost touched. The resemblance was uncanny. *Was it him?* Had I been passing him every day on my lunch breaks and never noticed? I imagined bringing Dad here, making him face the poster of his own father. What would he say then?

I hadn't heard Grandad mentioned in his presence for years. Not since I was about twelve, so two years after Grandad disappeared. It was the summer before Emily was leaving for university in London, and she was always coming into my bedroom, asking me to come downstairs or out for a walk. I can only imagine she was trying to make the most of things before leaving. One night, Emily and I were watching a TV film together. She'd picked a fantasy with strange monsters and labyrinths. There was a bowl of popcorn between us on the sofa, and Mum and Dad were upstairs. They had been shouting, but now all I could hear in the quiet moments of the film were rustling sounds and the odd bang, as if they were moving furniture around. I hoped they weren't in my room.

During one of those quiet spells, Emily wiggled her fingers in the popcorn bowl to make it crackle. "Did Mum tell you I'm bringing Neil home tomorrow? For tea."

I sighed and kept staring at the TV, confused as to why she'd think I'd find this interesting.

"It'd be nice if you'd make an effort with him. He said you blanked him this morning at the corner shop, when he tried to say hello."

"No, I didn't." I thought back and was sure this'd never happened. In fact, I could only remember the back of Neil's head. His stupid little ponytail.

"Davey, you were rude. You need to try harder."

"I wasn't rude. He never spoke to me. I don't even know what he looks like up close."

"Don't lie. He was hurt. He didn't say so and he wouldn't say so, but he would be hurt."

"I didn't do anything to him!"

Emily let out an exasperated groan and flung her head back into the cushions. "Get a grip, David. I'm not going to be here much longer, and you can't always have everything your own way."

How could she say that? What exactly was meant to go my way? I reached into the bowl, deep below the light, sweet bits of fluff to the marble-like kernels ringing at the bottom of the bowl. Emily's hand was a dog's jaw around my wrist.

"Listen to us, David. Listen to us."

I tried to ignore that familiar burn up my arm. "*I do listen. Why does everyone keep saying that?*"

Emily released me and rubbed her forehead. I focussed on

the TV again and the adverts flicking by. Exercise machines, disinfectant, job centres, the Samaritans.

"When are you going to bring some little squirt home for me to be all nicey-nice to, anyway?"

I couldn't think of anything worse.

"Please, pleeeeeease bring a friend back so we know you're not a sociopath. We'd all be so relieved." Her voice was light, but had an edge to it. She grinned. I think she was joking. "Though, you'd have to tidy up your room first. What was all that stuff on your chest of drawers?"

She'd been in my room. "What… stuff?"

"The black stuff. Looked like soil or something. It smelled smoky."

I shook my head and stared at the screen. It had just been a test. Something inspired by my book on hibernation. I'd been trying to make a nest for a field mouse I'd found by the cow fields, but it hadn't worked. The grasses and greens had fallen from my mould like skin from a snake. It just wouldn't come together. The whole thing made me very frustrated. It was as innocent as that, but even then, I knew I couldn't tell her. She wouldn't get it.

Emily sighed. "Oh, David. Seriously. No wonder Mum and Dad freak out about you. You make even boring things seem dodgy as hell."

There was an especially loud thump from upstairs, and even Emily looked up to the ceiling this time. After a while, I looked back at the TV but I didn't know what was happening. I'd missed too much of the film and lost the thread of it all. I didn't know how to rewind.

"I saw Dad crying last night," whispered Emily, her hand dipping into the popcorn again. She swirled the mix around slowly and sensuously. "On the wall outside."

I glanced through the open curtains at the back garden. I could just about make out the wall in the darkness. The moon hung low above it.

Emily let out one long stream of air. "He's just not happy anymore, is he?"

Dad and I lived in silence. We acknowledged each other when we were together, but that was it. And though in some ways he'd become as distant to me as Grandad was now, even I could see that he was a shadow of his former self. Dad had become a physical part of the house, a living amenity, working from home most of the week and working long into the evenings at his drawing board. He drew his architectural maps and plans slowly, as if he had to summon them from a far-away source, one unrelated to instinct. Builders and contractors came to the house to see him, not the other way around, whereas Mum, in contrast, seemed to go out even more. As his clothes grew softer and slacker, hers had become tighter and sharper, like a crisp butterfly fresh from its chrysalis.

Emily pouted, following my eyes out the window. I had her for a moment; *this was my chance.* I whispered softly, delicately, "Do you ever think about Grandad?"

She didn't stop looking out the window, though her brow furrowed, like I'd seen it do when she was stuck on something. "No." She seemed surprised by her own answer. "He's gone, hasn't he? What is there to think about? I can hardly remember what he looked like, now. As a real person. He's just someone in photographs. Is that odd?"

I tried to picture him, but even for me, the sense of him as I knew him was fading. It pained me to think of him. He who had been my favourite person in all the world, my warm and awe-inspiring Grandad, who wore colourful jumpers that you couldn't get in normal shops, was transforming into the Grandad in the photograph I'd taken from his house. A man I hardly recognised, grim-faced, clad in waterproofs. Alone somewhere I'd never been and would never see. He had lost his joy and had become solemn, grey, with a will of steel. Selfishness. But perhaps this was just because I was starting to understand him better.

Emily turned to me then, her voice lighter. "I do think about Grandma, though. More than Grandad. I remember her laughing when I danced for her. I mostly remember her being ill, but she still smiled for me. I cheered her up." She looked puzzled for a moment. "You know, I don't even remember Grandad being there in the hospital when she died. But he must've been. He would have been there for his wife. I mean, I know he was there, but I just can't see him. Funny." Emily looked thoughtful and then looked back at the film, nonplussed. "Dad doesn't talk about it. He's never talked about it. But he talks about Grandma all the time. It's been years and he still can't talk about Grandad. Perhaps it was just too much of a shock for him. And the fact that there wasn't a funeral... That's pretty weird."

I pinned my mouth closed. Dad never talked to me about Grandma. I coughed into my fist. "I wonder if Mum talks to him about it all?"

Emily shook her head, not at me, but at something she was thinking to herself. "Mum told me that Dad feels betrayed. By Grandad. Can you imagine?"

Just then, two things happened at once. Something throbbed inside my head so sharply that I winced. And then just as I turned to Emily, Dad walked in and stood in front of the sofa.

"What did I just hear?" His voice was quiet. Slow.

Everything was too bright, it burned. I wanted to say so many things and look Dad right in the eye, but my tongue filled my mouth, heavy and thick. Silhouetted by the TV, he looked like a mountain.

Beside me, Emily smiled at Dad. "Nothing, Dad. We were just talking about Grandma." She popped some popcorn nonchalantly into her mouth. She always knew what to do.

"And Grandad." I finally managed to blurt it out. My voice sounded different – scratchier, throaty. "Emily said he betrayed you."

"David!" Emily shoved my shoulder hard, but I didn't care. I didn't know what I expected Dad to do. I was well past the point of expecting him to tell the truth, but I suppose I wanted to push him enough to tell another lie. To sell himself again. To justify my anger. I wanted him to be angry too, because nothing can be more satisfying than anger meeting anger. But instead, Dad... shrank. It was horrible, like watching a snail force itself into too small a shell. Emily had her eyes on him too, her mouth agape.

"He did," Dad whispered, slowly. "He betrayed all of us."

I couldn't help myself; I reached for Emily's hand and squeezed it as hard as I could. She shot me a sharp look and then turned back to Dad. *This was it.*

"He..." Dad stumbled. "He didn't take care. He didn't listen to medical advice, or me. He didn't take his medication, he didn't rest. He went on his ridiculous expeditions, looking for magical doorways in hostile places. He made himself sicker and sicker looking for things that don't exist. Things that had him laughed out of his office and ended his career. He spent everything doing that. It left your Grandma on her own. It meant he had nothing left. And then he died. He did it to himself."

"Oh, Dad." Emily stood and wrapped herself around him. It was then that I noticed that she was practically as tall as he was. This just made him look older and sadder. He pulled her into his chest and stared at me over her shoulder. His eyes were cold. "I don't want to talk about him again. Not ever. You understand? You understand, David?"

That was fourteen years ago. And there I was, face to face with Grandad again. Could it be? It was an older man; I was sure of it. He had the same little round glasses. He wasn't smiling. Still holding my face inches from the lamppost, something dark and fluttering drifted upwards and into the air, just to my right, but when I looked there was nothing there.

Was he coming back to me?

The next few steps along the street felt odd, like I weighed less than before. In my hand, my plastic bag crinkled louder than it should. My fingers traced the wall as I walked, but I couldn't even feel the brick. It was as if my hand was passing through the surface, *I was that thin*. I needed something solid, something real to hold onto, and one face came into my mind.

Agatha.

Even just the thought of her skin, the soft curves of her cheek when she smiled, round as a pearl, brought me back. I needed to see her, I needed to speak to her. She might understand. But staggering into the arcade, I caught my reflection in the window of a suit shop. Between the pristine mannequins, I looked ridiculous. My soaked t-shirt clung to my skinny torso, and my jeans were heavy and dragging when I bent my knees. My curly fringe was flat to my forehead. I looked drowned. It was perhaps a good thing that Agatha wasn't at work today; I didn't want her to see me like this. Like I was.

I spent the afternoon shift hiding. To Paul, I was behind the desk, as present as ever. But I wasn't. I was somewhere else.

When five o'clock rolled around, I grabbed my plastic bag and waited at the entrance to the arcade. Sam was already there, sitting at the bus stop opposite. He was leaning against the bin, one hand fiddling in his holdall, while the other waved above at the fluorescent light. Seeing him there, I wasn't surprised that he was so often approached by the blue people. He looked the type. They'd approach him slowly, craning their heads to see if he wore the blue forget-me-not, offer him a leaflet or two. It normally ended with him taking a deep swig of whatever he had with him and proudly telling them to "fuck right off, you fucking do-gooders."

As ever, that day he looked crooked, as if his shoulders stuck out of his front, and his sodden overcoat hung off his chest. His beard dripped yellow, and his hair was pale, fine, and hung steel-straight like a plane of sheet metal. It was the hair of an old but well-kept woman, not a man who spent most of his time sitting between two bins. I'd never known his age. It hadn't mattered. He was probably in his mid-twenties, like me, but his hollow cheeks were so deep that they could've been shaded in. I found his earthiness comforting. It reminded me of the silent men and women who dragged their whole worlds down our village street, all those years ago. He moved deliberately, as if he always planned two steps ahead.

He spotted me standing under cover and strode over to me, his bag slung over his shoulder. "All right?" he grinned. One of his teeth had gone black.

I nodded.

"Fuck me," he muttered, his eyes on my hands. "You must be fucking freezing. You're shaking like a sodding leaf."

"I'm all right. Bad day."

"Aye. I know that." Sam stared down the street at the woman in the dressing gown. She'd gone silent and was staring at the ground. "She's collecting water now," he muttered. "Coming?"

I gave him a single nod before stepping out into the rain. Sam strode off ahead of me, head down against the torrent. And in the darkness of the street, I saw him as I saw the mudmen, lost in their own world and life strapped to their back as they trudged down our row to the gap in the fence and the empty cow fields.

10.

Outside the block of flats, a row of black skips overflowed with plastic packets and ripped up cardboard. By a fence, someone had abandoned a cream armchair with little black circles burnt into the arms. It had been there a long time.

Sam jabbed on the lift button a few times with his knuckle. The button made a little rattling noise when he pressed it, as if it wasn't connected to anything.

"Broken," he muttered under his breath, then he led me through a side-door and up six flights of stairs to a landing with glass doors in the style of an old porch. The only light was from a fading yellow bulb hanging from the ceiling, and the walls were lined with a carpet I could hardly resist digging my nails into to hear the sound it made.

Sam led me to his front door, number 662. It looked more like a door to a shed or garage than a door to a flat. He fussed with his keys, jamming the wrong one in so many times that I wondered if they'd finally kicked him out after all the threats. I hoped not. I didn't want to be on my own. Eventually he found the magic combination and stumbled inside, leaving the door ajar. I stood in the doorway for a minute, acclimatising to the smoke and musk before heading inside.

All along the hallway floor were empty plastic bags, tipped-over glass bottles, and little crumples of paper. Two empty cigarette packets, still half-wrapped in film, were wedged in a pair of dirty trainers. The walls had probably been white at some point, but now they were streaked with dirt, as if someone with oily fingers had spread his arms and dragged his hands along each wall. The air smelled like too many people, as if lots of bodies had been too close to each other for too long. Body on body on body. Skin and hair. There was something else, too, this time, a smell I knew from late trips home on the bus. It came from the back seats, where the floor was gritty and the poles made your hands black.

My mouth started to fill up with saliva, so I swallowed it down. This was a place where people never came out the same. But I knew that. I could just tell.

I followed Sam into a small kitchen-living room littered with more plastic wrappers, bottles, and takeaway cartons. But unlike the hallway, there was something more artful about it here. There was a window at the far side of the room with a blind pulled almost down to the windowsill. Along the shelf were twenty or so glass bottles, all crowded together, some perched right on the edge. The stormy light shone through them like stained glass, and someone had even dropped some cut grasses and flowers in one of them. It must have been a long time ago though, because the stalks were sticks, the blooms dried up like used tissue.

Opposite a long, three-seater sofa covered with a zig-zag throw was a black leather armchair. I could only see the back of it. Sam leaned over the arm, whispering slowly. Reclined on the chair was a girl with her knees up and over the back wing, her hair shining like a white waterfall down her jacket. The skin on her shins was bone white, and her toes were bare, the ends painted plum. It was difficult to pin an age to her; she reminded me of girls Emily had been friends with as a teenager, but her skin looked thinner, more fragile. *Old skin.* She watched a television that had a long crack down the centre of the screen. There was no sound coming from it, but on the screen were a group of women dancing, their faces fiery.

Sam leaned over her, breathing his own brand of alcoholic fumes into her hair, but she didn't look disgusted, or even uncomfortable. If anything, she looked bored. Her eyes focussed on a space in the air between us as she listened to his muttered words.

Sam looked up at me, but stayed bent over the girl. "Drink?"

He shuffled off out of the room before I had the chance to answer. I couldn't see where he'd gone. The fridge was in here. The girl watched me, chewing her tongue. She made a strange mewling sound before shifting her frame so that her hands rested on her chest. She stared at her body with a strange askew smile and started to pick her fingernails. Though I had the feeling that I was interrupting something, she didn't seem at all bothered that I was there. In fact, I couldn't help but feel that she enjoyed having someone there looking at her, watching her as she watched herself.

I was still standing there, not knowing where to look, when Sam came back in with a Tupperware box. He set it down on the coffee table and used it to push aside the glasses and plastic. He didn't signal to the girl, but at the sight of the box she swung her legs to the ground and sat cross-legged on the floor. Here I could see her properly. She was definitely a lot younger than Sam. Maybe only fifteen

or so. Sam was at least my age, maybe even thirty. She had
the same pale translucence as him though. Was she his
sister? His friend?

While Sam pulled three bottles from his pockets and took
off his overcoat, she prised open the box with more strength
than I'd have thought were in her thin arms.

"Sit down, man," Sam said, patting the long sofa with a
heavy hand.

I chose the far end of the sofa. In the definite 'in circle,'
but also close enough to the door that I could leave when
I wanted to. I'd met Sam a few months earlier while I'd
been waiting for Agatha to finish work. He was inside the
art shop, making her laugh so much that all her white teeth
were on show. He made me think of something that lived
underground, by water banks. He didn't wear a mask, a false
face, like most people did. He looked me in the eye when he
spoke to me, even when his stare became too much and my
eyes sought rest on the floor. I could see him for what he
was, with his pockets full of clinking bottles and plastic bags.
I understood that that stuff helped when you knew things
that were too much to handle.

Sam sat back and smiled broadly, as if he was genuinely
thrilled to have me there. He handed me one of the bottles
with a black label, fizz still escaping from the mouth. The
neck was grubby with dust, and I could still see where Sam
had gripped it. I took it and held it low between my knees,
secretly rolling my thumb around the lip.

Sam held up his beer to the girl. "I've got us a private
musician here tonight." He took a swing and sat back,
grinning at the ceiling. The girl continued to sort through
the box, which was filled with little plastic bags. Sam's gaze
settled on my hands, and as each moment passed, I felt less

and less in control. What did he mean? My mind started to race. I knew that feeling all too well. All my thoughts were running alongside each other, sparring, fighting to take different paths. *Fight or flight.* And bits of Sam and even this girl were seeping inside me, through my skin as if by emotional osmosis. I could hear him, in my head, singing quietly like he did sometimes on the bench when I watched him from the shop. Words that didn't make sense.

I squeezed the bottle. *He wasn't singing. It wasn't real.* All was silent apart from the rustle of the girl's fingers inside the box. She was separating out little white and brown pills onto a sheet of paper. She reminded me of a witch casting a spell.

I took a small sip from the bottle. It tasted like chemicals. Like it was wrong. No one was speaking. Sam was still leaned back in the chair but had slumped a bit to the side, his eyes half-closed. The girl had laid three white pills on a mirror. Each one had a black cross scored on the top. They looked like little berries. Like mistletoe.

Sam choked on something and picked at the chair with a dirty hand. "We got any food in, Lara?"

The girl shook her head, her hair swinging like wet leather. She tucked some long strands behind her ear and looked up at me from under her eyelids, both shy and knowing. A lurch, deep down. Even Agatha had never looked at me like that.

At the thought of Agatha I closed my eyes, but I still wanted to watch the girl. Something had locked between me and her, and watching her fingers roll one of the pills on the mirror set off the intense squeezing again. I didn't even know if it was good. It was like when you realise how hungry you are, and it's all you can think about so you become angry. A hot fist inside my chest, all want.

The girl pulled a roll-up from the plastic box, stuck it to her bottom lip, and lit the end. I watched the hot glow and wanted to press my palm against it. The girl opened her mouth wide and did this strange trembling gasp from the back of her throat. I looked down at the bottle I still held in my hands. Practically untouched.

"Is Agatha coming round at some point?" My voice seemed too loud.

Sam emitted a strange grunt. "Who?"

"You know. Agatha. From the Arcade. The art shop."

Sam's brow was a nest of ditches. "What, with the purple hair? Nose-diamond-thing?" He pointed to his nostril.

I nodded.

"Why the fuck would she come round here? Know her, do you?"

I looked back at the thin girl. Was she smirking? Sam blew a note into his bottle. "Bring her round if you want. Open house here, pal."

No fucking way. "No, she'll be at home. She lives miles away."

But Sam had already moved on, and was watching the girl intently. His eyes were hungry, but also soft, like a young boy waiting for the sweet shop to open. She leaned back against the chair with her arms outstretched like Christ. Ash flaked from her fingers onto the carpet, not caring what they burned. She took another drag and passed the roll-up to me. Sam watched me now, and his eyes, dark brown and huge, were those of a dog. I saw the pink rise of his wet tongue between his lips, and as I took the roll-up I had only one thought: *Fuck you, Emily. Fuck you. Wherever you are.* Smoke filled my mouth like a house on fire. I panicked, and I gulped, swallowing it like you would a mouthful of hot coffee.

It burned.

I thrust out the roll-up to Sam while I held my chest in perfect stasis. I knew that if I breathed in or out I'd cough, and possibly be sick all over the living room. The girl smiled. Her two front teeth were missing.

"You've never done it before," she whistled. "Cough it up."

At her command, my chest compressed like old bellows. Half the beer in my bottle ended up down the leg of my jeans, but I could hardly tell as they were already soaked through.

Lara leaned forwards and rested her head on the backs of her hands, which were flat on the table. "Poor little bug. You *are* a bug, aren't you? I can tell."

My throat was slick with bile, but I managed to gurgle a reply. "I've done it before, but it didn't taste like that."

Lara chuckled and closed her eyes. Sam, his breath rasping, slumped to the side so that he leaned on my shoulder. His eyes were half-closed and looking at something on the ceiling. Very quietly, he muttered, "I can feel it. I'm changing." I followed his gaze but there was nothing there.

Lara reached over and dropped one of the white pills into my palm. Up close, it looked more like a dried-up old berry than a man-made pill. What I'd thought was a black cross was actually where its skin had wrinkled, like an old berry.

Lara crawled around the table and pressed her cheek against mine. Something stirred and I gripped the chair. *Too close.* She purred, "These… are… my… little… secrets. They show you what you were meant to be," then parted her lips to show me the white held delicately between her teeth.

I closed my fingers around the pill. I think a part of me knew that something like this would happen. A way out. And here it was. My heart flapped against my ribs.

"Do you think it's real," the girl whispered, "what the white coats say on telly? About other worlds?" Her head rolled back on her shoulders, all muscle control gone. "Sam, maybe in one of them you have no bones, or I'm all feathers."

Sam blew into his bottle. "Maybe they'll go there in a space ship to find out."

"No. They'll send a nobody. A man they won't care about if he's split in two."

"Aye, maybe."

"A sack of sticks. Skin and bones in a bag."

Sam made a strange sucking noise with his mouth. "Maybe that's what happens in the hills."

The girl closed her eyes. "I want to go."

"It's just fucking words, Lara. Means nothing. All talk. Just like every fucking thing."

The girl sobbed and rubbed her eyes. When she lowered her hand, it was smeared with black. "But I want to go home."

I couldn't stop looking at the girl's eyes, trained on an invisible point. It was like she was trying to solve a magic eye puzzle. She raised an ash-streaked hand and prodded the air, twisting her wrist as if grasping a handle.

Sam's voice was soft, far away. "Do it now, pal. Play something. While I'm flying. *Make me seen.*"

"That's your coin. Show us somewhere," the girl said. She looked drowsy. Drugged. "Help us."

"I can't help you," I whispered. "I can't play anything."

"Play." Was Sam shouting? Everything here was out of proportion. "Do what you're for. You work in a fucking music shop, don't you?"

"I don't know what to play. I haven't even got an instrument."

"Play any mother-fucking thing. Just fucking do it." He slipped a pill into his mouth, "Take us away."

For a moment, both of them just sat with their heads flopped back. I didn't know what to do. For me, flying was getting the hell out of there. But when I looked into the girl's face, I understood what she wanted. *I understood her. But I couldn't help.*

The girl stared at me for a moment, her eyes wide and white, before leaning over to grab my arm. Her mouth hung open, her red tongue dagger-like behind her teeth. "Your skin," she whispered, "it feels funny. Like moss or something." The girl's voice shook. She looked like she didn't know what to do. All I knew was that I didn't want her to let go.

"Sammy." The girl shook Sam's arm and his eyes fluttered open. "Touch him. Touch him now. He's not right."

Before I had a chance to even flinch, Sam gripped my wrist. The skin on the back of his hand was dry and swirled with faded green marks. He sat like that for a few seconds, his eyes on the floor, before suddenly reaching up to grasp my neck. "You don't feel... right, kid. What are you? If you're not a music man, then what are you, eh? Why are you here?"

"Maybe there's another reason he's here," the girl croaked. "Yeah, I think there is."

Sam let out a snarl and pushed me away from him. My hands trembled. He hadn't squeezed enough to hurt, but I don't think I'd taken a single breath while he'd held me. Sam sank into his chair and his face took on the look of a little boy, crushed. When he spoke again, it was so softly that it could've just been to himself. "I had a guitar once." He held up his hand, the dirty back, the fingers that would barely straighten. "It wasn't mine," he added, as if he knew what I was thinking. "My Pa actually listened. But school took it back. Never understood the symbols."

"Notes," I whispered.

"Aye, whatever. I left and they kept the guitar." He stared again at the ceiling, his fingers twitching round the bottle.

"I want to go home," the girl whispered. She tried to climb back onto her chair but her arms couldn't support her weight. Through the window with the glass bottles above, I could just about make out something black fluttering against the glass. A leaf, perhaps, but whatever it was battered itself against the pane time and time again as if trying to break in.

It had wings.

Beneath it, the girl curled in on herself and sobbed, "This isn't home." Then, using what little strength she had, she crawled across the floor and flipped her legs onto my lap. Her bare toes traced up and down my side. It should have been ticklish there, but it didn't tickle. She raised the roll-up, lip-end towards me. It looked greasy, smeared with pink. I took one long, slow drag. And then another. And another. I watched the little fire burn the white paper away. Sam's eyes were closed.

"I *am* a bird, you know. Underneath my skin," she whispered, just for me. "My bones are bird bones. Thin, like reeds. I'm in the wrong body. I want to eat worms. I want to lay eggs. I want to be somewhere else. I know I should be somewhere else. Like the white coats say." And her eyes were more white than blue, then, like a crow. I could see it then, though it didn't make sense, that this was the truth. This thin, twig-like girl *was* a bird in a girl's skin. And I knew what that felt like, and I knew why she was here. But Sam wasn't a bird. He was something else. *She was like me.*

"Yes, I know…" I whispered. My heart was flapping around in my chest like a trapped bat.

The girl brushed my arm with her toe. "You. You're in the middle. A man. But with wings. They're all curled and crumpled, but they're there." She stuck her heel hard in my stomach. "They're black and leathery. I can see them. I have the gift."

Just then, Sam stood up and shuffled out into the hallway, his eyes still closed, holding up a hand as he did it.

"Why are you here?" The girl's whisper was as soft as moths.

The hush of my breath soared in my ears. A tide, rushing. "To see you."

She sighed. "Hmm, I thought so. All the beetles and bugs come to me, you know. Like I'm the queen, and I keep all the little secrets."

"Yes." I inched closer to her, my mouth open. All the air in the room was disappearing.

"You wanna know what's true?"

She had my heart in her hand. It thumped and pulsed and twisted to be free, but it felt so good to be held tight. Safe. Even though she was just this little bird with white hair.

The girl mouthed, "Help me up," so I held her hands and pulled her onto the cushion next to me. Her hands were so small that they were hard to grasp. She held her face inches from mine and took a deep breath in, eating my heat. "Sing me something. Something just for me, please."

And then I did it. Something I hadn't done since I was eleven. *But it felt right.* Under my breath, I started to click, to tut, to flick my tongue off my front teeth.

She gasped as if I'd touched her, and then she started to

click back, making odd little whistles between the tuts. What we did sounded like a song, and every time we clashed, she giggled, as if it was all a cute joke. Her translucent little face was all points and corners, but it also drank in the light, like silk. Everything tingled. It didn't even matter that I had no memory of what the clicks meant. It wasn't about words.

Her hand crept over and pressed on my thigh, at the top, near the pocket. Her fingers curled a bit. I could feel her hum vibrating through her palm into my leg. Warm and living. Her eyes were half-closed, and closing more with each note. She pressed down with her hand and I stopped clicking.

I pressed my mouth onto hers, my hand wrapped around the back of her skull.

She squeaked and pulled out of my grip. Her mouth and eyes were wide. I took a few shallow breaths as the room dipped and spun. The girl spluttered onto the table and started to laugh this thick and gluttonous laugh.

There was spit on the table. There was spit on my jumper.

"Get off her, you cunt."

A hand on the top of my head, and Sam was standing behind me, grabbing me by the hair. His face was balled up like a fist. "You don't do that to her. You don't do that. She's fucking mine." He shoved my head forwards towards the table and then let go. The girl was still laughing, now with her hands clawing at her lips.

As I struggled to rise, my legs weak and pathetic, I retched over the table. When I reached the corridor to the front door, I heard Sam's voice behind me. "That's right," he growled. "That's right. Run. You can't help us. You talk shit. That's the door. Shut it behind you, you fuck."

I grasped the handle and yanked the door open. The cold

night air hit me in my soaking clothes and I stepped through the door and back into the strange orange light, dropping the pill into the weeds.

11.

By the time I reached my flat, I was shaking so violently that I could hardly get the key into my front door. On the doormat lay a blue package, about the size of a shoebox. My address was printed across the top. I hardly ever got any post, really, so I searched my neighbours' doormats to see if they had packages too, but theirs were bare. I picked it up tentatively and was surprised by how light it was.

I entered the flat, and once I was sure the door was locked behind me, I dropped my carrier bag and the package, and slid down the wall into a heap like I had no bones at all. The skin under my soaking sleeves itched, and nothing helped, no matter how much I scratched beneath the wool. I pulled off my jumper and let it fall to the ground with a wet slap, my arms wrapped around my bare chest.

What had just happened? How had I got it all so wrong? *She was a bird.* And she said I had wings. Not Sam. *Me.* We spoke to each other. She understood the Verbatinea. Grandad's special language that he taught me. She spoke it back to me. I thought back to the little black book I'd thrown away, and felt like I'd thrown away the secret to the universe. There was no getting it back. And Grandad had kept the master version. I'd never know what she said to me, before it had all gone wrong.

I crawled into the small space at the bottom of the bed, like I'd done in my bedroom at Mum and Dad's house, and pressed my face into my knees. Above my head, the bones of my creation creaked a little. I looked up into her folds, dark and soft. Wide enough for two. Light from the bulb on the ceiling still glowed through her skin, but that was OK. I still had a month or so until Midwinter. The first frosts hadn't even arrived yet. I reached out and stroked the wall closest to me. I knew to be gentle. It hadn't been easy to get it to this point. It seemed to resist being made to exist. For every layer I added, half a layer flaked away. My touch brought disaster and decay. Beneath my fingers, its surface was almost soft, velvety, as if coated in very fine fur. The surface shifted and swayed like a curtain, and I pulled away. It wasn't nearly strong enough yet. It needed to hold itself up – I couldn't risk that it might collapse, slipping away like boiled flesh off a bone.

I'd add today's harvest to the skeleton later.

Beside me on the floor were several books, their pages fanned open. One on black and white marbled salamanders sprouting back legs and crawling from the water. One on sea-stars losing parts of themselves but growing them back. And my favourite: one on the *turritopsis dohrnii* jellyfish, that doesn't age and just transforms itself back into a juvenile state. 'The immortal jellyfish.' I rested one hand on a book and one on the carpet. I longed for the ragged red pile to come alive and grow over me. For once, I'd actually reached out for something I was sure was right, *out of pure instinct*. It'd been as simple as breathing or using my tongue to taste. It was biological. Animal. I struggled to remember any other time when I'd acted on impulse like that. It'd felt right, and she'd said it herself: we were winged things. But if even the birds didn't want me…

Inside my pocket, my phone buzzed. Seven voicemails from Mum. I took a deep breath before listening to the most recent one. It was Dad, his voice crackling. He must've been calling from his walk with the ramblers. "Hello. It's your Dad. Emily called in; she's fine. Your mother is fine. Hope you're doing well." In the background, I could hear Mum speaking in a sing-song voice. I guessed that she was talking to Emily on the landline, like she hadn't a care in the world.

My chest felt tight again. Almost, almost, this time. I knew Emily would be fine. It made no sense for her to go anywhere. But even now, she had me by the stomach every time she 'forgot' to call. The truth was, I wanted to forget her. I hadn't seen her in two years. Her life was a London life – she very rarely looked back to us. As a kid, I'd have wanted nothing more than to fall under the hot scent of Emily's breath and to be wrapped in her arms. She'd always been a stabilising force. She told me what to do, what people expected of me, and she showed me the path of least resistance. But Emily was unpredictable now, a loose cannon, and thinking about her made me feel sick. She'd moved away without so much as a glance over her shoulder. She'd left us. Me. But it wasn't even that she'd become was a stranger; it was more that, from this distance, I could see her fully for what she was now, and it flitted from shape to shape. Flaky. Unreliable. Inconstant. I'd seen her as stone, but if anything, she was a butterfly skimming the surface of a pond. Delicate and raw. Breakable. And she made the world seem breakable around her. That was the thing I couldn't cope with.

My stomach rumbled.

I deleted the voicemails and opened my messages. Agatha's name was there, at the top of my chats. At the thought of her I remembered Lara's smell, the feeling of her lips in the split second before she pulled away. *What had I been thinking?* Had I cheated? It'd been so impulsive, and nothing like that had ever happened with Agatha.

I pulled my little black book from my carrier bag and flicked through a few pages of things I'd recorded there. At the sight of Agatha's name over and over, I felt calmer. Agatha was still there. She hadn't gone anywhere. And nothing had happened, after all. There was nothing to tell.

I replayed back everything I could remember the girl saying and inked it onto the page. Most of it felt fuzzy around the edges, even though it'd only been a couple of hours ago. But she had definitely said, "I want to go home." Where had I heard that before? It tickled a place in the back of my head, like a dangling string.

The box by the door caught my eye and I crawled across the floor to inspect it again. I didn't have anything sharp to open it, so I tore at the packaging until finally I could see inside. Something rattled around the bottom until it settled on something soft. I stuck my hand in and pulled out a blue T-shirt and a strange round whistle with four holes. The label dangling from it read, 'Express yourself with an ocarina.' I lifted the t-shirt, my arms outspread to the width of it. You could've fitted two of me in there. Across the blue was written, 'I belong here.' Who would have sent me this? I double-checked, but it was definitely my name on the top. There was no invoice, no return address. Perhaps it was a mistake? I put the items back in the box and left them outside on my doormat.

From there, I crawled onto the bed, opening up the news on my laptop. Scrolling up and down, nothing particularly caught my eye. The usual 'Economy Slumps' spelled out in different ways. Public disruption – this time a man who'd knelt on the mainline from Edinburgh to Newcastle. There was a photo from CCTV; he looked like he was praying. Long gone were the days of reporting disappearances like they were unusual. They were still there of course, hidden deep down in the menu, but only the mass disappearances were listed now in the style of a roll call. A duty, rather than a spectacle.

But there, further down the homepage, were the physicists. I clicked. The girl had mentioned believing what the 'white coats' were saying. The worlds upon worlds. The layering of light. The girl had shone when she'd mentioned it. But what did it matter, really, what lay out there? It didn't mean anything to us. We couldn't touch it. It was just air and light. This article was headed with the quotation: "Could this be the greatest scientific breakthrough of our lifetime?" Two of the physicists beneath the banner looked smug, sitting on tall chairs like bar stools. But the man on the right, a bald man with black-rimmed glasses looked defiantly down the camera lens. He looked vaguely familiar. As I studied his face, I could hear his voice. It was loud. Angry. Rude.

I closed the laptop. My arms were scored with nail marks now. An allergic reaction maybe? I picked up my little black book and made sure to record the spread of the itch, before turning off the light.

Other than the structure in the corner, my flat was bare and clean, and I liked it. Everything pointed towards that corner. Now that I'd started to add more of my cemetery finds, the skin was finally thickening. If you climbed inside and looked up, the canopy barely even glowed beneath the ceiling light. But it still wasn't strong enough. Lying in the dark, I'd listen to it creak as it shifted from side to side, trying to find its balance.

I'd been in my flat a year. It'd been part of my plan, you see. I needed the room. The privacy. The space to think, build, dream. I could never sleep the way I needed to at my parents' house. How I'd need to sleep, to escape.

Mum and Dad had said they didn't want me to go. They'd said it with their tongues, but the rest of their bodies had stayed still as stone. I hadn't told them I was going until the day I'd collected the keys. I packed a 'Bag for Life' with all the clothes I owned, a few books I needed, Emily's old laptop, and left everything else behind. My bedroom was an egg I'd finally had the courage to hatch from. Now, I was ready for the next stage.

On the way out, I handed Dad my house key.

"Son, you don't need to go. Your mother will worry. She worries enough as it is."

As I pulled on my trainers, one of my books slid from my carrier bag. Dad picked it up and glared at the cover. It was a picture book, entitled The Cold Dark Night. Dad's brow creased and he flicked through the pages. He paused on a spread showing a lone queen bee digging into the soil on the side of a bank, her eyes already closing as she prepares for the big sleep until spring. Her hive all dead. Over the hill, winter approaches.

"What's this? I don't remember you reading this as a kid."

I snatched it from his hands. "Agatha gave me it. It's a private joke."

Mum and Dad watched me in silence as I strode to the bus stop, liberated, and already thinking quicker than I'd done in my whole life.

My life was finally beginning.

I chose the place because it felt enclosed, and as it was on the third floor, no one could press their face up to my window. If I peered down through the glass, all I'd see were brick walls and windows, and unlike Mum and Dad's village, the curtains were always closed. I never saw anyone in the narrow alley beneath, and it pleased me that I wasn't near a bus station, main road, or – even worse – a supermarket.

Inside, there were few distractions because I kept it that way. Most twenty-six-year-olds might've had collections. Art. Exercise equipment. Games. Stuff. *Things* everywhere. But I had no interest in any of that. Even though my flat was a cave, it still didn't feel like home. I only had one box of things which were precious. A plain plastic storage bin, only a quarter full with some old clothes I didn't wear, the books I needed for my research, and the materials collected for my project. My little black book would fit in there too, if it needed to. A few of Agatha's things lay around the space too, and I hadn't the heart to pick them up. I liked them being there. A hair tie by the sink, a silk scarf tied to a door handle. It was like she was always there, even when I was at my most alone.

But my favourite thing about that flat was that my neighbours were faceless. If we passed each other in the corridor, they'd scuttle along with their heads down like beetles. Only twice after moving in a year earlier had there been a knock on my door, but neither time did I answer. No one knew me there, so it must have been a mistake. At one point, after I'd been there a few months, a series of handmade posters went up around the building, with 'Get to know your community!' scrawled on them with a black Sharpie. There was no other information on the posters – no names, flat numbers, or contact details. So – like everyone else, I imagine – I turned away, no closer to my neighbours than I was before. The posters were taken down a week later, and replaced with the building policies and foyer cleaning schedule. From what I could tell, no one read those. But what I could've really done with were instructions about the front doors. The access code to the building seemed to change every fortnight, and I couldn't keep up with it or understand what the rules were. I'd often get locked out, and have to wait in the rain or wind for another resident to enter the code so I could follow them in like a shadow.

I also liked that on winter dawns – like the morning after visiting Sam's flat – my breath would plume up to meet the beam of yellow light through the window. The cold made me feel more alive. But that morning, as I sat up and peeled my still-drenched jeans from my legs, I shivered a bit too much. It wasn't that delicious electric tingle that meant I existed; it was a shudder originating from beneath my skin. I flexed my fingers, stiff and white, before rubbing them up and down my legs. Everything felt cold and damp, like I hadn't dried from the night before. As I dressed, the fabric felt rough on my skin and my arms began to itch again. I tried to ignore it, pulling on layer after layer of t-shirt, then jumper, then jacket, all in the hope that it'd stop my shivering.

All the way to work I trod carefully, my feet skating with every step. The rain had frozen into slush, but no one else seemed to slip. They glided as smoothly as ghosts as I clung to the walls, struggling to stay upright. My legs weren't my own. What was happening to me? I paused outside a charity shop to catch my breath. Like so many other shops, the window display was set up like a low-budget episode of Star Trek. A toy microscope in a battered old box, a 'make your own clock kit,' and an old zoetrope were set around a huge second-hand telescope, pointing to the sky like a black cannon. Spread around its feet was a display of science books. The one at the front featured that same bald man I'd seen on the news: *The Road to the Stars* by Dr John Gray. And beside it lay a red book, a red book that made my stomach squeeze with such force that I could taste acid. After all these years, there it was: *Hidden Worlds* by Dr Francis Porter. Battered and bruised, the cover was torn, but it was sitting there, inches from me. I hadn't seen a copy in the flesh since Dad had torn Grandad's copy from my arms and thrown it across the room. The shop wasn't even open yet, but I pressed my hands against the glass and held it in my gaze, just in case it disappeared. I couldn't let it go. Not this time. When eventually a thin man in a blue polo shirt unlocked the door, I raced inside, hardly breathing. As I lifted it from the display, a faint clicking tickled my ear. I quickly flicked around to see where it came from, but of course there was no one there. But I couldn't stop my tongue from replying. Standing there, holding Grandad's book in my arms, it was like I was holding Grandad. Or more like he was holding me. The bristle of his orange knit jumper, the iron smell from his hands. I squeezed it like I'd never let go, but at the thought of opening the cover I felt sick.

It was then that I looked down again at the book with Dr John Gray on the front and I realised where I'd seen him before. He was the man who'd come into Grandad's office at the university, the last time I'd been there. The one whose voice had been too loud, and had told Grandad to leave. Grandad had seized up when that man had come into the office. He wasn't a good person. I knew that then, and I felt it again now.

I left a few minutes later with the book stowed away in my carrier bag, alongside my black notebook. My heart was fluttering inside my chest, weak and desperate. Suddenly, eyes were everywhere, and I wrapped my arms around my middle, holding myself together in one piece. Every so often, I glanced over my shoulder to see if someone was behind me, but there never was. I couldn't have felt more visible if I'd been setting off fireworks.

The girl in Sam's flat, the poster, and now the book. It was as if I'd been living in darkness and now all the lights were switching on. All these things, these connections, they had to mean something. After so many years of being lost, so many months meticulously planning my special project. Perhaps someone was trying to find me. To draw me along another road.

Thankfully, I was just around the corner from Flynn's, though I was already late. I ran into the shop and stowed my bag under the counter. Paul appeared in the doorway to the stockroom. He held his hands in front of his chest, palms up, like he expected something to be there. "I give up," he announced. "She's there, in my head. But her face is gone. Her name is gone. All that's left is flowers. She had something to do with flowers." He rubbed his fingers together, pinching the air. "Her voice is still here though. I remember that like it was yesterday. You'd have liked her, David. She wasn't as good at reaching the top shelves as you, but you remind me of her a bit." Paul scrunched his face up. "You... smelled the same. Like wood." He pulled a roll of receipts from his pocket and scuttled over to stand beside me. "Look, look." He pointed at the slips of paper, handwritten in a curly script with bright blue ink. "She wrote these, I found them in a box in the back." He held them like unearthed bones.

It was the first time Paul had shown me anything like this. They must have belonged to the woman who'd shoes I'd filled when I'd started working at Flynn's. She'd disappeared, like so many people had, and it'd taken Paul a year to accept that she wasn't coming back. He didn't wait long to share what'd happened to my predecessor. In fact, it was on my first day that he'd told me – with a strange furtive glance – that his last assistant had asked to finish early one afternoon and never turned up the next morning. He never mentioned her again, but for months he ended every day with, "And you'll be back tomorrow, yes?" But now, years later, he couldn't even remember her name. It made sense, though. Everyone knew that those who disappeared had 'problems.' And when they removed themselves, spaces just made more sense. Life was easier. I suppose it explained why no one seemed to care so much anymore about the missing, and why only the mass disappearances were reported on the news.

Paul crinkled the receipts between his fingers before looking up at me. He squinted with his mouth slightly agape for a few moments before speaking. "Are you all right, David? You're very white."

I intended to answer, but all the wind had been knocked from me, so I just nodded.

Paul sidled up to me and looked up at my face, as closely as he could manage. "You look like wax."

"I'm fine." I whistled it, more than said it.

He didn't say anything else, but he stood next to me for the next thirty minutes as I went through the usual routine of setting up change in the till and cleaning the glass counters. He watched me like he was testing me, waiting for me to reveal myself as an imposter. At one point, he leaned in close to me and said, "What are you humming? Stop humming." But I hadn't been doing anything, so I just shrugged and carried on as if everything was normal.

Whatever Paul's test was, I must've passed, because eventually he shuffled back into the stockroom, mumbling under his breath. Not long after, after the sound of a few boxes moving around, he called out, "Watch for shoplifters, David. I did stocktake last night and we're missing more sheet music since the last time I counted. At least two hundred pounds worth now since the summer."

All the while, the book screamed beneath the counter. I had to keep going back to check that it was still there, crinkling the shopping bag as little as possible. Paul couldn't know it was there. He couldn't touch it. Of that I was certain. And with each minute that passed I became more light-headed, more nauseous. When I moved my arms and legs it felt like directing a marionette, rather than my own body.

An hour after opening, I called to Paul from the desk. "Paul, I need to go. I'm not feeling right after all." That was met with silence that lasted for so long that I wondered if Paul had left the shop and not told me. But after ten seconds or so, he called back, "All right. All right." I didn't wait for him to appear, and just grabbed my coat and bag and left, running on legs that didn't belong to me anymore. Legs I could barely feel. Legs that were alien and too long and utterly, utterly wrong.

As I ran, I could see the top of Agatha's purple hair from inside the art shop. She was alone today, standing behind the counter and fiddling with her phone. Without thinking, I staggered in her direction. She was wearing a black top with lace that tickled her neckline, and her hair was up in two knots on top of her head, like ears. When she saw me, she lowered her phone and slid around to the side of the counter, a soft smile on her face. Her eyes widened and her mouth opened to speak when I felt my phone vibrate in my pocket. I whipped it out and Emily's name flashed across the screen. No. No time. I swiped her away. With everything else in the world fading to grey, acid burned the back of my throat. Agatha paused, her mouth still open. She was only feet away, almost close enough to touch, but it was as if there was a sheet of thick glass between us. I couldn't move forwards. My mind was with the book in my carrier bag, and all I could see was Grandad's face, but not in the mountains with his yellow rucksack, like in the small picture of him I kept in my box of treasures. It was his face that time he slumped in Grandma's armchair, with the map across his lap.

All my lights were on, fireworks behind my eyes. Her skin was close enough now for me to press a palm to, but I couldn't stay. She may as well have been miles away. I mouthed, "I'm sorry," and turned away. The last mental snapshot I took before leaving her was of her standing straight-backed by the till, one hand gripping the edge of the counter and the other squeezing her phone so tightly that her knuckles had gone white.

Outside and in the light, I turned into an alleyway between the arcade and leisure centre and squatted on my haunches behind a bin. Being low helped my light-headedness, and I

was able to take some deep breaths. I felt more alive than I'd felt since I was little. The sky crackled blue. The wind sliced across my face. Everything was *loud*.

I was ready.

I opened *Hidden Worlds*. I was ready to hear from Grandad.

A Personal Foreword from the Author
Dedicated to my grandson, who understands our game more than the rest.

The road to writing this book has been long. Research has taken me from the CERN collider in Switzerland to the night sky over the Highlands of Scotland. As yet, the human race has only been able to creep a little each day towards understanding the true nature of our universe. It has seemed that the more miles we travel, the slower our steps.

But this is not the case, and all my roads have led to one question: What space lies beyond our world? Or should I be asking, what world lies beyond our space?

The Multiverse, of which our sphere is but one of many clustering worlds, opens up possibilities for wormholes, where space-and-time warps to connect different realities. There are many researchers currently active in the field who speculate that perhaps, one day, if life becomes untenable in our present ageing universe, we may be forced to leave it. Similarly, current astronomers now realise that if the universe continues to expand and accelerate as it does today, the human race will face the prospect of a 'big freeze,' wherein the universe will be plunged into darkness and cold, and all intelligent life will die out.

But this prospect is a far-away concern. What is this 'big freeze,' to the lives of everyday people?

I believe there are more vital, urgent reasons to explore the Multiverse theory. Reasons that relate far more to our modern mindset than any distant future threat. Research thus far suggests that answers might be found within dark matter – an elusive material of which little is known but makes up around 26% of all matter in the universe. And herein begins our journey into black holes, portals, and doorways.

Many miles must be walked in order to understand the cosmos. And in understanding the cosmos we can finally understand ourselves and our true natures. Who we truly are and where we belong. For our universe is a game with movable pieces. We are not designed to stay in one spot. We are made to explore and find the place we can truly call home.

I will leave you here with this image: Did you know that dark matter bends starlight, like water or glass? Imagine how the other things we love might transform… if the sun rose in a different sky?

I do this for my family. I do this for my grandson, who is still so small in the scope of the world but already shines with a different light. Our children will always need guides, when we're no longer around.

I do this for us all, as human beings.

Yours,

Dr Francis Porter

Superstring Theory and Dark Matter Studies at University of York, December, 2010

12.

The more words I consumed, the more I could hear Grandad in my head. The book had been written for me. All of it; I was certain of that. That's why Dad didn't let me keep it. He didn't want me to follow Grandad. The book was an instruction manual. The pages were dense with text, punctuated with sporadic diagrams and star charts. I found that I'd finish a page, move on to the next, and immediately forget what I'd just read. I couldn't understand it; it was like it was written in code. That was very like Grandad, but why hadn't he written it in a code I could understand, when he'd predicted that he wouldn't be around to help me?

I read until the sun went down and the pages turned dark. I tore at my hair, my teeth clenched. I didn't understand what I was meant to do. I flicked back to the photographs at the beginning, Grandad standing in front of the strange purple mountains. Beneath the picture in tiny type was written, 'Doorway near Glencoe, Scotland.' I crawled across the carpet to my box of treasures and dug out the matching framed photo I'd taken from Grandad's house. What did he mean by a 'doorway'? A doorway to what?

My head was thick, and I spent the night drifting in and out of consciousness. Every few minutes I'd wake and clutch the book to my chest as if it was falling away. Above my head, black shadows fluttered around in the darkness. Watching them eased the blood pumping through my head until I'd fall asleep again for a few minutes, waking up as I imagined the *click click click* of Grandad's tongue against the roof of his mouth. Our language. He was talking to me from wherever he was. Another world. Another universe, perhaps. Why hadn't I listened, that last time I saw him at the university? Hadn't he told me that he'd found something, and he needed to explore it before he could tell me. He promised that I'd be the first one he'd tell, and perhaps this was his way of doing it. Our special language. The Verbatinea. We were two of a kind. Different from everyone else. And now he was coming back to me. After all these years.

The next day dawned grey. I felt stiff and cold. The book was open to the acknowledgements page. At the top, was the name John Gray.

> *My greatest thanks go to my collaborator, Dr John Gray. Many of these findings would not have been possible without your grounding nature and familiarity with the landscape of Western Scotland. You are an expert in your field, and I hope this book helps you to understand that science has the ability to shapeshift, just as we do.*

A quick internet search told me that John Gray was still at the same university Grandad had worked at. He was a professor now, teaching dark matter principles to postgraduates. In all the photos I could find of him, he never once looked happy. I scrolled for a long time looking for the same purple hills in the background, but all I found were the usual blurred

lecture theatre photos and generic headshots. He looked
bored.

I jotted down the address and left with *Hidden Worlds*
stashed in my carrier bag. The sky was dark, heavy with rain,
but it still made me squint in the daylight. The university was
only a bus ride away, and I sat at the very back, shielding my
eyes from the light. A few other passengers gave me strange
looks over their shoulder, but I couldn't understand why.
One of them, a woman wearing a black bobble hat, was
tapping her fingertips on her chin, then her nose, then her
heart. Another, a man wearing a hi-vis jacket, moaned with
every exhale. I could hear him from halfway down the bus.
I sank low in my seat. My hands were sticky from holding
the poles and I wiped them on my jeans.

The campus was far greyer than I remembered. Far fewer
flowers, and the bins overflowed. Benches were missing slats
and all the signposting had been removed. I didn't need it,
though; I knew the way. The physics building was towards
the back, a small cubic block. I measured it up, the steps that
led up to the revolving door, the number of windows lit by
yellow lights. It felt… sad. Sleeping. When I used to peer out
of Grandad's window, there were men and women in white
coats everywhere. Groups of gangly students would sit on
the steps talking or tapping on their phones. But now, only a
few men and women drifted through the quadrangle, heads
down and feet dragging across the pavement. I wondered
if they'd put weights in their shoes, anchoring them to a
place they knew. No one looked up, and the only spark of
life was a crudely drawn piece of graffiti beneath a lower
window. I stared at it for a few minutes trying to understand
it. It looked like someone had started writing something in
red, then changed their mind and started writing something

else. This must have happened a few times because it had become a mad scrawl with only the outer edges of the letters visible.

The door wasn't locked, and inside the corridors were just as barren. A poster told me that Dr John Gray's office was on the third floor, so I made my way along the corridor to the lift. Occasionally, I passed an office with an academic sitting at a desk, typing or staring into space. I ducked underneath the little windows in their office doors and carried on to the third floor. Where was everyone? It didn't make sense. The news about the department's research was on TV all the time. Shouldn't there be more of that buzz here?

I stepped out of the staircase on the third floor, face to face with Grandad's old office. I laid a hand on its surface, and in that second had the mad feeling that I would open the door and see him sitting at his desk, his yellow backpack at his feet. I gave the door a gentle push.

"Who are you?"

I turned to see Dr John Gray standing in the middle of the corridor. The top of his head barely met my shoulder. He wore the same expression he did on all the news reports, in all the online photos. His hands were deep in his pockets and he looked me up and down as he spoke. "Are you here to see me?"

I nodded. "Yes." My voice was hoarse, like I hadn't spoken for days. Dr John Gray didn't seem perturbed by it. He opened the door next to Grandad's office and strode inside, without looking back. I followed him into a surprisingly small room, much smaller than I remembered Grandad's office. Papers were piled high on every surface. When the doctor sat behind his desk, he disappeared into it as a rabbit would in a warren. My breath was coming out in ragged gasps as I tried to stay composed. This was Grandad's colleague. He could tell me everything.

I sat down on the chair opposite, right on top of the paper folders. Dr John Gray looked at me, his face completely impassive. I couldn't read him at all. "Are you a student? You don't look like a journalist."

I nodded my head.

"Are you my student? I don't know your face."

I pulled out *Hidden Worlds* and held it up to him to see. His expression didn't change, but his face went white.

"Do you remember this book?" My hands were shaking, but not with fear. This felt like *euphoria*.

"Where did you find that?" The doctor's mouth hardly moved as he said it.

"My grandfather wrote it." I spent longer on the word 'grandfather' than I would normally. It rolled around on my tongue. I hadn't spoken about him in such a long time, but he was still there, living in my head.

"Oh," he leaned back a little. "Oh. I remember you now." He nodded towards the book. "Well, it's an interesting read, I'm sure you'll agree."

"I've tried, but I can't understand it." Suddenly I didn't want to wait. I *couldn't* wait anymore. "It's instructions, isn't it?"

"Oh, I really wouldn't know about that. Francis wasn't all that clear towards the end." His voice was very flat as he said that. I couldn't understand what he meant.

"He put his instructions in this book; I know he did." I pointed at the cover. "But I can't follow them. I don't know how to follow him."

"What do you mean?"

"He found a doorway or something. Another world,

maybe. I don't know. I was young, only ten. But it makes sense now. He vanished, on one of his research trips. And he quotes you" – I pointed to the book – "in this. You worked with him. What happened?"

Dr John Gray sat back in his chair. His mouth became a tiny slit between non-existent lips. "Have you... talked to anyone else about this?"

I shook my head.

The doctor exhaled slowly through his nose. "I have nothing to do with that book. I don't approve of that book. I don't condone it. I don't even like that my name is mentioned. He certainly didn't ask my permission. I'm sorry, I can't help you."

My lungs shrank in my chest. *No*. "Your name's in it. You can."

"No," he said, "I can't. That book was written against the work of the department. My research with Francis explored the *probability* of multiverses. Your grandfather's ideas were experimental and wildly theoretical. Almost druidic in their sentimentality. They had no place here."

"He credits you. In the back."

The doctor waved his hand as if swatting a fly. "He goads me, I'm sure. That's what he usually did. He knew that I found his passion for this stuff an embarrassment. He never won a single grant for this pursuit, and yet he used the department like his own personal piggy bank. His last efforts were carried out completely independently, against our wishes. That's why he lost his job here. Didn't you know that?"

This didn't make sense at all. "But it's all over the news. You've proven it's all real–"

Dr John Gray laughed. "Just the likelihood of existence

of other worlds, not how to travel to them! What do you think this is?"

I looked down at the book in my lap. *Secrets. Why must there always be so many secrets?* "You know where he is."

"What?" The doctor's eyes opened wide, and I was surprised to see that they were such a bright shade of blue. The rest of him was so very grey.

"Where he went. Where he tried to go. Where he never returned from."

The doctor's forehead wrinkled. "He's dead."

No no no no no. I stood up, towering over the desk. Dr John Gray shrank inside his nest of paper. "Why are you saying that? Why are you protecting him? From me? He wanted me to follow him. *Why is everyone stopping me?*"

"I'm sorry," the doctor wheezed. "I just know that he died, years ago. A stroke, I think. Wasn't it?"

I looked down at John Gray, this beetle of a man. I saw him telling Grandad that he had to leave the university. I saw him on the news, talking about his research into multiverses. I saw him for what he was: *A thief.* And then, there, on the windowpane behind his head, an unmistakable *click click click click click.* The doctor glanced behind him briefly and turned back to me, nonchalant. He might've once been in on Grandad's research, but now he had no idea what was happening. It was beyond him and his piles of paper. I smiled. "He isn't dead. He never was. And you know that."

John Gray rose, but even he seemed to realise that this didn't have the effect that he wanted it to. He continued to shrink. "I can't help. That book is a fiction. It was published by the only back-alley place that would accept it. A bunch of charlatans. I'm sorry, but this is something I can't and won't lie about."

And that was that. Dr John Gray had his eyes and his ears shut. As I'd done so many times before, I took a few deep breaths to calm my beating heart. I wouldn't reply anymore. This man wasn't what I thought he was. He was either a liar or Grandad kept secrets from him, too. In the end, it didn't matter; he was useless to me. And I'd wasted so much time before finding that out. I walked through the empty campus, my ears ringing. All around me, the walls and the pavement clattered like steel on steel. The artificiality of it all felt like daggers in my ears, and with every step, the pavement sent shockwaves up my legs. How could this have ever felt like home? It was a dead planet. The only place I'd felt like everything made sense, was now an ache. Cold pulled at my bones. At the bus stop, a poster showing a man and woman embracing at their front door lit up as the sky darkened. In big blue letters, 'Home is where it starts.'

Without thinking, I let the bus to my flat leave without me, and I crossed the road to the train station.

When Mum answered the door, Dad stood inches behind her. She had his right sleeve in her left hand, and he grasped her left sleeve with his right. Her wrist was scabbed with a ladder of scratches, presumably from Bosey. Her mouth opened wide at the sight of me, and they stood there for a few moments, like a human barricade.

"David! What–"

"Can I come in?"

Mum and Dad continued to stare. Mum's squinting eyes ran up and down my body as if checking and double checking me against some quota. Behind her, Dad... well, he just looked sad. They stepped back into the house and I followed them in, leaving my jacket and shoes on. My nose and throat immediately began to burn. They led me to the living room, where I stood awkwardly for a minute, my carrier bag pinned to my side under my arm.

"Sit down," Mum whispered. *But where?* They still gripped each other's sleeves, as if afraid to let go. I sat in the armchair by the window. It was narrow, and I liked the way the sides squeezed my legs.

"Would you like a cup of tea, David?"

I didn't like tea; never have. But I nodded. It's what you're meant to do, isn't it?

Mum smiled. She looked relieved. "Oh, good," she gasped. "It's supposed to help, isn't it? So silly, but it's what they say on TV." She scuttled off into the kitchen, dragging Dad along with her.

As soon as they were out of sight, I heaved myself from the chair and climbed the stairs as I used to do when I was little, on all fours like a spider. Bosey was lying on the landing, flat on his side, sensuously licking a flank. His eyes were half closed, and he didn't even pause as I stepped over him and into Dad's office. I pulled a carrier bag from my pocket and started filling it with the usual fare: spare printer paper, glue, and an old bottle of black fountain pen ink. I saw that Dad had ordered several new sketchbooks. The paper was thick and warm, but he'd notice if I took it, so I placed it back carefully on the desk. Before heading back to the landing, I ran my hand behind the radiator, *just in case.* Suddenly my wrist burned and my fingers stiffened. *Not now.* I needed to be quick. I scoured my skin against the carpet in an attempt to satisfy the intense itch. I was just about to go downstairs when I heard Mum and Dad whispering. Mum's voice was hushed, shaky. "He's looking more like Francis all the time, isn't he?" A grunt from Dad followed. I stared at the open doorway to their bedroom. Dad's bedside lamp was on, and cast a dull orange glow on the mess strewn across the floor. Every surface was packed with ephemera, from porcelain ornaments and strangely whittled pieces of wood to half-used toiletries. Some were clustered very deliberately in a group, like a circle of lipsticks on Mum's dressing table. But other items were lying on their sides, leaking into the carpet. The floor was littered with packaging and torn postage labels. I knew that if I touched something accidentally, everything else would fall, like a train of dominoes. *It was all so very, very loud. All the stuff was shouting in my head.*

Carefully, I stepped through the swamp, setting my feet down wherever I saw carpet. When I reached Dad's wardrobe, I began moving the stacks of cardboard boxes blocking the door. *Gently, gently.* They felt strangely empty apart from the one on the bottom. I peered inside to find a harmonica, still sealed in its packaging, and an instruction booklet. The invoice was dated over a year before.

Once inside the wardrobe, I started digging around on the shelves and at the bottom, where I knew Dad kept things he didn't know what to do with. The rail was so packed with shirts and jumpers and trousers that it was near impossible to see anything. I pulled out my phone to use the torch and noticed that Emily had called me three times. She'd also messaged me. I was about to swipe it away, but it was so short that the preview said it all, really. It read, 'David. FFS. What are you doing? Call me.'

I shone the torch into the cubby at the bottom, and saw something shining black. I was actually surprised. I'd judged him right. A bin bag, tied with a red cord. The one he'd taken from Grandad's house, the day we went there after he disappeared. I'd seen him fling it into the wardrobe and close the door, like he did with everything he couldn't handle. And though I'd predicted it, I couldn't quite believe that it was still there.

The red cord was tied in a triple knot, so took a painful length of time to undo. I could hear Mum and Dad talking downstairs. Hopefully they thought I'd gone to the bathroom. That would buy me just a few minutes.

As I opened the bag, history plumed from its folds.

That smell. Red iron. Almost a bit sour.

It took me straight back there, to Grandad's house. But it was changed, too, like it had rotted. It carried the musty weight of an attic or basement. *I had to know.* I stuck my hand in, feeling around for something, anything, that might help me find him. Maps. Diaries. Anything. But everything was soft and insubstantial. Clothes. It was all just clothes. My fingertips brushed against a fabric particularly scratchy, and settled on something hard and cold, about the size of a pound coin. I dragged it from the bag. Orange knit. A ludicrously kitsch brass sparrow on the collar, sewn on with brown thread. Grandad's orange jumper. For a few moments I couldn't breathe. My chest felt compressed by the weight of the thing clutched to it. I pushed my face into it, scoring the rough stitches up and down my face, rubbing my cheeks until they were raw. I was holding a ghost. Grandad had become black and white, but now burst into technicolour. This is how I always saw him, wearing this. This horrible orange knit, the one Grandma made fun of. His favourite. The one I'd been so sure he'd taken with him when he'd travelled. But here it was, in my hands. Left behind. Still on this earth, and now passed down to me. A gift.

AFTER

~

When I wake in the lilac light, the hand and the face are gone.

For hours I'd watched it. Occasionally, it would vanish as if swept away by the moths, but then the hand would be back again, pressed so hard against the glass that the wooden frame creaked and groaned. The sight of it yanked the muscles deep inside my chest, but I just sat there, hunched on the corner of the straw mattress, doing nothing. A wisp of recollection occasionally stirred in the back of my head. A memory, but one I couldn't reach. A ghost.

But do ghosts beat at walls? Do ghosts try to clamber inside?

It's a while before I brace myself enough to fling open the cupboard door to see if the worm still coils inside. I nudge it open with a long branch, but find the compartment bare of anything except a heap of something broken, reaching up to my knees. Like a huge eggshell, splintered and shattered, the shards burned into a blackened pile. Feathers and leaves and skins. I nudge a shard with the end of a shoe and it rolls onto a ridged and rounded edge. A brown bit loosens. It smells like rot.

There's no sign of the worm, so perhaps it flattened itself

enough to squeeze beneath the heap and bury itself in the earth. I sit back on the mattress and peer at the glass in the window behind me. Where else am I supposed to go now? I've tried the mountain face, I tried moving the blockage, but I couldn't do it. Not alone. My stomach groans. I haven't eaten in three days. What was the last thing I had? I strain to remember the last flavour that passed my lips, but I can't. I'm changing. Perhaps when I fell down that ravine, I hit my head harder than I thought? Still, it doesn't matter. I can't look back. Only forwards now.

Perhaps it was a clementine? Yes. A clementine.

What if the person pawing at the glass was stuck here, just like me? Michael's words had been, "No one who stays in Mothtown lives there long. Everyone passes over."

But what proof did he have? What if she – something about the hand and face makes me sure it's a woman – travelled here with the same goal, found the way was blocked, and couldn't go back? Could it have been the same woman who I'd seen in the mouth of the cave, as strange and contorted as she was?

Then, the most awful thought, one that's been gnawing at me for the last day, opens like a terrible flower: What if no one has *ever* found the door, and they're stuck here? All of them. But surely, Michael wouldn't keep sending people here if there was nothing to find? Nothing to do but die? Waste away, or fall down a crevasse, or into a bog. But then again, if that did happen – no one would return to ever tell the story. To warn the rest of us.

I shake it off. That's a dark road. I can't go there now.

The woman at the window: she, at least, was real. Perhaps she needed my help? Michael never said that the statute of secrecy ended when we reached Mothtown. It was the first rule of door-seeking: delegates could only make it through if they travelled alone. She shouldn't be here. So even if she did need help, I can't help her. But what if the shadows were pursuing her, too? What was I meant to do? What if I'd strayed too far, after being lost in the marsh, and this was somewhere else? No. This has to be the right place. I'm doing everything I was told to. I sink back into Michael's office in an attempt to remember the moment I knew this was the way. As ever, he was sitting on his leather chair and looking up at something I couldn't see. But this was early on, during our third lesson. Back then, my clothes were still clean and my hands didn't shake. But as I often did, I was fighting a crippling headache that would black out the following day. Once it came on, there was little I could do.

"So," he said, reaching a hand across the table as if he was about to take mine. "We need to find your way out."

"I already know what it looks like," I said, as casually as I could. "I've seen it. In a photograph."

"Oh?" Michael's jaw cocked oddly to the side. "Where? Near where you live? Yorkshire, isn't it?" He pulled a little golden key from his pocket, swivelled around on his chair, and used it to unlock a long wooden box on the cabinet. "No one ever knows their way out before I tell them."

As Michael filled his arms with scrolls, I sought perspective through the window. That day, there was no one at the bus stop, and traffic – nose to bumper to nose – crawled along the road. The bright blank of sky sparked a sharp pain through my temples, so instead I focussed on the soft violet plant on the windowsill. The soil twitched with bluebottles, disorientated, stuck on their backs.

The air in the office was thick. My head throbbed.

Michael dropped the scrolls on his desk. "These are the

doorways we know about so far. There are nine. The dots are the in-use doors. The crosses are doors we can't use anymore." He started to pull the elastic band from one of the largest. "These maps are the shortcuts. This doorway's the closest. I'd suggest this one for you."

"No." I shook my head. "There's a mountain, and heather. It looked cold, and wild. In Scotland. Near Glencoe."

"Where did you see that?"

"That doesn't matter."

Michael's eyebrows raised "It does." He tutted, the tip of his tongue coming to rest on the edge of his teeth. "You can't just follow someone else you know. What works for one doesn't necessarily work for another, everyone's path is different. Your body is different. Your mind is different." He gestured to the row of rolled up papers. "That's why I'm here. To teach you what you need to do to survive, and to find the door with the right shape to let you through."

Why wasn't he listening?

"I know the place. It's the only one that will work."

Michael raised his eyebrows again and shook his head before selecting a roll from the pile. It was a map of the UK, with nine green circles distributed across the isles. I hardly needed to look at it at all before I pointed to where I needed to get to. A doorway that stood alone, with not another one for hundreds of miles. "This one. Is that a mountain?"

Michael squinted. "Yes. And a valley, here." He traced the faint blue line without touching the page. "I've not sent anyone there for a long time, it's the furthest journey, geographically, for most. And most don't want to suffer more than they are already. They want it to be easy. They need it to be." He combed his fingers through his hair, so pale that I could see his scalp. "But I hear this is the best one for seeing the stars." His eyes glittered. "You think that's the one?"

I nodded. "I know it is. It's where I'm meant to be. It's where I'll find… home. What's it called?"

"Doras Mountain. But the road to it, that's Mothtown."

The door in the mountain isn't a mouth now; it's an eye. I even see it when I'm not looking, when I'm trawling the crags around its root, looking for another way in. The chalk shimmers with a fresh layer of frost, and I leave footprints from my too-large shoes. I hobble as best I can with my arms wrapped tightly around my chest. Behind me is a copse of copper trees and cherry buds. How can it be both autumn and spring, when it's winter? I left in winter. *How long have I been here?*

Since I first emerged empty-handed from the mountain, I count two nights in the cabin. If it wasn't for the rivulet down the slope behind the shack, I would have nothing to drink or wash the salt from my eyes. Somehow, the colder the stream gets, the easier it is to swallow. Submerging my foot in the flow numbs my ankle enough to keep searching, walking, *crawling*. My face itches. The heap of skin and bones on the doorstep disintegrates every hour, as if it was never meant to last the light of day. I step over it when I come and go, wishing it would be carried away by the night wind, but not wanting to lose the only remnants I have of something living. It is mostly bones now, broken down by the sun. Insects crawl and leave trails in the ash.

Everything repeats. The trees, the chalk flats, the cracks in the earth. No matter how far I stumble, I always end up back at the cabin just as the sky begins to bleed. I don't even engage my mind anymore; I'm simply a machine trying to get from A to B on too little fuel. But every so often, I snap back to the present and I feel a huge weight on my back, anchoring me in place. It's like I'm trying to knit things together, and each dropped stitch jolts me awake. The soundlessness of the place is loud in my ears, and my steps echo across the valley. I look for shoe tracks in the dirt, poring over tread marks to decipher whether they're feet to follow or signs that the hunters are close. Increasingly, I'm doubled over, my jumper stretched over my raw and swollen back. I've given up trying to speak, and the fire that'd burned my vocal chords until now settles down into a dim ember, aching in my lungs.

And now, as I approach the third night with a stomach that bites at its own walls, I fall to my knees and stuff a handful of the white berries from beside the trail into my mouth. In my desperation, I try to swallow even before I've chewed; but I can't. It's as if my oesophagus had healed over almost completely, like a layer of skin shaped like the bottom of a cup. The berries taste sweet but artificial, like cough syrup, and the sickly flavour lingers long on my tongue even after I lean forwards and let them fall from my lips. I kneel in the copse, too exhausted to rise, but too terrified to lie there. I imagine how it would feel to have a warm blanket weighing down my back. Or for a hand to feed me something warm and soft. Something kind.

I remember him.

I see the back of him, standing straight against the mountain. He doesn't move any more than a portrait does; he just stares at the road ahead. It's the landscape around him that shifts, breeds, and grows greener and greener until the figure is small and obscured by grass stems as tall as lampposts. And even so, I'm looking up at him, because I'm even smaller.

I hope he made it. I can't imagine that he'd suffered like this.

It starts to rain, and I hold my face up to the clouds. Even though I'm shaking, I savour the jolt of each drop on my tongue. The painting falls away, and I'm here again. Alone. The backs of my hands look grey and dry enough to be stone. I want to cry, "This isn't what I wanted." But instead, all I can do is release a low moan like an animal. I clutch at my chest and then for the cold, blunt grasp of brass at my collar, anything to bring me back to earth, but my fingers are lost in the mass of holes.

No. No. No.

It's gone. Grandma's brass button. The sparrow. I grab a handful of wool and curl my head down to my knees. *It's all falling away. All of it.*

There's a noise, as light as a footstep behind me, but it hits me like a sonic boom. And this time I don't feel the urge to run at all. I squint through the trees to see who or what it is, but my head is too fuzzy to make anything out. Even the trees look as if they're walking towards me.

It might be the woman with the face like a moon.

Wings flutter inside my chest. I search through the trees for her, try to taste her on the air. *If only I could shout.* What if she's stuck somewhere or starving? Wouldn't it be better to suffer with a hand to hold? We can't step into each other's heads but maybe we don't need to. If we're both here, we're both the same. We can help each other. I open my mouth and shout a name… and what comes out hawks the air. It doesn't even sound human; it's mechanical, but it's all I can do, so I call again and again until, exhausted, I fall forwards onto my hands in the litter.

Can she hear me?

But when I look up, the trees have shifted to the side

and there are two figures, dressed in grey, standing between the voice and I. It's them. Something about their clothes; I recognise them now. All-in-ones, all loose and baggy. Each one has something clipped to their chest. I can't work out how, but they're part of the same story as the woman with the swollen middle. I can see them together, somewhere open, and they were coming for me then, too. Everything was loud and people were screaming. Neither of them move, and although their faces are as featureless as the sun, I know they've come for me. It's time.

No.

I scramble to my knees and crawl, but it's not fast enough. Over my shoulder, the two figures take a step towards me, their arms held slightly out from their sides. There's something tentative about the way they move, and it disconcerts me more than if they rushed towards me.

It's too late. I can't go back now.

I don't know where the energy comes from, but in one, final, desperate burst, I stagger to my feet and race through the trees. The cabin is just ahead, though the hunters are close behind, crushing the undergrowth with each stride.

I slam the cabin door and heave the desk in front of it, but it won't be enough. I drag the straw mattress against it too, and tug at my hair as I work out what else can be used to bar the way in. In a moment of madness, I try prising the cupboard door off its hinges, but they hold fast. Heavy fists hammer on the door, and I feel like I'm being shaken in a box.

And then I see the heap of dead things.

I fall into it, pulling it apart and spreading it around me. Feathers and leaves and more shredded skins. *Hide, hide, hide.* I'm wearing it like a coat and I feel heavier all the time. But then I see what lay beneath the broken mound: a tunnel, which drops a few feet and twists sharply to the right.

Towards the mountain.

The tunnel smells sweet, like pears, and as I lean closer, I see the soil is twitching with shining particles like glass. I press my finger to one, but it doesn't hurt – in fact, it's warm. All the blood rushes to that hand and my eyes roll back in my head with relief.

Behind me, the cabin door buckles against the furious slamming and the desk legs squawk a few inches across the floor. I shed the skin, swing my legs over the edge of the hole and, with one final breath, lower myself down. There's just about enough room to crouch while I close the cupboard door behind me and slink like a worm through the shimmering opening ahead.

BEFORE

13.

Wait. Stop. It's my turn to ask *you* something.

This glass, littered around my feet. It's not the way I remember it at all. This room, his room... It was always neat, everything in its place. Instruments sat in their corners, metal settled like stone. Glinting in the window-light, like old stars.

The glass. The glass is not just glass. There's skin there, thin smoky strips like damp paper. What is it? Should I know? Can't you tell me?

Back at the flat, I stored the orange jumper and a few other shirts I'd taken carefully in my box of treasures. The box was half full now. As I peered in over the edge and surveyed my collection, I felt fuller somehow. Like the more things I put in there, the more rounded I was myself. I'd never shown anyone else what was in the box. Why would I?

I spread the materials I'd foraged from Dad's office on the floor along with the last bag of leaf matter from the cemetery. In the centre of the pile, I placed the mouse and a small, feathered body I'd found by the side of the road a few weeks earlier. The skin had already rotted away, leaving just fuzz and bones. It might've been something as plain as a sparrow, but as I traced the skull with my fingertip, it was as beautiful a bird as any I'd ever seen.

Beside my bed, the canopy groaned and a thin waxy layer of matter hanging loose fluttered to the floor. My stomach squeezed. The days were passing quickly now, and the glue wasn't sticking. How could it fulfil its purpose if it couldn't even hold itself together? The structure was me, and I was it. Perhaps it needed to breathe, to beat like a thriving heart.

Perhaps the structure was missing an ingredient.

I pressed a fallen leaf to my tongue and then back onto the wall, but once again it drifted to the ground. Blood? Would that work? Perhaps foraged natural matter wasn't enough; maybe there needed to be a bit of me in there too. *But the size of it.* The structure must have been seven feet high, at least. Midwinter was only a few weeks away now. I couldn't leave it another year, I couldn't. I couldn't see another year in, not in this shape. And if I wasn't careful, my window would close.

And so, as the night fell, I rolled up my sleeve and sliced my forearm with a pair of kitchen scissors before settling down beneath the structure to paste a fragile layer of skin, feathers, and bone with dripping garnet.

KNOCK KNOCK.

I woke up curled on my side. The wooden floor felt cold against my face. The light through the window shone silver, and the faint call of the dawn chorus could be heard as birds passed through to greener places. For a moment, everything was peaceful. I heaved myself up into a sitting position and crouched there awkwardly, all knees and elbows. In that moment, I couldn't see how it might feel to hold yourself and not be disgusted.

I pictured Dr John Gray, squatting in his nest of paper. He hardly moved his face or body at all, as if he didn't need to. His body was his fortress. I shuddered. Just the thought of him still flooded my heart with disappointment. I'd surprised myself by having such high hopes for the visit. Why was I so shocked that I'd met another dead end? Hadn't it been locked doors and lies that'd cut short my search for Grandad when I was a child? I'd been left with no one to turn to, no one to trust. Recently, I'd drifted. How could I have forgotten that I was always going to be on my own?

Whatever Grandad had done, it was thoroughly off the academic grid. I slid *Hidden Worlds* across the floor so that it lay between my knees. Dr John Gray had said that Grandad had published with a bunch of charlatans, the only ones who'd touch the book. *A "back-alley place," he'd said.* I turned the book over and found the logo in the bottom corner. An orange bird, spread-eagled and soaring like a phoenix. It almost disappeared into the book's red cover. Beside it was the name of the publisher, Melius Est.

I opened up my laptop and typed it into Google, but all that came up were Latin Dictionaries and translation sites. So I added *Hidden Worlds* to the search and there it was: the phoenix with feathers sticking out at all angles. Melius Est was a publisher, but more than that, they looked to be a collective of books all based around New Age principles. I was surprised to see books on Tarot cards and palm reading side-by-side with books on astronomy, but I didn't dwell on it and quickly searched the menu for a list of FAQs. My eyes flicked past the history of Melius Est and how far they'd come, and came to rest on a tiny link at the bottom of the page, a button that took me to their community forum: The

Institute of Homefinders. My heart started to race again and I squeezed it back into my chest with my hand.

Homefinders. Homefinders. The girl at Sam's house had said she wanted to go home. And that hadn't been the first time, had it? I squeezed my face in my hands as I rewound my brain back to where I'd heard it.

The library. The mudman. He'd said they were all going home. My throat tightened. How could I have forgotten that?

I opened up the forum, and a welcome message filled the screen. *Could this be it?* It read:

WELCOME TO THE INSTITUTE OF HOMEFINDERS.

We began as a small co-operative, determined to find a road to a better world. The world we were born to join.

It used to be that it was only those who had nowhere else to go came to us, finding us through paper flyers in internet cafés and libraries.

Dislocated folk.

But now, we're growing. We're a movement.

It's time to discover your true home. The place you belong.

Welcome to your doorway.

Doorway. *Like Grandad's doorway.*

I couldn't catch my breath. Was I falling, or were the

walls rising? I was gripping my knees, but it didn't help; I was still spiralling down. I locked my eyes on the screen and watched as the welcome message faded, and a bright orange phoenix soared across the top of the page. It was a login page. It looked like you needed a username and a password. The only other option was to 'Request Membership.'

No. No. No.

I needed to get in. I clicked the 'Request' button and desperately filled in my name, email, and home address. The last box to fill in was for 'any additional information to consider.' I didn't even pause. Before clicking submit, there was only one thing I could write:

I DON'T BELONG HERE. I WANT TO GO HOME.

The confirmation email had said my request could take up to a week to be answered. I must have sat on the floor clicking refresh for hours before I finally gave in and left the flat. The air in there was thick and tasted stale, and I was finding it hard to breathe.

When I opened my door onto the corridor, on my doormat was another package, the same size and shape as last time. How long had it been there? I stared at it for a few minutes before picking it up and tearing at the cornflower-blue cardboard. It seemed tougher this time, my fingers tangling in the tape. Eventually, I pulled out a set of coloured pencils, a sketchpad, and a small pin, printed with 'Introverts unite separately.' Again, there was no return address, but this time a little slip had been included in the package. It read:

Hope you enjoy this gift. We are beside you, always.
The Blue Pilgrims.

Everything went cold. Who was with me? What was going on? I dropped the open package on the doorstep and stepped over it to the staircase. My skin was starting to itch again, around the wrists, and I clawed at them as I descended the metal stairwell. As I reached the ground floor, a woman with short black hair was inspecting the small letterboxes for general mail. She didn't seem to notice me in the doorway, and kept squinting at the door numbers as if she couldn't quite make them out. But I did notice one thing: her blue fleece. The blue forget-me-not embroidered onto the shoulder. I turned quickly to head out of the fire exit. Were they watching me? Why? Suddenly I needed to get out. The walls were all watching me, flickering like blue irises. *Why couldn't they just leave me alone?*

On the street, passers-by were hurrying about on their lunch breaks. I stepped into the throng. Many were shovelling food straight into their mouths as they walked. Others leaned against walls or sat on benches, their thumbs flicking wildly across their phone screens. On one corner, I passed a man in a blue checked shirt and a white apron. He was standing with his back to the street, his hands spread wide across a brick wall. Every few seconds he ran one hand down the wall, and then the other. Even against the street noise, I thought I could hear the grating of nails against the clay. His eyes were cast upwards towards the sky, and his lips mouthed words I couldn't make out. It looked like he was trying to climb the wall and hadn't realised that it wasn't happening.

Normally I'd have just walked by like everyone else, leaving him in his bubble. But this time I approached him and placed a hand on his shoulder. I stuttered as I tried to voice something, *anything*, to help bring him back down to the ground. But the words wouldn't come, and as he stared right into my eyes I felt not even a single shred of recognition. He muttered a few words under his breath but they didn't make any sense at all. It was an entirely different language.

"I'm here," I whispered. "You're here."

The man yanked his shoulder from my grasp, almost as if he was frightened. I raised my hands and then, in one mad and unplanned moment, I began clicking my tongue against the roof of my mouth. But, his forehead a map of creases, the man backed away from me, making a strange chirping sound as he did so. Soon he disappeared around a corner and I was alone again, my heart cold and my skin prickling. Reaching up my jumper, I raked my nails down my side but it didn't help. Standing there, I could've quite happily torn off my skin. I smiled. *Not long to go yet. Not long.*

I pulled up my hood before entering the arcade. It was busier than usual. I didn't want to hold my head up too much in case Paul caught sight of me; after all, I hadn't been back to work in two days. He hadn't even messaged me. But I needed to keep glancing up to avoid the walkers striding about. No one else seemed to want to budge. Luckily the central bench was empty, and as I sat on it, I spread myself out so no one would try to share. I didn't want the hassle, I couldn't deal with the distraction.

Inside the art shop, Agatha was sorting through a cardboard box on top of the central glass counter. Every so often she'd raise a little bottle of what I supposed was paint up to the ceiling lamp and peer through it before placing it carefully back in the box.

At some point very soon, I was going to have to tell her the truth. I'd put it off for far too long. But every time I'd thought of doing it, I'd shut it down. And now there were too many things to say, and they swarmed around me like flies. What'd happened with the girl at Sam's house. The plans I had for Agatha and I. And now… the Homefinders. I'd known exactly what Agatha and I were going to do, but now… everything was upside down. It was as if my sight had cracked, and now Agatha existed on the other side of the mirror. The thing is, I'd always thought she was just like me. An outsider, with her ever-changing hair and unusual smile. It'd been what drew me to her when we first met in the art shop. She was standing alone in the corner of the store, her hands wrapped around her middle. She'd given me this huge grin, her mouth shining like a crush of pearls, and my stomach just *flipped*. She saw me and understood me. But I suppose the more I'd learned about her, I'd discovered that she wasn't *quite* like me. Like Emily, she integrated in a way that I didn't. And she had a family that she lived with. A mum who brought her cling-filmed tuna sandwiches and a paper bag of cherries that stained her lips purple. A little brother who came to visit her sometimes in a black hoodie and jeans, his face low and self-conscious. I'd never actually spoken to him, but I often smiled as he passed me on the way out of the arcade. He'd normally give me a little side-look as if he shouldn't be speaking to me and then scurry off down the road. I wondered what Agatha had said about me to make him so embarrassed.

But still… the sight of her purple hair anchored me there. I felt my breath deepen and my body fill the bench. She always did this to me. She made me feel real. Like anything was possible.

I was still watching her when a man and woman dressed in blue fleeces started to approach me from my left. Their eyes were fixed on me, and the woman wore a huge smile, her lips tight.

No time for that shit.

I heaved myself to my feet. Surely they wouldn't follow me down the street? That's not the Blue Pilgrim way. I whispered a goodbye to Agatha before striding as fast as I could towards the exit.

"Please sir, please stop." A hand on my shoulder. Her voice was soft and clear. It had a sing-song quality to it that made me want to hear more, but I knew I couldn't. Talking to the Blue Pilgrims once they'd picked you was a slippery slope. From the safety of the counter at Flynn's, I'd watched people being led away, always gently, to the blue cars parked outside. And then presumably to a blue house and locked behind those cloudy shutters. Some were faces I recognised, gaunt men and women who found themselves on the benches regularly, just sitting in silence. Some were the men and women who poured themselves out onto the street, desperate to be heard. They'd tried to take Sam a few times, hadn't they, but he seemed to make sport of attracting them and then fighting them off. But I had no energy for that.

I twisted from her grasp, and as she let go I felt this strange violent lurch in the pit of my belly, and I fought the urge to be sick. Holding my breath, I staggered from the arcade as quick as I could, my head down. Outside, it had begun to snow, and the street was a moving tableau of dusted black umbrellas and jackets. Somehow the snow made everything out there seem quieter, and I leaned against the wall behind the arcade, my arms wrapped around my jacket. I was suddenly aware of being massively hungry, so much so that I leaned over as far as I could to get some blood back into my head.

Not remembering if I'd brought a card to pay for anything, I reached into my pocket. I let out a little groan as that confirmed that I'd definitely left all my money in the flat.

Out of habit more than anything, I pulled out my phone and sank to a crouch.

A reply from the Homefinders. *Already*.

Inside were the login details. Fumbling with the icons, I found the welcome page again and entered the username they'd issued me and the password. After a few terrifying seconds where all I had was a white screen, a whole world opened up before me. Hundreds and hundreds of chat groups. Messages popping up every minute in conversations about missing people, dark matter, and doorways. 'How to find your doorway.' 'How to prepare for the wilderness.' 'Are there directions in the night sky?' 'What do you think lies on the other side?' One forum was entitled 'Doorway search.' I opened it and scanned down the thread. Users were posting photographs of places they thought could be doors – mostly caves, crypts, and in one case, a sewer drain. No one was sitting back. Everyone was doing something to change things, to find their origins.

Above my head, something *tap tap tapped* on a glass window.

These people, they were all in the wrong skin too. Never meant to fit in. Just like me. Just like Grandad. But no… that wasn't quite right. Scrolling through it all, I couldn't see anything to indicate their plans were the same as mine. They weren't trying to change their skin; they were trying to change their place. Just like Grandad did.

My project. I'd been going about it all in entirely the wrong way.

A burst of colour in my head, red and orange and purple, and suddenly it all made sense. I wasn't born in the wrong skin. No. I was born in the wrong world. And I needed to find my way out of it.

14.

It was surprising, even to me, how rapidly I became words on a computer screen. All I wanted to do was lie on the floor and scroll through the forums for names and places I might recognise. Very quickly, I spotted a picture of the long street in Mum and Dad's village which led to the broken fence and the cow fields. It was posted in a forum for locating missing 'nomads,' as they were called, and was accompanied by a photo of a woman with thick curly black hair that fell in coils around her face, and a desperate plea: "Gabriella Wilson. Last seen near here, Yorkshire, England. If you've seen her, please contact us. Reward offered."

Other users posted photos of similar streets, decorated with moulting bouquets. But the more recent the photo, the fewer the flowers. No one posting seemed to say what the importance of these streets were; only that someone who may or may not have been their friend had last been seen there, trudging downhill, somehow familiar but not quite themselves. And since no one in the forum lived on these streets, no one could confirm or deny if the person listed had been seen. The story looped on and on. I scrolled down the forum for a long while before I gave up. The last message I got to was posted seven years earlier, but the posts

went back way further than that. A few times, my fingers
hovered over the keys, ready to share that I'd lived on that
street, that I'd seen the lonely figures trudge down the road.
The mudmen. But doing that would've opened me up to a
world of vulnerability. For the first time since those early
years of my life when I sat by Grandad's side in his office,
I felt safe, hidden in the darkness of my flat. To tell people
where I was from would've felt like tearing open my heart.

I looked up at the canopy in the corner of my room,
unfinished folds of black skin dangling from the frame.
Several pages of sheet music stuck out from the bottom
edge, not yet glued properly to the tissues and feathers and
matter. I hadn't worked on it for days. I had another goal
now. But its dark silence was still so inviting. I crawled into
the chamber and imagined it closing around me, like hot
hands pressed over my ears. Staying hidden for now was
too warm, too delicious.

For the most part, I watched as uncountable users discussed
parallel lives, the paths people choose to travel, potential
maps to doorways. About a third of the conversations were
dedicated to sustainable living and survival tips, everything
from which plants were best for kindling to edible mushroom
identification. I scrolled past those quickly, but mentally
logged that they'd be important to me later, once I'd made
a plan and built up my supplies. Instead, I began trawling
through the other discussion boards in earnest for mentions
of either *Hidden Worlds* or Grandad. None of the suggested
reading lists included the book, but these lists were scattered
across the site, so it was potentially impossible to check them
all. In fact, nothing I could see explicitly connected to the
ideas in *Hidden Worlds* at all, but I had to be patient. There
were thousands of different discussions going on, and I just

needed to find the right one. That was all. But I constantly fought this red-hot urge in my head to scream, *'There's no time for this.'* I wanted to find someone, an administrator, someone who could guide me through the ever-growing family of posts. There was a 'donate' button in the corner and a guide for 'Forum best practice,' but no site owner, no contact details. Even the users were anonymous, having been given randomly-generated usernames when signing up. So even though I was now part of a community, I still couldn't quite find my way in.

I spent a lot of time scrolling through the digital boards where missing people were posted. Unlike news broadcasts or posters on lampposts, these notices didn't aim to get the person back. Each one had a thread of comments beneath with "Congratulations!" and "She did it!" and "I wish she could tell us where she is now." Often there'd be a list of that person's favourite hangouts and places they would've been, a description of the last set of clothes they were seen wearing, and anything that was missing from their cupboards. And sometimes, users could comment with possible sightings or their suggestions for which locations they thought the clues added up to. Some users even uploaded blurry thumbnails where they'd taken a sneaky photo of a silhouette they believed was the missing person. In my eyes, the blurry photos could've been anyone, but they did always wear a lot of outdoor gear and a rucksack, as if on a long journey.

I scrolled for hours, looking for his wonderful, round, bespectacled face. Hours, going back as far as the discussion board would let me, twelve years... Four years after Grandad had disappeared. But still, at that point in the timeline there were few enough faces to check them all to see if Grandad was one of them. And of course, he wasn't there; I didn't really expect him to be. The idea of Dad getting this far was outlandish at best. So who would have posted Grandad's photo there, other than me?

I kept a silent watch over the more intimate discussion groups that talked about *why*. Rarely would a user get emotional over someone that'd already disappeared, and I supposed that any family members who were using the Homefinders only to find a loved one were weeded out before long. I got far more satisfaction watching everyone else discuss, debate, and argue than I would've done by participating. I even started to recognise some usernames, like Violet239, who posted regularly on the digital noticeboard with possible sightings. I wondered how she could possibly be in so many places at once. Users commenting on her posts to say that she brought them hope only resulted in more photos and more sightings. The photos were always grainy and composed of the person's back or side. No one ever debunked them.

I needed to reach out. I needed to take a risk.

With my heart pounding in my chest, I set up a new discussion thread and named it 'The Multiverse Theory and Doorways.' I didn't know how honest to be, so I posted under the header just to say that someone I'd known had disappeared, and they'd known something about the multiverse theory that wasn't common knowledge. That I needed to know the truth, so I could find him. I don't know what I was hoping for… just someone, anyone, who could help me get to the next step. Someone who knew or had helped Grandad. I stared at the post for hours. It was only when a whole twenty-three hours had passed since posting, that a single reply, short and blunt, appeared.

Shouldn't this be a missing persons post?

I didn't reply. I closed the discussion and instead took to mindlessly refreshing the site so whatever posts were 'new' floated to the top like cream. My eyes began to sting, clouding with floaters, so every few hours I would lie back on the bed and rest them. Whenever I stood up to go to the toilet or open my mouth beneath the kitchen tap, it was as if my legs were made of water. They wiggled and moved in ways I could hardly control. A few times, I almost stumbled and fell, and for a brief second wondered if I would hit the floor with a thud or disappear with a splash, nothing left but a puddle.

I left my phone plugged into the wall and ignored the frequent vibrations. If it was Paul, it didn't matter now anyway. How could I go back? If it was Emily, I didn't want to speak to her. The only person that tempted me to look at the screen was Agatha, but I fought against it. I'd been distracted for far too long. Now, my eyes were on the horizon. I could see the light. I couldn't look away now, not yet. Not until I had all the puzzle pieces in my hands. Then it'd be time to talk to her.

One of the usernames I was starting to see regularly was Jamestown42. He often posted on the more scientific areas of the site, and didn't need to soften his words with 'please' or 'thank you' His logic was a solid gold circle. He referenced textbooks and online journals, he linked arguments to similar arguments in other groups, and, most importantly, he led a forum about the multiverse theory. I scrolled all the way back to four years ago when Jamestown42 had set up the thread, looking for mentions of anything that mentioned Francis Porter or even just photos of places that looked similar to the photograph of Grandad in *Hidden Worlds*: the wide valley, the row of crags like angry teeth. Anything mentioning Glencoe. But I found nothing, and instead started following closely whenever Jamestown42 posted something. If ever he wrote more than a couple of sentences, users fell upon it, showering it with 'thumbs up's and replying in their droves. I got the feeling he'd been a member for a long time, even before he set up that thread, and though there was never any hint of superiority or clue to his being more than a member, I trusted what he wrote. Whereas a lot of the other users often got carried away with what I considered to be wishful thinking, he kept it real. He *was* real.

Late one night, as I lay on the floor with the laptop blowing hot air on my stomach, I opened up Jamestown42's profile and sent him a direct message. He must've been logged in too, as he replied immediately with a short message saying hello, and asking if I was new. It'd only been four days since I'd first logged in, but I couldn't let him think I was completely green. So I told him I wasn't new, but that I'd been spending the time researching and learning as much as I could about the rules before I posted. As I waited for a reply, I noticed a strange taste in my mouth. Looking down at my fingers, my index fingernail was gnawed to a stump, pooling with bright blood. I wiped the back of my hand across my lips and then watched the red smear as it dried into my knuckles. By the time Jamestown42 replied, it was already started to flake.

Why are you here?

Finally. Time for the truth.

Have you heard of Francis Porter?

There was a pause.

No.

I realised that I'd been holding my breath and I released it.

> He wrote a seminal book called *Hidden Worlds*. It's
> not in print anymore.

There was an even longer wait before he replied with a link
to a second-hand bookshop site.

> Is this it?

There it was. I could hardly believe it. It looked to be a slightly
different edition, but it was definitely the same book. The
price was low, only a few pounds. I typed my reply.

> That's it. He worked on the Multiverse Theory. He was
> a Doctor of Physics. An expert.

Jamestown42 told me that he'd order a copy. That the book
wasn't seen as 'canon,' so he'd overlooked it. But it didn't
make sense that he hadn't heard of *Hidden Worlds*. Not only
did it explore everything that The Institute of Homefinders
was about, it was written by an expert on multiverse theory
who had actually gone and followed his own research. It was
even published by Melius Est. So how could Jamestown42
not even recognise it? How could he think the book wasn't
'canon'?

Before he signed off, Jamestown42 typed,

> Are you coming to the next gathering? Michael might
> help you.

I sat up. An actual meet-up? In person? And who was Michael? I clutched at my ears, blocking out the *loud loud loud* clambering grind of thoughts. I blew out one long breath through pursed lips. Calm hands. Calm fingers. *Type slowly. Carefully.*

No. Who is Michael?

I waited for a reply, one hand still on the keyboard and the other buried deep in my hair. Had he gone? Panic squeezed my throat as I felt my grip on Jamestown42 loosen. I typed again.

Could I be invited?

The little dots that meant Jamestown was typing flickered across the screen, so I released another breath and clamped my hands in my armpits.

Michael is the founder. He helps people to leave this world. But there's a price.
Michael keeps the maps.

He forwarded me a link to a short webform. At the top read:

**You've been invited to the Brick Lane Homefinders' Gathering
on Saturday 14th December**

This weekend. Three days away. I could manage it. I spread my hands across my chest and lay back on the mattress. Above, the ceiling, the lamp, the walls… everything spun.

This was it. Answers were coming, from Michael. The name burst from my lips. *Michael. Michael. Michael.*

"David." She spluttered when she said it. I pressed my phone hard against my cheek. I had to sound... *cool. Calm.* "David. Where have you *been*? I thought–"

"I've been busy, working. You know."

"But David, I've been calling. Mum and Dad said you were–"

"I'm calling you now, Emily."

"But David," she let out this strange, dry laugh. "Mum's been talking about a blue house–"

"I just saw them recently, everything's fine. I'm calling you back now. Isn't that OK?"

The end of the line went silent for a moment, the soft wave of Emily's breath just about audible. She sighed, and then whispered, "You can't keep doing this to people. We're trying our best."

I wanted to ask her what she expected of me, what she thought I was doing. Why my doing nothing was such a trauma for her. I wasn't bothering anyone. What it mattered, when she had her own world to fill. In London. But I couldn't. I couldn't be honest today.

"I want to see you," I said. "Can I come down?"

Again, she went silent. Was I supposed to fill the gap? I was just about to speak, but instead, Emily spat, "Really? You want to come here?"

"Yes."

She took a deep breath. "What's happened?" Suddenly, her voice seemed very small.

"No. Everything's fine. We just need to talk, that's all."

"Have you told Mum this? She's worried about you."

"Can I come, Emily? I can buy the tickets tonight, before they jack up the price." This bit wasn't a lie. My ticket to the Gathering had almost cleared out my account. I could just about afford the train fare to London. But after that, I didn't have many options.

"David…" Emily sounded weak, weary. I felt my insides brace. I knew this was coming.

"Are you embarrassed?"

"No!" She shouted it down the line, but the word was drawn out unnaturally, so I knew it came from somewhere manufactured. "How could you say that? You're my brother."

"Will Jed be there?"

"No, he's away until Monday. A sales fair." She tailed off. "Maybe it'll be better if it's just us anyway, more room. We can talk." The end of the line rustled. "Like old times."

I'd never seen Emily where she lived, not since she first left home at eighteen. I still thought of her as a fixture at Mum and Dad's house, cradled in an armchair with her legs swung over the back wing. The idea of seeing her somewhere else twisted my stomach into knots. But that wasn't important anymore. I had a purpose.

When the time came to leave on the Friday night, I packed only a few things, but made sure they were my cleanest things, and headed to the train station. I just needed to get through that evening with Emily, and then I'd have most of Saturday to myself. Emily had a theatre appointment that afternoon, and though she'd offered to cancel it, I told her I'd happily spend that afternoon seeing some of the sights.

I took a window seat and set up my laptop straight away on the little folding desk. I ran my hands through my hair to ease the tickle inside my head. The world outside roared by, green on green, and I took a picture before sending it to Agatha. "I'll be back soon," I messaged. "I'm sorry for staying away from you. I'll explain when I'm back. I promise." I scrolled through some pictures I had of her and stopped on the one in the little café, from a year ago, when her hair was more bubble-gum pink than purple. Her head was down over a wide cup of coffee, her ears hidden beneath a pair of huge black headphones.

She was so beautiful.

I didn't like the cold, creeping feeling that had started to slink up my spine, so I put my phone away and pulled *Hidden Worlds* from my bag. Most pages were a blur of small script, but I knew the pages with the photographs by heart. I flicked to the photo of Grandad in the mountains, near Glencoe, and laid it side by side with the small photo I'd taken from his house when I'd last visited with Dad. Perhaps a geographer would've been able to match them, but to me, a mountain looks completely different from each angle. But what couldn't be ignored was the great peak in both of the backgrounds, one side layered with jutting crags like teeth. A little valley, perhaps, to the right of the mountain. The glint of a stream down its centre.

"I'm coming," I whispered.

Compared to the muted, mauve tones in the photographs, the land outside my window looked fluorescent, but flat. I could see for huge stretches, but those dull, cultivated miles held very little to keep me. Man-made and man-kept squares of green, controlled and utilised. And beneath the silver veil of frost, not all of it looked to be thriving. One copse of oaks near the horizon looked scorched, the bark burned black and all the leaves fallen into the dirt. Through the trees, I could just about see a round white tent smeared grey, and three little caravans with their wheels removed. A low picket fence circled the space and separated it out into pens. There were a few animals – pigs, perhaps – and three women crouching by a blackened patch on the ground. The remains of a bonfire, maybe.

I trained my eyes on the tent until it disappeared behind the trees. Perhaps that was a bunch of friends, starting again? Or perhaps they were Homefinders too, searching for a doorway. And in that moment, I knew three things for certain: One was that they hadn't wanted to be seen. Another was that they were only visible due to the damage to the trees. And finally, that if I'd ever travel on that track again, the little commune would be gone.

Emily met me just past the ticket barriers at Kings Cross. She was dressed all in black: tight black jeans, a fluffy jumper, and a stiff suit jacket. She had one hand on her bag and the other was rubbing her stomach as if it pained her. Behind her was a street performer on a pedestal, painted grey and marbled, as if he was made of stone. People brushed past him in a hurry but he never wobbled or flinched. Everyone was in a hurry. Everyone.

Even from a distance, Emily didn't look like herself. Her skin sapped the light, her eyes pink and small. She smiled a tight little smile, which only slackened when I stumbled over my own feet as I approached her from the platform. The skin inside my nostrils stung, so I held my arm across my nose while I acclimatised to the London fumes. Looking around, though, no one else seemed to be bothered by them.

Emily pulled me into a hug and I didn't know what to do with my arms because she seemed so much shorter and rounder than I remembered. But as I leaned into her and her soft hair brushed against my face, it was as if I'd fallen and landed into a cushion. We stood like that for some time, as I watched the news-screen above our heads reveal today's headlines: 'Record number of bodies dredged from Thames,' 'Compulsory therapy for undiagnosed malaise to be rolled out,' and lastly, 'Fourteen backpacks found abandoned in Scottish woodland.'

My heart leapt.

15.

I'd always imagined Emily's flat to be made of wide, white spaces. All light and air, glass and magnolia. A place you could swing your arms and not knock anything down. But as if turned out, it wasn't all that much bigger than my own flat. Furniture jutted from doorways so the rooms overlapped, kitchen pans hung on the wall above the sofa, and you could only get to the bathroom through Emily's bedroom, as if she slept in a passageway. But despite the clutter, every surface was spotlessly clean, and every knick-knack fit to its shelf like pieces of a jigsaw.

As she directed me to sit on the sofa, I noticed that the air smelled like aftershave – rich, oud-y, expensive. On the coffee table was an open laptop beside a scribbled-in notepad and pen. The handwriting and set up looked so familiar to my own that instinctively I leaned across to see what research she'd been doing. But no; it was all just hollow marketing jargon. Emily must have taken work home. On the other side of the laptop was a pile of A4 pages, about eight inches high. Sections were held together by bulldog clips, and as I flicked through the pile, I saw that they were all stamped with 'Audition Script.' When Emily saw me looking, she picked them up and brushed it off with a, "Just something

I'm trying out, not that I have much time." I was surprised that Emily needed books of words to tell her what to say.

I couldn't tell which bits of the flat belonged to Emily or Jed. The walls were hung with abstract posters and prints of things that didn't seem to hold any resemblance to real life at all. Colourful squares and inky triangles. Emily caught me looking at one of them when I first walked in, a moody sequence of vertical columns. "Do you like it?" she asked. "It's one of Jed's. It's a painting of the London skyline. See here," she traced one of the tallest blocks. "That's Big Ben." I kept looking long after Emily had turned away. I could only see bodies walking in every direction, all alone. Some had more than two legs. Some had wings.

The sofa was already made up for me with a coverless duvet and bristling woollen blanket. There was a book on the pillow, *RSPB's Birds of London*. Emily pointed it out to me. "I thought you'd like a book to read in bed. You always had your nose in a book." She reached up and tweaked my nose as if I was still too young to do anything about it, but I twisted away from her grip. She looked abashed, so I smiled to let her know it was OK, really. I didn't want the weekend to start badly. I needed to be here until at least tomorrow night at the earliest. I'd keep it light.

I sat on the sofa while she clattered around in the kitchen. With her back to me, she didn't even try to fill the silence that pulsated between us. Every time she turned around, her eyes glanced around the corner of the room before turning away again. It was as if she kept forgetting where she'd left me. I didn't say anything either, just watched her cook as I thumbed through the book of birds. Pigeons. Jays. A drawing of crows and carrion. The longer Emily cooked, the pinker her face became. I'd never seen her flush so much before. Her skin had always been porcelain. Snow under glass. Never melting.

"It's so good to have you here," she called, even though she was only about ten feet away. Steam rose from the hob. "I mean, I can't believe you actually came."

I shuffled in my seat. "Right."

"You're actually here."

"Yeah." I laid the book on my lap and pressed the pages open on a chapter on starlings. I ran my finger down a dark wing speckled with iridescent purple, gold, and jade. "Where's Jed, again?"

Emily dropped a spatula onto the kitchen floor. "Shit. Oh, he's already gone. He won't be back until Sunday night, so you'll probably miss him entirely."

"Right."

"Right." Emily ran one hand through her hair before she doled out the pasta into bowls. "He's away a lot. Life in the big city, David. It's hardcore."

She set a bowl down for me on the coffee table, a huge pile of fusilli, olives, grated cheese, and a mysterious creamy sauce. It burned my palette, and soon my tongue felt numb. *So much salt.* After a few mouthfuls, I struggled to swallow.

"Do you like it? It's Jed's recipe. I fudged it, really."

I swallowed and smiled. Emily pouted and looked at her knees. "What do you eat? At home? Are you cooking?"

"Sometimes. Simple things."

"It's just… you look… *thin*. Dad told me you were losing weight, but I didn't think it'd be this much."

I didn't know what she meant; I felt good. Better than I had in months.

"David," Emily said, her voice low. "We're all worried."

Here it was. My mouth still full of pasta, I tried to keep my voice low to match her own. "Why?"

Her shoulders sagged. "You don't talk to anyone. You haven't answered the phone to me in months. You're cutting yourself off–"

I took a chance. "What do you think's going to happen?"

She sat back as if I'd pushed her into the chair. "I don't– "

"What do you think is going to happen, Emily? Do you think I'll be one of those faces on the news? A bag of bones, found on a cliff edge? A backpack, tossed down some gully in the Highlands? Or is it something else? No one cares about those things anymore, do they? Faces down. Eyes shut."

"No! No! Of course not. But Mum and Dad know you're stealing from them. You only visit to take things. Weird things. Paper and glue and fur from that bloody cat." She pressed her hand across her eyes. "Why?"

My chest heaved. There wasn't enough air for me. There wasn't enough air in the room. I remembered the year before, when she'd seen me packing a carrier bag in Dad's office. I'd been on my knees, pulling the grey formless fluff and fur from behind the radiator. Dust, skin, and dead-life. As I rubbed it between my fingertips to pull apart the dust of skin, I'd held it to my tongue, my heart longing for warmth and smell of home. Comfort. Familiarity. But the disgust on Emily's face was something I could never forget. Eyes wide, mouth twisted. She'd looked at me like I was something rotten. "Why did you have to tell them about that?"

Emily shook her head. "I had to."

"Are you all talking about me, behind my back?"

"For fuck's sake, David. We're trying to help. Trying to bring us together. You won't even let Mum or Dad into your flat. You don't answer the door."

I hissed under my breath.

Emily stared, her bottom lip sucked behind her teeth. "For fuck's sake. Talk to us. We miss you." She reached over and pressed her fingers on the underside of my wrist. My skin burned beneath her touch. "Dad even comes to the arcade sometimes to see you. Did you know that?"

Did I know that? I pictured the arcade, floating bodies milling around rubbish bins, trudging from shop window to shop window, slumping on benches. Had I seen him? No. But something teased in the corners. A shape I never looked at. Wearing a black bomber jacket and a grey hat.

"Did you know that, eh?" Emily was louder now. "He said he was there just the other day, but you were looking into the window of that art shop." She swallowed and placed her bowl on the coffee table, practically untouched. "We're worried you aren't looking after yourself. Not eating is one of the first signs…"

I shoved a forkful of pasta in my mouth. It tasted rubbery and refused to reduce.

Emily squinted as she focussed somewhere on my torso. "What are you wearing?"

I pulled at the loose threads dangling from a sleeve. "Why?"

Emily tipped her head to the side. "It's just… I recognise that shirt, but not on you. Is it Dad's?"

I shook my head and shoved another forkful onto my tongue. "Grandad's."

"Oh!" Emily pressed her hands to her cheeks, stretching the skin from her eyes downwards. "That's nice. He'd have liked that."

She had no idea. It was like putting on Grandad's skin, and even though the sleeves ended halfway to my wrist and the body hung formlessly around my chest, it still felt right. I held out my arm and she stroked the tawny stripes. Now that Emily had softened, I needed to keep it that way. Just for the next two days. "I'm all right, Emily, really. I'm OK."

She gave the slightest nod between casting her eyes back to her pasta bowl. Her hands twisted in her lap. I forked another few pieces of pasta into my mouth where they sat beside the others, still unswallowable.

"Well," Emily said, followed by a strange giggle. "Mum and Dad are tethering each other down; that's something, isn't it?" She then gave me the strangest look. Her eyes bulged a little and her lips pinched together. Her skin had gone bone white and she looked like she was about to be sick. "Can you just wait a minute, David?" She rushed out of the room, and I quickly slipped a page from her audition notes into my pocket. I know I didn't need it anymore for my project, but old habits die hard.

When Emily returned a few minutes later, she looked much lighter, as if something wicked had been purged. "Sorry about that, Davey." She smiled. Her skin shone. "Where were we?"

"I don't know."

Emily pressed the back of her hand over her mouth. "Right. Right." Her eyes were far away, as if looking right through me. "And Agatha! I've not heard how she's doing since you told me about her last year or so! Are you still close? I'd love to meet her one day."

"She'd love to meet you, too."

"Next time I come up to the village," she said, her voice soft. "Next time."

The rest of the night didn't flow easily. I felt Emily was as conscious as I was that I didn't sit well on her sofa, or fit in with the décor. Even my voice sounded strange and tinny, as if the flat was built from steel rather than brick. She went to bed soon after, leaving me with a little pile of printed leaflets and ideas for what I could do on my afternoon alone the following day: the Tate, a matinee on Shaftesbury Avenue, street music in Covent Garden, Madame Tussauds.

Before she went to bed, Emily offered to turn on the TV but then almost immediately changed her mind, tucking the remote deep into the pocket on her dress. She looked up at me through burned black lashes and tucked her hair behind her ear. "It's all just depressing anyway. The news. You're on holiday… time to think of happier things."

"I wouldn't mind watching it."

Emily pouted, unmoving. "Why? What good will it do?"

My throat tightened. My whole body was tense. "I saw there were more disappearances. Backpacks found in Scotland. It was on the screen at Kings Cross."

"Oh, right." Emily bit her lower lip. "I didn't know they'd found anything yet. Joseph… Gonzalez? Consuelez? Something like that. That was one of the names they've released on the news."

Hearing one of the nomads named felt electric. "Yeah," I whispered. "It's exciting."

Emily's mouth widened and she stood stock still. "Why?"

I couldn't believe what I was saying. I felt like a seed suddenly splitting, a sproutling inching towards the sun. "They're doing something exciting, aren't they?"

"No David, they're not. They're lost and alone. The whole thing is just very sad."

"Don't you wonder what happens to them? The bodies?" I sat bolt upright. Even I could tell that my voice was oddly loud now. I was on fire.

"Nature does... strange things to people, David. It could be animals. The weather. People doing weird rituals. The list goes on." She breathed heavily, gripping the remote control in her pocket. "It's not exciting. It's just very sad."

And then we were back *there* again. In polite, restrained quiet. Emily went to bed not long after that, taking the TV remote with her.

I did wonder what she'd have said, if I'd told her the full truth. When we were children, I'd have told her anything. She was everything. She was the sun. But now she stumbled and tripped just as much as I did, and it didn't sit easy with me. She was meant to be the example of everything I wasn't. A person perfectly suited to her world. A chameleon. Dad's favourite. She'd always shaped things around her, like a flame melting wax around it. But tonight, she didn't look well at all. And she couldn't even meet my eye. And so our minds, once linked as intricately as Russian nesting dolls, were finally exposed to be what they had been for years: brutally and irreversibly apart.

Emily left early the following morning, leaving me a key on the dining table. The flat smelled of burned eggs and bitter coffee. I was still curled beneath the duvet on the sofa, and had been awake since well before dawn, lying tense and terrified for hours.

Before leaving, Emily had tangled herself in knots trying to explain the Tube system, but once I made it to Seven Sisters station, it seemed perfectly logical to me how to get from A to B. Every direction I turned had a sign telling me where to go. Around me, the station thrummed with bodies rushing in every direction. Even standing against the white tiled wall, I knew I was in the way. Everyone got too close. I could taste their breath in my mouth. Old meat. This close up, I became aware of the oddities of different gaits. Quick and jangling legs. Slow and heavy, like marionettes. Occasionally a passer-by would flash me a wary look before looking back at their phone. Soon I felt like I'd forgotten how to co-ordinate my limbs, so I concentrated on the sharp edges of Emily's oyster card in one hand and the crinkling of my bag in the other. Everywhere I looked, back-lit billboards advertised everything from stage comedies to energy drinks, and the huge one above the escalator even advertised admission to a blue house. A renovated period house with a cornflower roof, perched on a cliff overlooking the sea, it could've been a holiday resort. But of course it wasn't. I couldn't get over their *gall* at tricking people like that.

The trains themselves meant that I had to stand very close to other passengers. Their shoulders and elbows jutted into my chest and midriff as the carriage sped through the dark. I raised my head as high as I could to avoid the smell. Over the top of everyone's heads, I saw the occasional blue-shirted individual smiling softly at the people standing next to him or her. I couldn't understand it at first. All the faces around these people looked down or up or sideways, as if determined to not engage. And yet the blue person kept smiling, occasionally touching someone on the shoulder or arm, but even then no one engaged. It wasn't until we stopped at a particularly busy station and the blue person was left almost alone in the standing area that I realised that this was a Blue Pilgrim. I quickly turned to face the opposite direction, a note of panic plucking away in my head. Up north you could avoid them, you could escape. But here, there was nowhere to run.

***

The gathering building wasn't actually in Brick Lane, though I walked through its streets of lurid graffiti and jingling market stalls to find it. It was a relief to be outside again, with the sky above my head. Despite the crisp December air, the street smelled of warm spices and skin. Some of the walls were so layered with spray-paint that it made me think of a crowd all scrambling on top of each other to be heard. At one point, I passed a church, its broken windows boarded up and plastered with overlapping posters. Workmen were carrying in sheets of metal and pointing down at a tangle of pipes in a hole. A big red 'SOLD TO PRIVATE OWNERSHIP' hung from a lamppost.

I'd pictured the gathering's venue to be something grand and exclusive, but when I finally found it, it was an old warehouse, only accessible by an alleyway. The red brickwork and windows might've looked impressive in their day, but now they were crumbling, stone by stone. Three of the large rectangular windows were smashed, cracks bleeding out towards the frames like snowflakes. Beside the entrance, a dead rat lay sprawled beside a skip so full to bursting with plastic and cardboard that the lid was suspended in mid-air. Fading posters for pub crawls and music festivals from years before were pasted to the brick.

This wasn't what I'd imagined at all.

The wide green door to 11b Hoxton House looked impenetrable. Even the letterbox looked screwed shut. Pressing one hand to my chest, I rang the buzzer.

A metallic, inhuman voice. "Hoxton House, how can I help you?"

"I'm here," I said, my mouth dry. "I'm with the Homefinders. The gathering."

There was a pause. "Name?"

"David. Porter. David Porter. I got the invitation–"

A furious buzz like a wasp in my ear, and then a click. "Come on in, David. We're on the third floor. Hope you're all right with stairs? The lift's out of order."

But before I could open the door, something sweet penetrated my nostrils. So pungent it was that it literally stopped me in my tracks. Suddenly, the alleyway became a stream of tangy nectar. Almost immediately, I knew that the source was a rubbish skip about twenty paces from the door. Inside it must be something *golden*.

It would only take a second. No harm done.

There wasn't even a choice in it, I had to see inside the skip, even if it meant pressing the buzzer again. It was more than a compulsion. It was hunger.

I peered down inside the skip. It initially looked like it'd be full of debris from construction, but passers-by had started to use it for any old thing as they walked past. The source of the zest found me, rather than I it. An open plastic bag containing four oranges. The skin of each had gone almost entirely green and puckered. Almost without thinking, I picked one up and pressed it to my lips. *Pure honey*. How did it smell so good when I knew it was rotten? I took a deep breath and swallowed the saliva pooling in my mouth.

Madness.

And then as quickly as the desperation had come, it dissipated. I dropped the orange into the skip and wiped my hand on my jacket. Tripping over my feet, I made my way back to the door. Luckily it was still unlocked, so I heaved it open, relieved to be getting away from what I'd almost just done.

It was like stepping into a tree. My heart was pounding. Inside, a narrow wooden staircase twisted up into the dark. At first I thought the walls were painted dark green, but on closer inspection it was wallpaper, thick and foamy, peeling at the corners. The landing windows were as narrow as castle arrow-slits and didn't let much light in. All up the staircase were photos of faces. Most of them looked fairly recent, and many were in groups posing in canoes, on mountains, in caves. Many of them could've been my age, and few looked over forty. Further up the staircase were photos of older faces in more sedate landscapes. In one, a group of three women with almost identical blonde bobs sat along a long stone wall. In another, a group of eight men and women who looked to be in their forties were fishing by a still lake. They all wore the sort of chunky gilets and plush jumpers that I recognised from Mum and Dad's village. *Comfortable*. All of the photos had a place name handwritten beneath them in scribbled black ink. 'Doorseeking, Filey Bay.' 'Doorseeking, Jurassic Coast.' One of the photos was of a mountainous landscape similar to Grandad's photographs. There wasn't that same violent crag, but something about the faded mauve hills and the hairy texture of the fields, that looked so much like the back of a giant, made me think it must be the same place. This photograph contained three men, two of which were wearing waterproof jackets and trousers, and the other was wearing a robe halfway between a business suit and a priest's cowl. He stood between the other two, his hands around their shoulders like a messiah. His face was thin, and even though he beamed at the camera, he looked tired and pained, as if his feet were too sore but he knew he had to keep on walking. I leaned in to read the tiny plaque beneath. 'Close to Glencoe, Scotland.' I scanned each and every face on the staircase, searching for that familiar old apple. But even then, even after coming this far, he continued to hide from me.

The third-floor foyer had full-sized windows made of that mottled glass used for bathrooms. One was open, and I welcomed the crisp air on my face after the closeness of the stairs. Here, the grey walls were pasted with posters stuck up in untidy rows. They all had the Homefinder's name in the corner, but bore different messages. One seemed to advertise an outdoor survival training course. Another, a woodland retreat. And a large banner stretched above the doorway revealed a woodland glade with a circle of white tents. Beneath the tents was written, 'Escape the machine. Discover freedom.'

At the back of the landing, a woman stood beside a table covered with a black tablecloth, a selection of Melius Est books, and a crudely hand-drawn sign with 'Book Sale' on it. She shifted from one foot to the other, gripping the sleeves of her black jumper low over her knuckles. Her hair was a dirty rust colour, and she had it tucked angrily behind an ear. In one wild moment, I imagined touching it, and could practically feel how dry and parched it was between my fingertips. She didn't look like the sort of person who wanted to be approached, and yet she was my welcome.

"David?"

I recognised her voice from the intercom downstairs. She sounded just as mechanical in person. She handed me a clipboard and asked me to sign in. I counted, and worked out that I was the sixteenth member to arrive. None of the names above mine looked familiar, but then they wouldn't, as people were signing in with their real names. I debated it for a few seconds before writing 'David Porter.'

"You have to leave your bag in the locker room," she said, pointing to a little cupboard behind the pop up. She tilted her head in what struck me as a patronising show of sympathy. "Sorry. Security."

I handed her my carrier bag but took out *Hidden Worlds* and my little black book first. She raised her eyebrows at that, but handed me a cellophane pack of leaflets anyway and directed me through the door and into the darkness of the conference room.

16.

My first thought was that the room reminded me of the community hall where I'd joined Emily at one of her theatre classes as a child. It was small, with parquet wooden flooring and long benches under each row of windows. Chairs were set out in a wide circle around the periphery of the room, and at the far end was a small elevated stage, just like the one Emily had performed on. A few pieces of technical equipment were already set up, like a microphone and stereos, and the stage lights beamed down onto a six-foot-tall sculpture of a phoenix, made of what looked like red and orange plastic – the type that you felt like you could've knocked over with the slightest nudge. The air smelled of wood polish and bleach-water.

I helped myself to a paper cup of water from the refreshments table by the entrance and sidled into the room, clinging to the walls like ivy. Several of the other attendees were doing the same, either staring down onto their phones or glaring at the contents of their paper cups. A few others were milling around in twos, but speaking so quietly that they could well have been miming. Though they lacked the long trench coats and the beaten-down complexions, something about them reminded me of the mudmen. They had the same slow gait, the blank expressions that could have been intense concentration or complete distraction. They stood heavily, like wet clothes on coat hangers. But they didn't have the purpose that I remembered the mudmen having. They had been men and women who doggedly strode their path, whereas these people were so very green. Any of them technically could've been Michael, but I didn't need to check. It was clear that they were all waiting, just like me. I squeezed *Hidden Worlds* to my stomach and focussed on the sensation of the hardback edge digging into my hip bone. Somehow, the pain pulled everything into sharper focus.

"Is it… Mothtown12?"

A man had approached me from the side. The top of his wispy grey hair only reached my shoulder, but his shoulders were broader than mine, and his stomach and hips were so wide that his t-shirt – baggy everywhere else – was stretched so thin that I could see the curve of his belly button. He didn't seem to have much neck, so his head had the appearance of being grafted onto his body. His skin was ruddy and had a complete absence of facial hair, which made him look like a fifty-something-year-old baby. His features faded quietly into his face; his eyes were so dim and watery that they were difficult to focus on.

"Mothtown12?" He repeated, his voice gurgling.

I nodded. I had no idea who this man was.

"It's Jamestown42," he mumbled. "I'm Jake."

No, surely this wasn't him? Jamestown42 was a leader. I bowed to him as a source of truth. He'd sounded like someone that knew this world inside out and *owned it.* But that wasn't this man. This man had little crusts of spit clung to the corners of his mouth. He smelled of grease and sweat.

Everything about this man horrified me.

He stuck out his hand, so I had to take it. It was hot and clammy, and I still felt sticky even after he let go. "What do you think of it all?" he rasped.

"It's good. I…" I stopped. I didn't know what else to say. Jake pressed himself against the wall beside me. *Too close.*

"I'm glad you came. You'll like it."

"Yeah. Thanks for inviting me."

Jake nudged my shoulder and pointed a stubby finger at my book. "I read that in the end," he said. "I wasn't convinced."

I pushed myself off the wall to face him, head on. "Convinced about what?"

His eyes quivered in their sockets. "Errrr. Just the methods he planned to use to find his doorway. It's all a bit… indistinct. That's all."

"Why?" I wanted to spit.

He shook his head. "Just, none of it stands up against the other texts, that's all. It's all completely left-field. And he's too emotionally invested."

"What?"

"Like he was doing it all for himself, or his son, or something." Jake sniffed, a long and wet noise. "I couldn't tell which, but he isn't doing it for the greater good, is he? Or for science."

Jake's outline quivered in front of me, his face shifting on the front of his skull as if it didn't know where to hide.

"I mean," he stuttered, "I looked up if he wrote anything else after that, but his publishing credits just stop dead. And that one" – he pointed to the book's spine – "is out of print now, so it must never have been a success. Maybe he was excommunicated or something."

I'd gone bone-cold, and my skin became this prickly

wool coat that I wanted to throw off and run away from. I kept my face as still as I could as Jake shuffled side-to-side and pulled at his ear. "Err... Do you know if he's writing anything now?"

I squeezed the book into my stomach again, deliberately jamming down the edge even harder on my hip. *Release.*

"He's gone. He found his door. He never came back."

That would shut Jake up and wipe that ugly, wobbling look off his face. That'd show him that he knew nothing about it. But instead, he just mumbled, "Really?" and looked over my shoulder to the centre of the room, distracted. Behind me, the noise of chairs scraping against the wooden floor meant people were taking their seats. Jake edged around me and found himself a seat at the far end of the hall. I sat in the chair closest to where I already was, mainly because the chairs on either side of it weren't occupied. I didn't want to speak to anyone else now, not if I could help it. But I needn't have worried; even where people sat in adjacent seats they couldn't reach out and connect because of the odd spacing of the chairs. The gaps between were so wide that each attendee was his or her own little island, rather than a link in the chain.

A minute or so after everyone had settled, a man strode onto the stage, causing it to creak with every step. He was dressed in loose red trousers and a billowing white shirt that reached almost to his knees. He raised his arms wide and smiled, nodding his head at each point in the circle as if acknowledging applause. The room was silent. A few people looked like they were poised to, their hands hovering in front of their stomachs, but no one brought them together. One woman dabbed at her runny nose, and another rolled her wedding ring around and around on her finger. Jake's hands lay flat on his stomach, which rose and fell with each breath through his nose.

The man seemed deaf to the quiet, and continued to nod and smile as he made his way down the side-steps from the stage to the centre of the circle. The ends of his sleeves were embroidered with something red.

"Welcome," his voice boomed. He had a little microphone pinned to the collar of his shirt, which seemed totally unnecessary considering how close we all were. "It's amazing to see so many people here today. And so many new faces."

I looked around the group. There couldn't have been more than twenty of us there. Every face was transfixed on this man. Up close, his face looked familiar, something about the pointed look. His delicate frame and springing steps gave him an air of youth, but his eyes and forehead were lined with wrinkles. Two distinct frown lines creased the space between his eyes, and made him appear concerned, despite the grin. He was a confusion. His face, a mosaic of different ages and emotions, completely threw me; as did his hair, a strawberry blonde mop flopping around in curls. As he turned to face each one of us in turn, his clothes ballooned and made him appear even smaller, like a snail trying to fill out a shell. It was a few more seconds before I recognised him as the central figure in the photograph on the staircase, the one near Glencoe.

"Welcome, everyone! It's wonderful to see so many new faces. It goes to show how many of us need more. More than this." He pointed up at one of the windows. I recognised the cracks in the glass from outside. "This grey, unhappy world. We aren't seen. We aren't understood. We aren't heard. The modern world is blind, deaf, and dumb."

Across the hall, Jake's eyes were closed as if he'd fallen

asleep. The speaker spun on his heel, keen to look each and every one of us in the eye. My head was starting to spin, and even the low light in the hall blazed in my eyes. I looked down at my lap, at Grandad.

"As many of you will have heard me say before, this 'Modern Problem,' as it's been coined, isn't a problem at all. They're saying it's depression. Loneliness. Isolation. Pressures of a work-driven world. How hollow. But then, how could they understand? This 'Modern Problem' isn't a problem. I'm telling you all this now. You need to know." The speaker brought his hands together in prayer as he addressed us, bringing them up and down with each syllable. As he turned, his eyes locked with mine and I couldn't pull away. My chest heaved. The man smiled delicately. "That's right. We should not be solving it. What's dissected in all the TV shows and mis-sold in those terrible adverts is merely a side-effect of our real condition." Michael pouted at the floor. "And don't even get me started on the Blue Pilgrims. White teeth and blankets, a pat on the hand and a phoneline. Tea and biscuits. That's all it is. Would a real doctor focus on curing the symptom, rather than the disease? No. He'd look for the root, the cause, the rusty gear."

The woman sitting next to me shuffled in her chair and one of her leaflets drifted to the floor. The shoulders of her black jumper were covered in loose grey hairs. Michael turned to her and leaned in, inches from her face. "Do you ever feel like you're being watched? Like there are people out there, stifling you. Weighing you down. Forcing you to conform?"

The woman nodded, her mouth agape. I thought back to my flat and the blue boxes. Hand-delivered to my door. Intrusive. Dangerous.

They were watching me, too.

Michael smiled and held the woman's wrist. "You're safe here. The Blue Prison Wardens will not find you here, under my protection. And they will never understand the fundamental truth of reality that we whisper to each other across the airwaves, through the undercurrents. And the truth is, my friends – and this is a truth that the rest find it so hard to accept – that some of us are born in the wrong skin. Why aren't the surgeons and the scientists trying to solve that? No. It's a blue house for you. And you. And you." The speaker spun around the circle, pointing at us each in turn. By the time he reached me, my face was burning. He kept his finger on me longer than the rest, I was sure of it.

"You don't need to fit into the shape society has cut for you. Friends, it's time to shed our skins, to emerge from the chrysalis, to rise from the ashes."

My chest squeezed, pushing out every inch of air in my body. *This was it. He understood.* For years, I'd waited for this, going it alone. And now here my saviour stood, arms raised, fiery feathers stitched up his sleeves in red thread. The microphone shrieked. "This afternoon you'll be hearing from speakers at the very heart of Homefinders. Essential lessons required to find your doorway. Teachings shared with thousands before you. Sworn to secrecy."

The speaker had been beaming all this time, but now his face fell. "But first. Now that we're emerging from the underground, you might get some stick for what we know. You might hear that this is all New Age bullshit. But this is no astrological clap-trap. This is physics." At that, the man strode over to the edge of the stage and pulled a paperback from behind the curtain. He held it up as if it was a holy relic. The cover was plain black, and in shining silver letters: *The Truth, by Dr Michael White.*

So, this was Michael. My attention bore into him, desperate to dissect this walking puzzle. "He keeps the maps." That's what Jamestown42 had said. He'd tell me where that valley was, near Glencoe, and how I could get there. Maybe if I showed him Grandad's face he'd even remember talking to him.

Could Grandad's map, the one that lay across his lap in his living room, have been one of Michael's?

Michael looked soulfully at the book in his hands. "This was my first exposé, and you can buy copies just by the front desk. It's sold over ten thousand copies over the last ten years, and that's not mentioning how many people have borrowed from libraries or shared it with friends. That proves that our community is waking up, and that they're hungry. More and more of us are embracing our differences and seeking where we truly belong. We're fish out of water. Sparrows out of sky. Friends, it's time to find the nests we were born to rest in."

With every word, the hairs on my arms pricked. I wanted to stand and shout, "Yes!" But at the same time, I wanted to disappear into his blood stream, to curl up in his beating heart. Michael wasn't only convinced that finding a route to another world was possible. He was that fact. He lived it.

Michael pointed to the phoenix on centre stage. "This is who we are. You are not invisible. You are not fading away. You are as real as I am, flesh and bone. Right now, you may be ashes, but that is going to change. Please, now," he pulled a silver box from behind the phoenix and passed it to the seated woman closest to him, "pass this around and know that your donation fuels a better world." The woman crammed a folded wad of notes through the small slot and passed it to the man next to her, already waiting with a slim envelope just the right size. Just as the box approached my side of the circle my hands started to twitch. No one said I'd need to give anything. I couldn't let Michael see that though, so down by my thigh I folded one of the leaflets from the front desk into a small square, ready to slot inside the donation box. As I passed the box on, Michael reached out to touch the feet of the phoenix, and it reminded me of how the priest at Mum's church, Father Douglas, had grasped the sides of the pulpit when he spoke. "Thank you all for taking this journey with us. Are there any questions?"

No one moved, every faced fixed on the phoenix. And before I even had a chance to contemplate the consequences of what I was doing, I raised my hand. All eyes were on me.

What was I doing?

Michael smiled, his cheeks rising up to hide his eyes. He did a little half bow before saying, "Yes, what's your question?"

I thought the words wouldn't come, but they did, dry and cracked though they were. "If you know all that, about doors, then why are you still here?"

The building creaked. Michael observed me beneath lowered lids, his thin lips now pouting so tightly that it was a miracle that words could emerge at all. "That's a very good question," he said, quietly. "No one's asked me that before." He spun slowly in a circle, addressing the whole group. "I got to this point because I felt just like you. I became a researcher and an academic, because I wanted to find a road to somewhere that made sense. But along the way, I realised that I can help more people by staying here, than by leaving. That's my meaning, my purpose. So it's my duty to stay."

The attendees nodded. Across from me, one side of Jake's

face had puckered. If he didn't like Michael's answer, I couldn't understand why. It made sense. But worryingly, it tickled the little nagging feeling within me that I had perhaps found a sliver of meaning myself. I saw Agatha's face, behind the counter in the music shop. At the station, waiting for her bus home. Beneath the hood of her parka, her eyes wide and cheeks pink beneath the fur. Agatha was there for me. I'd always planned that we'd find home together. But I'd already left her behind. It wasn't the same with her now. And if I was honest with myself, it hadn't been for months. Something between us had twisted. But what if Agatha was my meaning. *What if she was my home?*

Suddenly, Emily's face appeared in my mind, brighter and sharper than Agatha's. *No.* I pushed her away. She didn't get me, she never had. Agatha did.

I'd started to shake, so I sat on my hands as Michael welcomed on the first guest speaker, a tall blonde woman in a black dress and silver heels, who tore a sheet of paper in half and then said, "Today, is the beginning of the next phase of your life." The pieces fluttered to the floor and I tipped my head to get a better look at them. Both were blank. The woman then spent an hour talking fitness regimes and the importance of good nutrition when trekking. None of it seemed anything other than common sense, but she delivered each slide with her fingers pinching the air as if grasping something illusive. Next up was a twitchy woman dressed all in cream who gave us all a handbook advertising clothing to protect against adverse weather. I flicked through it as she explained each piece and my heart sank. There was no way I'd have the money for any of this. Looking around the group, it was impossible to tell by their expressionless faces whether they thought the same. All I knew was that

I couldn't let them see, in case Michael was watching. So, I held my head high, drinking in every word.

Finally, after the twitchy woman had finished, she was followed by a tall man dressed in a grey suit, who had previously worked for the Blue Pilgrims. He walked around the circle and gave us all a metal pin – a red feather on a black background. "Remember those forget-me-not pins people used to wear, before they forgot? No more. These are forever. Look out for them on jackets, jumpers. So far, we've issued over two thousand of these. Look for your brothers and sisters and you'll find them." Would I have noticed if I'd passed anyone wearing one? It was so very small. I inspected the pin before slipping it into my pocket.

There were three other presentations before the conference ended, each one primed with handouts and leaflets. I'd written down as much as I could in my little black book, and on my lap lay a hiking book catalogue, a short guide to navigating by the stars, and a strange postcard with a painting of a phoenix on one side and a list of suggested books from Melius Est. I think it was meant to be a bookmark. There wasn't much of a chance to speak to anyone or ask questions until the end of the presentations, and when five o'clock rolled around and the last speaker said his goodbyes, the attendees sluggishly pulled on their coats. No one spoke or looked at each other in the eye. Jamestown42 squeezed himself into a red and silver sports jacket before rocking from the room without saying as much as a word to me.

Was that all there was? What was I meant to do now? I picked up one leaflet I'd been given and touched the image of a walker, clad in camouflage and ascending a mountain before balling the paper in my fist. All of this, *it was just adverts. Sales pitches.* I remained sitting for a while and watched the group leave. All so ordinary and nondescript. I couldn't connect a single one of them to the usernames I'd seen on the forum at all.

I still had *Hidden Worlds* on my lap, and stroked the cold cover until the room was empty and I felt a hand on my shoulder.

"That was a good question. Can you believe no one's asked me that before?"

It was Michael, and he sighed as he lowered himself into the chair beside me. Neighbourly, but out of reach. I didn't know what to say. I was both overwhelmed and exhausted from trying to absorb everything I'd heard over the last four hours. And here I was, talking to Michael, *the man who keeps the maps*, and I hadn't any fuel left.

"I'm sorry if it seemed abrupt–"

"Not at all," he gushed. "I'll have to write that answer into the next lecture." He looked down at the book in my lap. "That looks interesting."

"It's my Grandad's book. He wrote it."

He lifted it from my knees and flicked through the pages, his face expressionless. "Ah yes, I think I read this years ago."

My heart almost stopped. "What did you think? Did he come to you?"

Michael released a strange half-laugh and shook his head. "I like to think I remember faces, but I can't remember all the faces. What's your name?"

"David. His name was Francis," I pointed at the name on the cover. "He was an academic too."

Michael nodded slowly, turning the book over between his slim hands. "You must be very proud."

I nodded. Michael began flicking through the pages, settling on a diagram of a six-sided shape, separated into quadrants. I knew that one by heart. The four sections were labelled 'Black Hole,' 'White Hole,' 'Our Universe,' and 'Parallel Universe.' Michael cleared his throat and traced the line labelled 'Parallel Horizon' with one slim finger, tipped with a tapering white nail. It was the nail of a cat, not a person. I couldn't take my eyes off it. "Where is he now, David? Is he a member?"

I took a deep breath. "He left. He did it. He found his door. But I'm not sure where. I think it might be in Scotland. The Highlands."

Michael titled his head and for a second, he looked at me like I was a little bird on a windowsill. "Did he?"

"Yes, when I was ten. Sixteen years ago. His wife died, and he left a year later. I thought you might… know."

Michael nodded slowly, his brow furrowed.

I leaned across and flicked through the pages until I reached the one of Grandad in front of the mountain. The one with teeth. "There's this photo here," I pointed to Grandad in the valley, "And the photo on the stairwell out there." I gestured out to the foyer. "You went to Glencoe. Is there a doorway there? In the mountains?"

Michael paused for a few minutes. "I went up there to assist two long-time members." He spoke slowly, the words dripping from his tongue. "And I'm afraid that what happens during private tutelage is confidential."

"You offer extra coaching?"

"I do, to those who have the resources to take it on."

Private lessons. A shortcut. How many others had done this? And those that had… *could I have seen them before?*

Up close, Michael's eyes looked sunken, and his skin was

so pale that I was half-convinced that I could see his pulse in his temples. For a moment, I felt sorry for him. He looked starving.

"You know," Michael's voice was low, purring, "I choose my students myself. Most of these" – he gestured to the exit – "won't make it. They'll never even make it out of their front door. Do you know why?"

I shook my head.

"Because they still exist here, even if they don't feel they do. But sometimes I meet people at these events who I can tell are from another place." He reached out and touched my cheek. I didn't move. His finger was like ice. "It's the skin. It's like no one else's. Soft, elegant, like wax. You're not real, are you?"

I shook my head. His eyes were almost yellow. I had to ask it. *I had to.* "What happens to the nomads in the mountains, Michael?"

Michael smiled, but just with the corners of his mouth. "What do you mean?"

"Why are they… well… half of what they were? Why are they only half gone?"

Michael sighed through his nose. "That's nature's way. Everyone's end is different."

"Did they do something wrong? Take a wrong turn?"

"No," Michael shook his head slowly. "They did what they had to do."

"But what–"

"Everyone's end is different. Don't question it. Don't think about them. Concentrate on you. Your journey. Your story."

Hardly thinking about what I was doing, I scratched at my left wrist and rolled up my sleeve. "I think I'm changing already, Michael. I don't know what to do."

His eyes flicked down to my arm and then back up again almost instantly. He cleared his throat. "I can help you with that."

"You promise? You promise me?" My voice shook but I didn't even care. A doorway was opening, right then.

"I can help you. But you must understand that it's a long road to where you want to be."

"Whatever it takes."

"The cost is high. Everything you have. And then stripped of everything you were, we'll provide everything you need. Simple, sustaining food. Clothes to help you hide."

"Maps," I whispered.

"Yes," he nodded. "And then you make the journey alone, in secret, and in quiet."

The Mudmen. The lone walkers, dragging their tired feet down our street towards the broken fence, the cowfields. Dressed like the earth itself. The mudman in the library had said they were going home.

"I grew up on a street where people disappeared. I watched them when I was a kid, silent, alone, their eyes focussed on a gap in a broken fence. There were a lot of them, for a while." I took a deep breath. The air tasted of dust. "Are the mudmen your students?"

Michael chuckled. "What's a mudman?"

"It's my name for them. The men and women dressed in rags who walked through my village. They don't speak. They had maps."

Michael sat back and clasped his hands together. "Yes. They're mine."

It made sense now. They couldn't speak because they knew a secret so overwhelming that it muted the whole world. When you're ready to escape our universe, what use are common words? They'd feel as dead as Latin. I looked down at Grandad's book again. "Grandad always said that we were the same. He made me feel like I was home. I need to find out where he's gone. It's where I should be, too."

Michael looked down at my shoes as if reading them, and I felt a hot rush of shame burn my cheeks.

"Tell me, please. Do some doors close? Forever?"

Michael cleared his throat. "I wouldn't say that. But some doorways became too notorious. Too much press. Too many flowers. Too many interruptions. Too upsetting. We abandoned them for more hidden doorways. Away from watching eyes."

"Like my street."

"Like your street."

This was it. The moment I'd waited for since Grandad first told me he was leaving, that Midwinter. The chance to follow him into the unknown. "I'm ready, Michael."

Michael reached into a trouser pocket beneath his shirt and pulled out a business card. "Take this. Let me know how much you can afford and we'll go from there. I can help with maps, with memories, with transformations – with everything. I will take you to your grandfather."

AFTER

~

Am I travelling forwards, or am I falling down? Can it be both? I dig the heels of my hands into the soil to stop me tumbling head first into the soft and sucking darkness, but it draws me in. A stone in a pond.

Furious hands behind me scrabble at the dirt, thick white fingers working their way towards me like maggots. I feel them against my left foot, the broken one, rolling their heat around my ankle, *once, twice*. Almost tenderly. I kick, kick, kick, and the brogues and socks are gone, lost to the mud. Blackened toes sink into earth, cold as cake, and now the walls are collapsing like falling flowers, embracing me on all sides from the waist down.

Reach forwards, to the glimmering light. It looks like a moon.

And there's a voice, a soft, crooning voice. Gentle. Like milk. A man's voice, "How are you today, David?" My name echoes in my ears. There's earth in my mouth. It's coming from the route ahead, the dip down into night. "You've been here long enough. Can you open the door?"

Michael? He's the same but different – calm, slow, anchored.

I only have seconds, before I am crushed beneath the weight of everything around me, everything I'm carrying.

Everything that's happened. The loneliness. I don't belong in this tunnel, in the ground, but it's eating me. "It's time, David. You've done all the hard work."

Then my hands are seized by the wrist and I'm drawn from the mouth into sweet, spine-bending *pain*.

BEFORE

17.

I'm starting to see.

These shards beneath my feet. The case in his office. The cocoon, cushioned in white cotton. It sounded like snow. I know now. Like an eruption. An earthquake. Detritus after the great shake. My glass ceiling… shattered.

Tell me, the others in this place. In the wooden rooms I just passed. They weren't quite like me, were they? I thought they would be. Same eyes, same way of seeing. Will my story help them too? It seems cruel to leave them where they are. I can't stop thinking about them. Are you helping them, like you're helping me?

When I got back to my flat, there was another package waiting for me on the doormat. This time I didn't even pick it up; I just kicked it into the corner and locked the door behind me. A sharp pain shot through my big toe. As soon as I dropped my things onto the floor, I pressed my face up to my window and peered down at the street below, searching for a flash of blue.

Perhaps they knew where I'd been. How close I was getting. *They weren't going to take me. Not without a fight.*

After sliding down the wall, I removed my shoe and

peeled off my sock. My toes were grey. I began to rub them between my fingers, but no amount of squeezing brought life back into them. They felt icy cold. I leaned in closer to get a better look at what'd caused the pain. My big toenail was turning black at its edge and was beginning to peel away from the skin.

What was happening to me? Was my time running out? I pulled my sock back on and tried to forget.

I kept Michael's card safe, tucked away in *Hidden Worlds*. The card detailed Michael's name, address, phone number, and email. I Googled the address while lying on my mattress, and Maps brought up a huge block of flats just outside Watford. It wasn't what I expected, but then I couldn't tell much from the roof.

Abandoned for over a week now, my project had started to rot. Up close it smelled like decaying fruit, and on the floor beneath it lay a shatter of dried leaves and a decomposing wing from a sparrow. Mud had turned to dust. Bits of animal hung from its bones.

I climbed through the opening and sat amongst the dust, hugging my knees to my chest. Both feet were freezing now, my toes numb. The walls of the cocoon were much wider than me, wide enough for two to squeeze in comfortably, if they stood wrapped around each other. Sitting there, it was like crouching within my own self. It made everything quiet. Even though I now knew that I'd never finish it, it still felt right to be there. I'd spent such a long time collecting the parts to make this bed – both living and dead. And by Midwinter, when the ice forms and the creatures sleep, I had planned to be ready to start growing my new skin. Becoming who I was meant to be. I stroked my fingers down to my ankles, poking from the bottom of my jeans.

Lumps and bones. Now I understood that this body, strange as it was to me, would make sense when I stepped into a new world. And Midwinter would be the perfect time for that, too. It was when Grandad left too, after all. At the pause "between endings and new beginnings." Wasn't that what he said? It seemed so perfect that it'd been my plan too – perhaps for different reasons, but that we had the same goal.

Under two weeks to leave this world forever.

Over the next eight days, my door knocked seven times. I wrote the time and number of knocks in my little black book. Sometimes there were even knocks up through the floor. I counted thirty-six, and I wrote those down too. Only four times were there knocks through the wall, always the left-hand wall, but I counted and wrote those down, in case they were important. *Knocks and clicks. Clicks and knocks.*

My face had started to itch, just like my wrists. A few days after the gathering, I'd noticed that my cheeks were red and flaking, and I fought to not constantly scrub it all away with my sleeve. I stopped looking in the mirror in an attempt to stop noticing the itch. To not start tearing at it with my nails.

My door had been locked since returning from the gathering. No one was getting in or out. Every moment was precious, and I needed to concentrate. To prepare. The day after I got back from the conference, I scraped together the total sum of what I could pay Michael, adding up my meagre bank balance with guesses for things I could sell. I didn't have much, but it would help. I wouldn't need 'things' once I was a nomad anyway. And I'd need to be out of the flat before the next rent was due at the end of the month. Only after I pressed 'send' on the email did I wish I'd chosen to receive a read receipt.

Next, I scoured the forums for as much advice about survival in the mountains as I could find. Where to find budget weatherproofs. What to eat. How to prepare for the walking, the potentially endless walking. Each time I found a suggested exercise regime, I followed it. Star-jumps. Push-ups. Weightlifting with books. Pull-ups using a doorframe alone. But with each day that passed, I felt weaker, not stronger. My heart thudded through my ribs like they were as light as twigs. After exercising, I'd hold it in place with both hands, as if trapping a desperate bird.

Had Grandad fought with his own body this way, in his last days here?

As I clasped my chest, I couldn't help but think of Agatha. I'd tried to limit myself to checking her social media accounts to just a few times every day. Seeing her interact with faces I didn't know and pose all-smiling with her arms around drunks and dancers made my skin crawl. That should be me. I hadn't seen her since a few weeks earlier, when I'd left her in the art shop. Our chain of messages had completely run dry. In that time she'd bloomed, her smile wide and white. In the photos posted online, she'd started to look directly into the camera more often when she grinned, less natural, but more direct. I couldn't help thinking she was looking at me. Her hair was dyed as stark and red as a traffic light now. As red as a phoenix. Was that a sign? Was she doing that deliberately, so that I would see that she understood? That she, too, was ready? Red was the colour for transformation, for rebirth. And hers had already begun. My beautiful Agatha.

Emily distracted me further. Since the moment I'd stepped

off the train from London, she'd been sending me more messages than she'd ever done before. Multiple times a day I'd receive something from her, asking how I was, what was I up to, had I eaten. Every message latched onto me like an anchor and made my thinking sluggish. I replied at first, but after a couple of days I couldn't stand it and left my phone plugged in at the corner of the room. Occasionally, the grind of my phone vibrating across the wooden floor woke me from a doze, but otherwise I paid it no attention. *Distractions. Distractions.*

I didn't have many supplies in the flat, but by the eighth day, I'd almost completely ran out of food. Half an orange, green and puckered, lay on the kitchen counter beside a third of a tin of noodle soup. But the truth was, I had so much to do and to work out that I didn't feel like eating. I'd read that hydration was vital in the mountains, so I made sure I drank a full pint every hour. It made my stomach ache, but I couldn't take any chances. Michael's reply would come any minute now, surely. I'd have to be ready to go.

There were only five days left until Midwinter, and it was difficult not to panic.

Dark thoughts had started to creep in. I squatted under the eaves of my chrysalis, the tissue turning to dust above my head, and covered my ears with my hands to prevent anything else from burrowing inside. It was like that time when I was a child, fallen in the crypt, and the flies were everywhere. In my head. In me. I could hear them buzzing, but this time they were speaking in clicks, like thousands of little clicking voices weeping in my and Grandad's language. So, lifting my face to the rotting canopy, I sang. I sang as loud as I could to burn out the ferocious energy inside my throat and to drown out the discord. But they didn't go quiet, and now the walls were banging on all sides and I didn't have my notebook to write them down.

Had I made a mistake? Turning away from my original plan?

I hadn't heard anything back from Michael. The nights were long and cold, with only the forum for company. That night, the eighth night, the rain pelted against my windows like it was trying to break in. My breath hovered in the air above me like smoke. My fingers looked thin and grey in the light of the laptop. I crawled to my box of things. It was almost empty now; most of what was inside had been used for the chrysalis, but a few of Grandad's clothes still lay at the bottom, scattered with a few pages of sheet music, Emily's audition notes, and a little purple bundle in the corner, tied with string. But first, I reached inside for the thing to start my transformation. Something warm and knitted.

And hairy.

There it was: Grandad's orange jumper. The one I always imagined him in. The one I'd searched for in the photographs of Glencoe. I hadn't wanted to touch it before; it was too much. But that night, I pulled it over my head and tugged the hem down. It was far too short and excessively wide. It still smelled like rust. The fibres scratched at my skin like the nails of a little creature, and each time I blinked I saw the bright orange phoenix with its wings outspread in the forum banner, at the gathering, on the spine of *Hidden Worlds*, in Agatha's hair. And now on me. Connecting everything. It was everywhere. Reborn from the ashes. *I'm not me,* I thought. *I don't have my wings.* The bronze sparrow on the collar caught the light like fire.

I watched dawn rise up the wall of my flat like a wave. I lay flat on my back on the mattress. All poured out. Just bone.

Beside me, the laptop lay open on the Institute's login page, and the little string-tied bundle poked from my fist.

I felt very strange.

I'd been drowsing, slipping in and out of dreaming so that I hardly knew whether the bangs and clicks and singing were real or imaginary. Sometimes the voices turned chaotic and I bolted upright, but then they would drift away again to a distant and delicate hum. At one point I could hear voices, speaking in English, through the wall, but it wasn't the grunting gravelly tones I was used to. The roundness of the words sounded like TV. I crawled to the wall and pressed my hands and head against it.

"Why did you go?" A plummy voice. Older, maybe.

"I didn't know who I was. I floated, not connected to anything. And being in nature, helped for a bit. I felt more alive." A man, young.

"What made you come back?"

"Because I felt more alive, I felt the loneliness even more."

"And then you found yourself in a blue house. Did you commit yourself?"

Silence, or words so low that I couldn't make them out. And then the plummy voice again. "And how do you feel now, David?"

"I'm not a new man. There are no miracles. But I'm less confused."

"And what would you say to other people on the brink of choosing the same dangerous path? To walk away from responsibilities and those who love them?"

"If you're unprepared, you won't come back. It still happens, though it's not big news anymore. Bodies on the side of mountains, their hair turned white. People floating in rivers and lakes like logs. It's cold and dangerous. And you're walking away from love, all to feel more human. It doesn't make sense."

"Why do some people never come back, David?"

A pause, in which the wall tremored. "They're still searching."

The words dimmed as the clicks in my head soared again. Every inch of my skin crackled, drying like a toad in the sun, tightening and pulling away from my fingernails, the corners of my mouth. My heart thudded against my chest and my stomach groaned. I hadn't eaten since the day before yesterday. I filled my belly with three glasses of water, one after the other, and then lay back on the mattress and closed my eyes.

Where was Michael? Maybe he'd never come back. There was only one place to be. And I knew it would be the last time I ever went there.

On all fours, I crawled through the hole into the chrysalis. The world was so loud, so bright. It screamed at me. How could I make it out there, alone and naked beneath a stark white sky? Wouldn't the mountain wind slice me into pieces? I wasn't Grandad. Perhaps I wasn't strong enough to do what he did. I'm weak. I'm nothing.

Perhaps changing my skin really was the only way for me.

Picking up a pair of kitchen scissors, I sliced at the scabs on my forearm and pressed my wrist to the sheet music and the audition script, pasting them as best as I could over the opening. Loosening the string on the tiny purple bundle, I pressed Agatha's hair to my lips. There were only a few, taken from the back of her cardigan while she worked in the shop. She hadn't even known they were there, those precious threads fallen from her head. I imagined her beside

me in the chrysalis, where she was meant to have been. Wide enough for two.

Moving my body became an abstract concept. As if manipulating a puppet, I felt removed. Curling up into a ball meant folding myself, and folding myself, and folding myself again, until hundreds of joints were so tightly packed that I became something else entirely. A fossil. Stone that no hands could break apart on their own. The soles of my feet rub against the bits of broken twigs but I can't feel a thing. My toes are pebbles in my hands, frost-bitten and grey. They look dead.

And something was happening to my legs. I could feel it, like bones gently breaking. The soft snap of old chalk. Coiled as I was, I couldn't tell which way each joint faced anymore. Where were my knees now? My elbows? I didn't want to look, because I was either being ripped apart and reshaped, or it was all in my head. I couldn't tell which would be worse.

With a shaking hand, I suspended Agatha's hairs from a protruding twig, before continuing to seal up the hole with blood and any scraps of matter that'd fallen from the roof of the cocoon. And finally, I embraced the darkness and the overwhelming sense of deep sleep falling on my scalp like snow.

18.

I don't know how much time passed before I jolted awake to furious banging. It sounded like war. It started and stopped, and as soon as it faded, I'd instantly drift back into the deep. But the banging came again, four times, and then a voice I recognised, clean and sonorous despite the walls. "David? Are you in there? Please be in there. I've got a key."

I couldn't place it at first, but then I felt Agatha's face in the bend of my neck and I knew it must be her. Agatha with the phoenix hair, ready to rise. "Agatha," I whispered, and opened my eyes. But I was still alone, curled around myself. I tried to move, but my arms had blended into my legs.

Sleep overwhelmed me again, and I let it take me. What was I meant to do? The cocoon shifted like a cabin in an old ship. Something was tearing. The surface clicked rapidly, like crickets in the grass. A strange pattern like words. Like the Verbatinea.

I was going. It was happening.

Light. White and pure. And hands grasping me around the arms, pulling me from my own body and wrapping me in my new coat.

"Davey."

She was warm and soft. I looked up at Emily's face. It was bloated, as if her cheeks were packed with cotton wool. Dark circles framed her eyes, and her stomach was swollen to the degree that it was grazing my own as she pulled me into her chest. Had she really looked like that when I'd seen her a week and a half earlier? She looked like a monster, and I retched a dribble of bile onto the carpet.

Again, Emily had made something from nothing. I'd never understand this magical ability. Never. How she was able to create, express. And why everything I touched became dust.

Before, I'd towered above her; but then, as she squeezed me still in her arms, I'd never felt so small. When the shaking started to recede, I straightened up so that I knelt on the carpet beside her, inspecting my knees, my wrists, the backs of my hands. But they were the same. Nothing had changed.

Emily had her hand on her stomach and her eyes were wide and bright white.

"David… what's happening?"

The air was so thin that I was struggling to breathe, so hoarse gasps were the only response I could manage. She reached across and lifted my arm, black with dried blood. "What have you done?"

I yanked my arm back and pulled down an orange sleeve. I turned to look at the chrysalis. No. Emily had torn open the entranceway, raking back paper and skin and bone. A rabbit skin I'd stripped from roadkill dangled from the canopy. The left side of the frame had buckled, so that already the skeleton had started to fold. Feathers and crackled leaves lay scattered across the wooden floor. All my work. Gone.

Emily covered her mouth with her sleeve. "David. What have you done?"

Words came out in jagged gasps. "It's rotting. It's dying."

My last hope was Michael now.

"What is it?" Her voice shook. She leaned over awkwardly and picked up a shred of torn up sheet music that'd come unstuck. "Did you take this from Flynn's?"

How could she ever understand?

I nodded. "It's language. It's special."

As she released it to the floor, she whispered my name again. Her face was hidden behind her shining black curtain. I crawled over and touched her ankle. *The crickets were back, and they were getting louder.*

Emily yanked herself free of me towards the door. "What is it?"

No need to hide now. The end was there, so close. *It was time.* "To be born." The words hung between us in the gloom. Emily's cheeks were sucked in, her hands clasped across her bulging middle. It was like we were children again, when she stood over me. No one had done that in such a long time. I couldn't stop staring at Emily's stomach, as it seemed to move and ripple in front of me. Before my eyes, she was transforming into a soft and enormous shell, in which something curled safe and warm. And it wasn't me.

Emily shook her hands clean and let out a long, hoarse groan. "This isn't right. Oh, Davey," she let out a little sob, "why didn't I come sooner?"

Leaves crumbled between my fingers. She'd destroyed my chance to transform. It was working. I'd felt it. My throat tightened. "I know what I'm doing," I whispered.

"And what's that?" she shrugged. "David, something's gone very wrong; can't you see it?" She grasped my shoulders, firmly but tentatively like you'd handle a bomb. "How long have you been living like this?"

I followed her eyes around the room. What did she mean? Emily held her hands in front of her, fending something off. "Davey, where's all your furniture? Where's the bed? Everything? Anything?"

I pointed to the mattress on the floor. That was all anyone needed. But Emily's eyes kept locking onto the chrysalis, in shreds and tatters in the corner of the room. "I don't understand," she whispered, her eyes wet.

That made me smirk. *How could she expect to?*

Heaving herself to her feet, she began to drift around the flat, kicking old pizza boxes and plastic bottles with her boot. "This is terrible," she muttered, so low that it couldn't have been to me. "This is squalor." She was getting dangerously close to my laptop, so I scrambled across the floor, surprised at the energy I mustered, and closed the screen. The sound made her attention snap back to me. "You're skin and bone."

I needed to get to my feet. *Why was I so weak?*

Emily reached over and touched my cheek. "You're... withering. You don't look well."

What did she expect, when she pulled me, half made, from my chrysalis?

"What are you doing, Davey?" she whispered. "You haven't been answering the phone to us. Mum and Dad have been knocking on your door all week. You know they were too scared to call the police, in case you'd done something. And look at you. Your arm. You can't even stand!"

She was talking like I was a child. But she was the child, now. Her world was so small, and mine was expanding every second. Every second.

"I'm leaving."

"No, you're not."

I laughed, then. *What did she think she could possibility do?*

"Emily," I sounded shrill. "You know nothing about it. The things I know now. The people I've spoken to."

Her head cocked to the side. "Who?"

Had I said too much? Michael had said absolute secrecy. How much was secret?

"People who can help me leave."

"I hope you're not giving them money."

Money? Why was this about money now?

"David, don't give anyone anything. There are charlatans out there who look for people with 'The Modern Problem' stamped across their foreheads and take advantage of them. Their loneliness. Not everyone is who they say they are."

"I know that."

"David. They will milk you dry and leave you in a fucking field somewhere. They prey on people like you." She had this really weird smile on her face. I couldn't understand it. It was like she was angry, but also thought the whole thing was funny. She gestured to the mess on the floor before striding to the window and flinging open the curtains. White light poured in like milk. "The only place you need to get out of is this shithole."

Cold trickled down my back. What if Michael hadn't replied because I hadn't offered enough money? What if he thought I'd had more and now he thought I was wasting his time? I could get more money. There could always be more money.

"David?"

Why was Emily so far away?

"David, did you open the boxes I sent? The blue comfort packages? The Blue Pilgrim subscription boxes? I sent them to help you."

What was she talking about? Her voice echoed from down

the tunnel. *Could she see me? Could she hear me?* She held out a hand, too distant to reach.

"David? Shall we leave?"

And in my mind's eye I saw that suited woman standing in the middle of the busy road, the day Mum and Doc took me to the doctor when I was ten. How the cars were parked up to her bloody and scraped knees but the drivers didn't even look. *How desperate the woman was to be seen.* Emily didn't see the woman, neither did Mum or Dad. *But I did.*

Something snapped.

"Let's go to Grandad's house, or his grave, shall we? Why don't we go there?"

Emily took a step back. "What are you talking about?"

"Why don't we go? Pay our respects?"

Emily's face was pale, her cheeks sucked in again so that her bloated face actually looked gaunt. The longer she stayed quiet, the more satisfied I was. *Yes. She knows. Dad would have told her, and she's kept it to herself all this time. So many secrets, so many lies. A whole little family inside a nut, with me on the outside, blind.*

And that was it. The truth was finally exposed, like a fleshy red tongue.

I reached to the side of the mattress and dragged *Hidden Worlds* across the floor. I couldn't lift it, but I didn't need to. I slipped my fingers between the pages, pulled out the business card I'd placed inside and tucked it in my back pocket. My eyes caught for a second on the chapter title, Grandad's question:

Who are you, in this vast multiverse?

And I knew. I finally, finally knew. Emily watched everything

I did, her eyes as wide and white as eggs, her hands pressed over her mouth. I didn't care. She watched as I struggled to my feet and grabbed my heaviest boots. She watched as I staggered out of the flat with a scrunched-up carrier bag in my hand without saying another word. She watched, fanning her hands over her stomach as I got close to her.

There was only one person left who might understand. And I planned to tell her everything.

19.

The arcade was a full forty-minute walk from the flat, but that day it only took seconds. Though my head rattled with things I needed to do, I had very few clear thoughts on the way there. I stuffed my hands deep into my pockets to stop them trembling, and I trained my eyes on the cracks in the pavement to help me move in a straight line. I didn't think about leaving Emily alone in the flat. What did it matter if she found my books or opened the laptop now? I was gone. There were only a few days left until Midwinter, and if I worked it right, I need never go back to my flat.

Just as I was about to turn the corner onto the high street, my boot slipped on a patch of ice and I fell against the exterior wall of an abandoned shop. It'd been painted to represent a bright red sunset, and I leaned into it, pressing my forehead against the cold. A moment later there was a hand on my shoulder, light and cold, like someone had rested a glass there. When I turned to look, it was a woman around my age, maybe a few years younger. Her auburn hair was plaited down one shoulder, and her nose was a nest of freckles. She was dressed all in blue, and a little embroidered patch on her polo shirt read, 'Solving the Modern Problem. Let's talk.' Her lips were wet.

"Are you all right, Sir?" Her voice was hardly more than a breath. "Can we talk?"

They *were* following me.

I shook her hand from my shoulder. She stepped back tentatively, but then moved closer again. "Do you need someone? We can talk." She placed her hands on my upper arms. "Feel my touch. I'm here with you. You aren't alone. Do you have somewhere to go home to?"

Why couldn't they just leave me alone? I'd always understood when they approached Sam, sitting there on the bench, mumbling into space. But why was this one talking to me? Couldn't she see that I was the only one here who actually knew what I was doing? I knew *so much more* than anyone else did about the nature of the world.

Who are you, in this vast multiverse, David?

She wore her face openly. White as a pearl and quiet, her mouth slightly open. She reminded me of a snowdrop. So many emotions flooded her face at once. Hope. Peace. Unease. Order. Perhaps a little bit of fear. "If you tell me where you live, I can take you there. You aren't as lost as you think you are." She let out a long breath. "All you need to do is talk; it's easy. See?"

I twisted from her grasp like a snake. "I know where I'm going. I'm late." It was only one woman. What could she possibly do to stop me now? As I turned away, her face fell and her hands folded across her heart.

Before I entered the arcade, I leaned into an alcove beneath the electric heaters and pulled out my phone. It was just a short email, but my fingers weren't working, so it took longer than it ought to.

Michael,

Ignore my last total. I have more than that. I will have
more.

I'll come to the address on the business card with everything
I have, and everything I want to take with me.

See you very soon.

David Porter

My hands deep in my pockets, I approached Flynn's. Behind
the counter at the back, a woman was slipping sheet music
into plastic sleeves. Tall and ashen-haired, everything about
her was fluid. She stood like a waterfall, wavering. Her head
hung low, her eyes pouring over the desk. It was strange,
seeing someone else standing in my space so soon. I'd only
been away for a few weeks. I hadn't even handed my notice
in, not officially. But I'd already been replaced.

Paul was nowhere to be seen.

In the corner of my eye, the silver corner glinted. Quickly,
I leaned into the corner and picked up the three display
models of the most expensive flutes the shop stocked and
slipped them into my carrier bag. I turned on my heel and
made for the exit.

"Can I help you?" Paul crouched by the spare strings
stand, his hands full of crinkling packets. He looked up at
me, his eyes shrunken behind his square glasses. I backed
away a few steps.

"Is there anything you want?" He squinted at me. "Are
you a regular, here?"

I shook my head and tripped over the toes of my boots as
I left the shop. My hands were so cold, and I looked down
at them then, silver and pale as they were, and they rippled
like the girl behind the desk. I couldn't feel the wiggle of my

fingers, just like I couldn't feel the heave of my chest as the air grew thin.

There was so little time. Was it happening already?

Just a few more steps and my hands slammed into the glass window. *There she was.* Why had I stayed away? Agatha stood behind the desk, flanked by two middle-aged men, laughing into her ears. Her arms were half-up in a faux shrug and her hair was aflame. She wasn't in uniform and was wearing a tight blue t-shirt with 'Punk is Queen' on the front. Everything else in the shop was grey.

Being this close to her again made everything go tight. My lungs had grown too big and strained against my ribs. Tears filled my eyes.

Why had I waited? Why had I been so stupid?

As I entered the shop, the three of them looked up, their smiles frozen on their faces. Agatha's chest heaved, and she mouthed, "Oh my God."

I ran up to the counter and, losing my balance at the last second, laid my hands flat on it. I couldn't catch my breath. "Agatha," I gasped, "Am I still here? Am I here?" Looking down, my hands were glass. "Oh, fuck. There's no time. You have to come with me now." I held out one watery arm.

And then everything warped.

The two men stepped closer to Agatha and one of them put his hand on her upper arm. The younger one, whose straggly beard reached down to his Adam's apple, cleared his throat. "What are you doing here?"

"What?" I shook my head. Suddenly, all three faces were difficult to focus on. The one on the right had something black in his hand and he pressed it to his face. Agatha swam in and out of reach, her hands were pressed over her mouth. Her eyes shimmered like diamonds.

"I said, what are you doing here?" His voice was a cannon.

"I'm not here for you," I hissed. "This is between us." I pointed at Agatha, who seemed further away and smaller than she had done a few seconds ago.

"No." A bullet, quick and sharp. "It's not. You're banned from this shop. You shouldn't be here."

I shook my head; they were wasting time. I'd already spent years planning my transformation and had been so close to making the wrong choice. How could I have ever thought that this was the right world?

Never again.

I reached across the counter to grab Agatha's wrist and knocked over a stand on the counter. Little pots of paint rolled onto the floor like rain. The other man, flushed and shuddering had lowered the black thing from his face. "Please stand back now," he said. "Please."

I ignored him. "Agatha, please. I know I've been wrong, but I know what to do now. You have to come, you have to let me explain. I know the way out now." My voice, only starting to sound like itself again went shrill before cutting out. My face itched so I scratched at it, and was shocked to find it was wet with tears.

And then, for no reason that I could understand, Agatha turned completely around so all I could see was the fiery back of her head. The clicking was back, and the room flickered as if I was surrounded in a swarm of flying creatures like locusts or moths. I craned my head up, listening.

What are you trying to tell me?

And as if whispered into a strong wind, I heard her say, "Make him go."

This couldn't be happening. I reached across again and the bearded man stepped between us. "Fuck. Off," he said, inches from my face, and then softer and over his shoulder, "Get in the back, Aggy. Go."

She disappeared through a doorway behind the counter and all the colour drained from the world. The bearded man held up his palms towards me. "She's told you before, leave her alone. You can't be here."

All the strength went from my legs and I fell to the floor. Was I water? A dull sensation in my knees came and went, and I rolled into a ball, my hands folding my head onto the orange knit on my chest. Inexplicably, all I could see was Dad, the night he told us that Grandad was dead and my world split into two. The before and after.

I scrunched my face as tightly as I could against the clicks. It was too much, too much now. And then firm hands were gripping my shoulders, and rather than lifting me up, they pressed me down further into darkness.

20.

So much of my life so far has been in black and white. A truth or a lie. And then suddenly, everything became grey. Upside down. Inside out. The boundaries between tearing, not neatly, never neatly, but rough and jagged at the edges.

I can't remember what happened when I was taken. I just see flashes of yellow and reflective silver, and I hear voices which started off loud and abrupt but became softer and gentler with time. I answered back, I functioned. I said what they seemed to want me to say. I shook my head and I cried. But when one man left and another came into my grey room, furnished only with a desk and two chairs, I couldn't remember which I'd met before and which I hadn't. They asked me about Agatha, and at the mention of her name my throat clammed up. To my left was a mirror, about six feet long. I trained my eyes on my reflection just in case my outline began to shimmer.

I spent the night on a thin mattress on a metal frame that creaked. My tiny room was painted pale yellow, like being inside a buttercup. The door was thick, and didn't have a handle on the inside. There was a little window at face level where men and women wearing black hats walked past every so often, sometimes chatting, sometimes looking determined. At one point, a man came in wearing a brown woollen suit and little round glasses. His pointed chin and gingery hair looked vaguely familiar. He held out his hand and introduced himself as Dr Rosenburg. His breath smelled like boiled sweets. He leaned forwards and said that everything we would discuss would be confidential and then asked me a few questions about nothing much: who I was, where I was from, why did I think I was at the station. I told him that I didn't know how I was, but that I was here because I'd upset someone. He didn't mention Agatha. When he stood up to leave, I felt my whole body relax.

All through the evening, the police station buzzed with activity. My room was dark, but I felt its electricity through the brick. Strange wails and shrieks sliced the night, and through the illuminated square of glass I caught sight of faces closed tightly when running, and once a scuffle, as they dragged an uncooperative someone along the corridor.

By the time the door opened and I was led from my room, I had no idea of the time. I'd spent the night fluttering between sleep and wakefulness, so that reality became almost more obscure than my half-dreams. I was told that I could leave, and a woman, only as tall as my shoulder, read from a piece of paper in a monotone. She sounded like a machine, and so I missed half of the words. Emily was waiting for me at the reception desk, signing various bits of paper. If anything, her stomach looked even more bloated than it had before. Could it have grown overnight? I fought the urge to run up to her and scream to her belly, "*Stay in there, don't come out.*"

Emily handed back the clipboards and the woman behind the desk handed her a clear plastic bag. Inside was my wallet and phone. I patted my pocket; I hadn't even noticed they were gone. There was no sign of the carrier bag and the flutes. My stomach clenched. Emily held my elbow and led me to her car in silence. I sank into the front passenger seat with her hands squeezing my shoulders.

We pulled out of somewhere grey and industrial, and within a few minutes we were on a country road surrounded by the green that I hadn't seen in a long time. The passing trees and shrubs were too difficult to focus on and made me feel nauseous, so I rested my eyes on the far hills, stark and crisp against the sky. Emily wore a smile, but her hands were white on the steering wheel. Occasionally she'd glance my way and then look back at the road again with a long, slow, blink. Only when we'd been driving for twenty minutes or so did she say anything.

"Can you hear me, David?"

I didn't turn to her, but took a long deep breath and slouched lower in the seat.

"Did you remember that she had filed a complaint against you before?"

The hills dipped and rose again. The sheep like clouds.

"Theft, too. Little things. Things I saw around your flat."

A blackbird darts between the trees. Shouldn't he have gone by now? To somewhere warmer? Kinder?

"You said that she was your girlfriend."

There were haybales, as big as cabins. A red tractor over there. Time for harvest.

"Do you remember when you were little, and Dad said you didn't speak? You spoke to me, Davey. You always did. And you can now."

The grass is a cold sea, that's all. Times are tides that drag us in and out.

"Davey?" Her voice cracked.

Grandad's in the sea, up to his waist, with the yellow backpack. But not the orange jumper. I have the orange jumper. His map is sodden. He waves.

"Can you hear me?" And then finally, she gave up.

The car pulled up onto the driveway. Mum and Dad stood together at the bottom of the stairs when we walked in. Mum's face was obscured by a thick mask of make-up, like camouflage, and her chin wobbled up and down. She had Bosey crushed to her chest, and the more he wriggled desperately to leap over her shoulder, the tighter she gripped him. Her neck was hatched with bloody lines. Dad stood slightly behind her and stared directly at me, his hand squeezing Mum's shoulder. While everything else was fuzzy and quivering, Dad's face was stone, all the contours of his wrinkles, the light shining from his grey beard.

Emily spoke a few soft words to them and led me upstairs. This was far easier than thinking. I held her hand tightly, so she knew I didn't want her to let go. She took me to my room. I hadn't been there since I'd left home, years earlier, and it was exactly how I'd left it, not a single thing changed. Two golden chocolate wrappers lay crumbled on the windowsill, and particles of dust danced in the light that beamed through the crack in the curtains. A mug on the dresser was green on the inside. Something about the room soothed me. It was like entering the belly of a whale that was entirely dead. I couldn't imagine anything more cold, still, or peaceful.

"Come on, lie down." She pulled back the duvet and pushed me onto the bed. There was a strange tugging sensation on my feet, a few mumbled words, and then silence. The longer I lay motionless, the swifter I fell.

I slept and I dreamed. I saw Grandad in a glen, his backpack a beacon on the mauve hills. He held a huge map sketched in a language I couldn't read. His fingers followed the tracks on it and ley lines appeared on the ground, stretching across the fells and back into the trees where I stood. And then Agatha was beside me, and every time I reached out for her, she stepped away and laughed, like it was all a game, like the pale girl had in Sam's flat. I opened my mouth to tell her that this was serious, but my voice had been replaced with the sound of hundreds of cicadas. She laughed even more and stepped even further away, her brow furrowed as if she didn't understand and her head cocked like a sparrow. Again, I tried to speak, but I couldn't remember any of our conversations, or even the sound of my voice.

Then, as I stood there, the ground started to groan and crack and I was falling into a darkness softer and more inviting than the light. Agatha turned and ran into the trees just as I slipped over the edge and down a steep wet slope. At the bottom, I hit warm earth, and the walls crumbled onto me like snow, covering my face and filling my mouth. I wriggled in the shadows, feeling my body stretch and contort in my chrysalis, completely without pain. I was soup. I was swimming. And Emily had no idea that it was me turning inside her ever-expanding stomach.

I awoke so tightly wrapped in the covers that they might've been wings. The mattress was soft and I had sunk deep into a hollow in the centre. The ceiling hung above me like the lid of a coffin. Had it all gone away? I thought of Grandad, alone in Grandma's chair after she died, and loss hit me in an icy tide. I let the feeling swell into all my limbs, and I bit down on my sleeve to stop myself from calling out.

Later, Dad brought in a bowl and sat on the edge of the

mattress. He sat for a while, watching as the steam curled and faded in the air. He placed a hand on my leg. As he waited, his hold became tighter, and soon I could almost feel Dad's heart beat through his palm. When the bowl was no longer steaming, Dad offered me some on a spoon and I let him trickle it into my mouth. It was warm and salty, but I could only stomach a few spoonfuls before my throat started to clam up and I couldn't swallow. Dad urged me to take one more, and this time he offered me a little brown pill from his pocket. He pushed it past my lips, but I couldn't swallow, so I let it dissolve down by my gums. It was bitter and foul, but once it'd started to break down there was nothing I could do.

I had to say it. "Where's my letter, Dad?" It was no more than a croak.

Dad paused, watching me sideways. "Which letter, David?"

"From Grandad."

Dad's mouth fell open. His eyes were wide, and beneath the heavy whiskers they glistened like I remember Grandad's doing. Like hundreds of jet beads. "It's gone, David. It's gone."

The ceiling seemed like miles away and waved through the tears in my eyes. "Why?"

"I'm sorry, David." His head fell into his hands. "Perhaps I should've given it to you. But he wanted you to follow him," Dad whispered. "Into bad places. Bad ways of thinking. I couldn't let that happen. He didn't care about helping you to understand the world. He was teaching you how to run when he should've been showing you how to stand still. God help me, I tried to do that. To undo what he did. But he didn't listen to me, and neither did you. You only ever listened to him."

I waited for the little brown pill to change me, or to make the room pull back into focus, but instead I fell into a deep doze again, until I was yanked back by movement on the bed. It was Mum, tucking the duvet underneath my body as if wrapping up pork for the oven. The curtains were half-drawn, and the daylight turned her flyaways silver. Her face was still a mask from a museum, deep like teak, with painted-on lips and eyes. It wasn't a human face; it was the face of a ghost.

Straining my throat, I asked her, "Where's Grandad?"

She stopped dead. The mask didn't change. "What do you mean?" She whispered back.

"Where did he go? I need to know–"

"He's not here," her voice quivered. "He's dead, David. Don't you remember?"

"I don't believe you," I whispered. "He's still here. No funeral."

Mum squinted down at me. "There wasn't any money for a funeral, David. Fuck knows where it all went, what he spent it on. We could've done with it, God knows. There was nothing left. He even donated all his bits of furniture to the Blue Pilgrims."

"Why?" The word was a gasp.

Mum's brow wrinkled. "Well, they did help him a bit, if you remember. When he really struggled. After Grandma first died. Oh, David…" Her fingers stroked my forehead. "You've always struggled to let go of him, I know. I'm sorry I didn't help you more. Your dad was the same. He hadn't been dead two minutes and your dad already had all Francis's old maps out on the bed, seeking to walk in his footsteps. To connect with him again. It took years for him to make peace with it, and now he spends all his time in the outdoors. He's found Grandad there, you see. In what he loved best."

I closed my eyes, and when I opened them, she was gone. My mouth tasted like poison.

After pushing the duvet aside, I staggered to my feet and stood, marvelling at how I no longer felt heavy; I was light, but weak, as if stitched from smoke. My boots were gone, and my toes sank into the deep carpet. As I gathered myself, I looked around the room at all the things that were mine, but from a lifetime ago. Posters of salamanders, *Transfigurations in Nature* on the chest of drawers, an old doll's wardrobe of Emily's in which I'd imprisoned a chrysalis that had never hatched. I picked it up, and found that the thing that'd been forgotten had turned black. It just looked like dirt.

It seemed too unbelievable to imagine my room had been untouched since I'd moved out. On the chest of drawers there were a few objects that I didn't recognise at all, but somehow I knew they were mine. A little box of toy soldiers. A notebook, half-filled with sketches of snakes shedding their skin. A tiny blue eggshell, perfect other than a small hole poked in the side. The room settled a little as pieces of the puzzle fell into place, one by one. *I always knew that I needed to go.*

The door creaked as I opened it and crossed the landing to Mum and Dad's room. Their voices wafted up from the kitchen downstairs, so I knew I wouldn't be interrupted. The room was still dishevelled, the duvet hanging off the bed and onto the floor, dirty cups and bowls stacked on every surface, opened boxes and knick-knacks crammed onto every surface. It smelled like damp. The wardrobe doors were half-open, so I started there, sorting through where I'd found the bag of Grandad's clothes. I didn't bother to be quiet. The chest of drawers held no secrets either; only underwear and other soft, meaningless things. The top drawer rattled loudly with hundreds of silver tubes and black cases, more of the sort that littered Mum's dressing table. Many of them still had a little sticky seal that meant they hadn't even been opened.

By now my breath was coming out in sharp bursts again. I hadn't the time to waste.

Dad's bedside cabinet. *Where all the secrets live, so you dreamed about them, remember?*

The door swung open to reveal only two things: a white box, slightly smaller than a shoebox, and a folded grey page, held closed with a bulldog clip. There was no sign of the letter, or of any of the other maps or papers I'd seen Dad with when Grandad first disappeared. *Perhaps the letter really was gone.* The clipped paper bundle turned out to be a photograph and scrap of newspaper. It was of Dad and Grandad together, when Grandad's face was rounder and he smiled more. They were outdoors, amongst purple hills and a mountain that looked like a face. *It couldn't be the same, it couldn't.* Both of them there... *together.* The torn-up piece of newspaper was the brief obituary that'd been published at the time Grandad disappeared.

And a box.

My heart thumped in my chest, and I covered my face with my hands. It was about the size of a shoebox. It was surprisingly weighty, all of its density in the centre. I flipped open the lid with my eyes closed, and only when I couldn't bear it any longer did I look. Inside was a sealed terracotta pot, about the size of a small rugby ball. I lifted it carefully. There was nothing written on the sides to give a clue as to the contents. It took all my strength to prise open the lid, and I held my breath as I peered inside.

Sand. Or dust perhaps? No, it was neither. It was bone white and coarse against my fingertips. A sudden alarm in the back of my head and I frantically wiped my hand on my jeans. I put the lid back on and held it in my arms while I let this discovery settle. My mind was blank, but tears streamed down my face. Before placing it back in the box, I took a tentative look at the base, but once I made out Grandad's name and the date he disappeared, I didn't want to read anymore, so put the box back in the cabinet.

Everything was black.

I rose and descended the steps to the front door. It was like balancing on fists. I walked as if in a dream, only stopping to reach into the kitchen bin and pull out a piece of old orange peel that throbbed and rang like a silver bell between my lips as I sucked it. Treacle and nectar on my tongue. Only a little bit sickly. Still, like heaven.

My toes were completely numb. At the front door, I reached for a pair of Dad's socks, left balled beside the shoe rack. My throat tightened as I pulled them on, and saw that I only had four toenails left. Where the others had been was now bald skin, burned and black. I stepped into a pair of Dad's brown brogues, thankful that they were too big, and headed out into the street. The air was crisp and stung my eyes. Only a few dried offerings remained, stuck to the gutters in the winter slush. The street towards the broken fence and cow field was narrower than I remembered, and everyone's living rooms were on show. Most were empty, but in a couple of windows a creased old face hovered, watching me weave my way towards the fence. The old woman across the road, who had so often stood at the edge of her garden to water her flowers, was now watching me from behind the glass. She'd picked a few of her flowers and had placed them in a vase on the windowsill. Something about the light today made them look gloriously, vividly blue.

Is it Midwinter today? Is that today? Mild panic. I didn't know what day it was.

When I reached the broken fence, I rested my hands on each adjacent post. My fingers looked silver in the shimmering light. I took three deep breaths the air through the gap. It tasted as fresh and crisp as a green apple. In the sky, the clouds shifted and split like a doorway, and the buttery sun poured through and slicked down my back. The grass on the other side of the fence was short and violently green. The air smelled of rain. Beneath the earth was the sound of drums as a turning mass of life twisted its way through the soil. *The ground was breathing.* My whole face tickled in the light, until it began to burn, as if flying in the face of an electric bulb. I reached up, fingers spread. My left wrist and hand were on fire, as if I held the sun in place. My legs were water again, pooling inside skin hanging in the wrong shape. Between the light and I, a dark shape flaps past and disappears into the trees.

A weight pressed over my back and a voice whispered in my ear, "Don't go, Davey. Don't go." Emily pressed her cheek against mine and tears met tears.

"What's through there, Emily? Do you know? Have you always known and kept it from me?"

Emily turned and looked through the fence. "It's just fields, David. Fields and grass and hills, just like on this side. There's nothing else."

She held me in a blanket as I folded up into my knees.

The hovering silver shimmer in the air had started to fade already. The sky was dark.

"I'm here with you. You're not on your own." Her voice dripped like honey. I wanted to stay there with her until the ground opened up and swallowed us both whole, but she – still very much of this world – had enough strength to hold us both up in the light.

Emily brought her car over to the broken piece of fence and helped me into the backseat. As the car bumped along the road, I concentrated on my hands, turning over and over in my lap. My fingers had too many joints. I was sure of it. Maybe I didn't need to go anywhere after all? Maybe this would happen anyway, if it was meant to be. Transforming like nature intended.

When the car stopped, she peered down at me between the front seats. "Can you walk?"

I forced myself upright. Beside my window was a white sign plugged into the grass.

ST CHRISTOPHER'S BLUE HOUSE
DR MICHAEL ROSENBURG CLINICS

I blinked, but the writing stayed the same. *They couldn't think...?* Behind the sign was a large, blue-painted house with grey shutters and a white front door.

The car's passenger door opened and a strong arm lifted me from the seat. I leaned on the car roof for support, and looked into Dad's face, creased and grey. I couldn't remember the last time I'd seen Dad in daylight. On the ground beside him was a packed yellow rucksack. Dad glanced down at it, scratching his chin. "We thought you'd like to take it with you." Just behind him, a busy main road roared. *Home-time.* He squeezed my arm and nodded a tight little nod. "Son," he said, "I understand."

My skin ached beneath his touch so I yanked my arm free.

"Michael is good," Emily coo-ed. "You met him at the station, remember?"

No. I backed away from them both. Once I was in there, that was it; they'd stop everything. I'd be trapped here. Like this.

I checked my back pocket. The business card was still there. It was all I had. If I could just make it to the address.

I showed Dad and Emily my empty palms. "I'm not one of you," I croaked. "I'm sorry. I can't be. I'm different."

"You are, David. You've always been us. We're family." Emily's hands pressed over her mouth.

"No," the words faded to a light rasp.

Emily shook her head violently. "Don't you think it's the same for me? Do you think life's so easy for the rest of us? Why do you think I read my scripts? Why do you think I perform? I need someone to tell me what to do, too."

"No. You've all lied to me, all this time." I looked directly at Dad. "Why didn't you make Grandad stay? I needed him. He was the only one that understood. Why didn't you follow him? Bring him back?"

He shook his head, his mouth hanging open. "I couldn't bring him back, David. No one could. He's gone."

In the distance, two figures dressed in pale grey scrubs were slowly approaching from the entrance to the Blue House. I couldn't make out their faces, but their shoulders were broad. Their eyes looked black. Almost entirely black.

Emily's hands pressed over her mouth. "David," she

sobbed. "It might feel like a storm, but the thunder can't hurt you."

I open my mouth, but my throat has closed.

"Please just talk to us," Emily cried. "Tell us what's happening to you. That's all you need to do; just talk to us."

The two figures were speeding up, their faces impassive. I turned back to Emily, her face a pearl and her eyes glittering, and shook my head.

This was the moment.

Using my last reserves of energy, I burst past Dad and Emily, but she caught my wrist in her hand. "Don't go, please," she whispered. But behind my eyes the clicks were lifting again and I shoved her away so that she fell onto the tarmac and didn't move again. I didn't mean that to happen, but I took the chance, my very last chance, to turn on my heel and run. And with only Michael's address in my pocket, I streaked towards the motorway, Dad screaming, the lights, the horns, and the roar.

AFTER

~

I'm being pulled apart... stretched, like my skin and my limbs aren't a part of me anymore. They're miles away, tethered by threads which *hummmmmmm* like electricity.

Bright white. Leather tethers. A scream like an owl shot from the sky.

Is this forever? The feeling goes on, and what happened before is another lifetime. Another trial.

I'm split. I'm blind.

But behind my back, there's something cold and firm. My hands slip across it and I fall to my knees with a terrible crack. I'm already so weak that this new pain is just a tingle, a warm current flickering up my thighs. But my spine; I can't straighten at all. Something is inside Grandad's jumper, squatting on my back, pulling the knit tight against my throat, and it chokes. But all is so bleached and bright that I can't see, and I can't reach to knock it away. Whatever it is, it's clinging to my vertebrae like I'm a stone to squat on, and I struggle to breathe beneath its weight. We sit here in the silence, the pair of us, breathing, existing, being. The thing heaves rhythmically. He is silent.

Something rises in me and I fight to straighten up. The weight doesn't lift, but sags downward inside the precious orange jumper, now tatters and dangling threads, so I just about manage to my feet. Gravity curls my back into a crescent moon.

I open my eyes. I'm in a long corridor, painted white with wooden panelling. *Or is it blue? I knew it would be blue.* A pale cornflower blue. It stretches on for at least fifty feet, curving off to the left. To my right are floor to ceiling windows looking out onto a small garden, drowning in fallen leaves in shades of red and gold that reach up to my waist. The garden is blocked off by walls which look to be part of the same building I'm in now. There are three trees, their branches bald. I lean against the glass and watch as the piled leaves shuffle in certain spots, as if creatures were tunnelling their way through them, but never coming up for air. There's this faint rushing sound. It sounds like applause.

On the left side of the corridor are a row of white doors, each with a tiny window and silver plaque. None of the doors have handles. The first panel is engraved, *Joseph Gonzalez*. Holding onto the wall for stability, I peer through the glass. Inside is a small oak room with only a bench at the back. It's like looking into a closed wooden crate. Hunched in the corner is a man dressed in a rough brown suit, stained with mud. The breast pocket is torn, the fabric hanging down his chest like a flag. He rocks back and forth in his hunched position, occasionally turning his face up to the ceiling and mouthing words as if in prayer.

That's when I see it, and my chest tightens.

The man's face is a mosaic... a smashed mirror. His eyes, brimming with tears, have split into more eyes, which circle his nose like petals on a flower. He covers his ears with his hands, stained black as charcoal, his fingers as long and brittle as twigs. He looks to be completely lost in what he's doing, until he looks up and sees me in the glass. For a moment, I'm afraid. I'm afraid that he'll come rushing at the glass and look right through me with those splitting eyes.

But he doesn't.

He holds my stare for a few seconds before twisting his face in despair and hunching over into a tight ball. With effort, he crawls around and faces the wall and is still.

Am I breathing?

The next plaque along is engraved, *Polly Watts*, and through the glass is a room identical to the first, but this time there's a woman in a long yellow dress, lying in the foetal position. All I can see is yellow and a mane of brown hair which splays across the ground. She is so very still, and so without thinking, I tap on the glass.

She should know she isn't alone.

The woman sits up and turns to me with the back of her head. No, it's not. Her entire face is obscured with brown hair. She flicks and turns on the floor, even raising a hand. She's blind. I tap again on the glass, mouth to her, "Don't worry. You've made it." But she can't seem to tell which direction I'm coming from, and the more I tap the more aggressively she turns, and soon the hand that once sought a hand is now a claw angrily swiping at empty space.

Am I breathing?

The next room, *Martin Bowness*, is the same, and this time its inhabitant writhes on the floor as if he cannot straighten. His black jeans are starting to peel from his body, and his face – though I can still see eyes, nostrils, and a mouth – is flattened and is blending into his neck. Unlike the first two, he doesn't seem to see me at all, and thrashes at the walls with his back and his heels.

Am I breathing?

I stagger along the corridor, and all the rooms are the same. I feel like I'm going to be sick and retch against a door with *Gabriella Wilson* engraved. I look up through the glass and gasp. This time there are three people inside the cabin. A woman with a mane of black curls – I presume, Gabriella – kneels in the centre of the room, her body a rippling mass of pallid palms pushing outwards. They all say 'stop.' Her clothes hang from her in tatters as the hands fight to break the seams. Her face is two hands locked together, as if in prayer, and she tosses her head blindly side to side. At either shoulder is a man dressed in pale grey scrubs. Each has a small watch pinned to his shirt pocket. *The hunters.* The man on the woman's left seems to be holding her still, while the one on the right's mouth is pursed, as if 'shushing.'

I bend over and retch again, but nothing comes out. *The weight is excruciating.*

Each door I check makes me feel worse, but I keep searching – *I have to* – for one name. A name I'm so desperate to find that I stop looking through the windows and only read the panels.

Please don't be here, Grandad. Please don't have been here all this time. Trapped.

So many names. So many people stuck in their cabins. Suffering. Alone. All of them are silent and turn away when they see me. And though I don't recognise a single name on the plaques, I don't feel much relief. All I can see are the rows of faces in the photos in Michael's office, all smiling, all full of hope.

By the time I reach the end of the corridor, I'm practically crawling. My arms jut out in front and my shoulder-blades won't lock back, so I fold my hands in front of my chest.

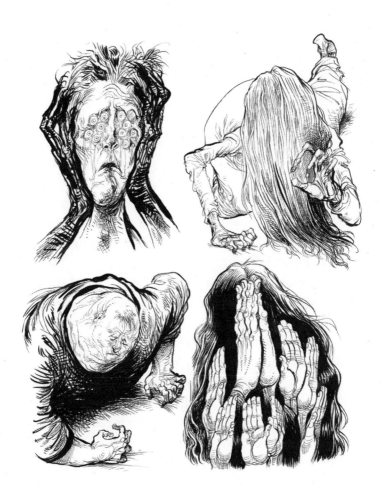

Finally, the last door in the left-hand row. I check the name and I let out a croak. *Emily Porter.*

No no no no no. She shouldn't be here.

My gut buckles, but I need to see. I step up to the window and with a deep, airless breath, I look through the glass. But this time the cabin room is empty, apart from a naked grey egg, as tall as my knee, in the centre of the room. Its shell is mottled and pitted like the surface of the moon.

I press my hands to my heart. *Thank you.*

Only one door left now. Set apart from the row and directly in front of me. The door is ajar, but only by an inch, so I can't see inside. This time there's no glass panel, only a golden plaque engraved with *David Porter*. There's no-where else to go.

I push open the door. It's an office, all wooden panels and velvet cushions. The walls are a deep green, wallpapered with huge flowers. There's a fish tank in the corner, planted with colourful corals. At the other side is a row of shelves, stacked with strange instruments with levers and gears and buttons and trumpets in all shapes and sizes. Most of the relics are big enough to pick up in your hands, but even if I did I wouldn't know which way to hold them up. Many are under bell jars, like they might be in a museum. Each one has a little panel beside it, but the type is too small to read.

On the two opposing walls of the room are two great mirrors, framed in bronze.

In the centre of the room is a desk, covered in a deep red tablecloth. In front of it is a low leather armchair, the sort which might eat you if you sink into it too deep, and behind the desk is a man writing with a black quill. He looks up from his huge piece of paper and smiles. It's Michael. Or is it? He's almost the same, that long pointed chin, the blonde hair, gelled in spirals. But he's wearing a grey suit this time, and a tie. A pair of little round glasses perches on the end of his nose. There's a little name plaque on the desk, which reads, 'Dr Michael Rosenburg.'

Michael rises, his arms outstretched. "Ahh, David. You made it. I'm so pleased."

I stagger forwards a few steps into the lamplight. I need to see his face better. The floor glitters with scattered diamonds.

"What a day, today is. Sit down, David. Emily's been telling me about you."

Glass. Not diamonds. Broken glass.

I drag myself up to the desk and lower myself into the leather chair. I'm flanked by mirrors. Michael smiles. "She's been trying to call you back to the world for such a long time. Could you hear her, I wonder? Did you see her, waving at your window? Despite you not wanting her in your room, she stuck around. Making sure you were all right."

"She's OK, isn't she? I pushed her. I hurt her. She fell in the road."

Michael's lips disappear. He looks like he might say something, but no words come.

"Is she OK?" I cry. "That egg, it was perfect. Surely that means she isn't–"

"Emily will heal, David. She's protecting herself now, but she wants you to get better."

A bell jar behind him catches my eye, it must be two feet high. Inside it, on a tall stone plinth, is a little black book, but I can't tell if it's the Verbatinea or the book I used to record Agatha's movements. A little white card in front of it reads, *Relic depicting David Porter's voice.*

The man taps his pen on the edge of the desk. There's something hidden in his other hand. It occasionally catches the light and shines. He rolls it between his fingers. "You know," he says, "if you disappear, you won't exist? Wouldn't you rather be here, full in body and filling the space? Owning your form." He places the little thing on the corner of his desk. A little brass sparrow. Grandma's button.

Michael points to the mirrors at either side of his desk. "Because you do, you know. You change every second, even now. You're centre-stage, right in the middle, exactly where you should be. In the perfect place."

I don't know how to answer. It feels like a trick, but I'm too weak to work it all out. He looks so familiar to me, but I can't figure out why. *Michael.* The doctor tilts his head and purses his lips. "Hmm," he says, before making his way around the table towards me with a small knife, pointing to my throat. I raise my hands, but the man pushes them away with hardly any effort at all and flicks the knife back and forwards across my throat. "There you are," he says. "You were halfway there already, I've just helped you along. A few days ago you wouldn't have let me do that."

I gasp, and to my surprise, *I make a sound.* I clutch my neck. Michael pushes me down into the red leather chair and sits himself behind the desk. I look down at my hands, no blood. My fingers curl towards the lamp, like smoke.

"You're ready. You're not squatting in darkness anymore. It's your time to shine." He picks up the pen again and holds the tip against the paper. My eyes sting with tears. "Tell me everything, David," he pushes his glasses up his nose. "Everything you've kept in all these years. From the beginning, when your grandfather died. How you got to be here. Everything that's happened to you, how it made you feel." He leans forwards, his little glasses slipping down the grease on his nose. "We're going to work out together how you connect to the world. And only then, will you know where you belong. Will you do it?"

My body is expanding to fill the space. I see the room multiplied hundreds of times, and two curls of hair flop in front of my face like ropes, but thinner and grasping around of their own will, feeling the contours of my face.

"Grandad," I whisper.

Michael looks up from his hands. "Yes, David?"

"He's not here, is he?"

Michael smiles, just with the corners of his mouth but it's a good smile. "No."

"He's gone."

"Yes."

"Really gone."

"Yes."

I let this settle for a moment, keeping myself still as stone as my body continued to swell and my legs twist, slipping from my hips.

"Who are they, out there?" My voice crackles, but the pain isn't as bad anymore.

Michael sighs. "They're stuck. It's very sad."

"They can't find their door?"

Michael squints. "Of a kind. They're stuck in their own heads. I'm trying to reach them, but they're still not talking to me. They will, sooner or later. When they're ready to. The nurses do good work, it just takes time."

"What do they need to do?"

"The same thing you're doing now. Tell me how you came to be here, ready to accept my help. Open to it. And how I came to be the one to help you. And I will help, David. It's time for you to cross over. It's time to set you free."

It's time. I feel it, in my marrow and in my heart.

I look down at my hands, or where my hands should be. That old itch is electricity jolting up each joint from wrist to shoulder. It's change. It's happening.

It's happening now.

I touch my face and my hands rest on eyes as wide and flat as pebbles. They're cold, and feel like water resting on stone. I open my mouth, and a long brown whip lashes into the air. My chest heaves, and in that moment, the back of what remains of Grandad's orange jumper splits and a pair of dark and fibrous wings uncurl, erupting from my shoulder blades in a cloud of white, choking dust.

And I talk.

ACKNOWLEDGEMENTS

Such a strange book to write, this. It all began with a midwinter walk in the Simonside Hills in Northumberland. A day-long walk under a freezing blue sky that we weren't altogether prepared for. We passed waterfalls, burial cairns perched on cliff edges, caves reputed to have been dwellings for tricksy brownies, and woodlands thought to be the home of the Will-o'-the-wisp myths. Mountains rolled ahead of us, clad in lilac, gold, and tawny hair. Utterly unreal, and yet existing beneath my boots. Simonside will always be *Mothtown*.

But that was only the beginning. I couldn't have written *Mothtown*'s story without the support of a forest of people.

The biggest thanks go to Ben, my husband, for listening to my mad ramblings while I wrote this story. And to Noah, my wee one; for even in the cradle, he had to listen to my thoughts on moths and mudmen. I hope he won't remember that.

To my friends, who've provided such excellent counsel and beta read this book from its confuzzled first draft to what it is today (hopefully not so confuzzled). Dave Lawrie, Russell Jones, Alistair Leadbetter, and Chris Panatier. Particular thanks go to my ever-wise friend Gabriela

Houston, for keeping me sane, and for being the rock I can always rely on.

Thanks (of course!) also go to Chris Riddell, for providing such incredible insights into David's mind with his illustrations and editorial feedback. Chris, you're a fantastic mentor, an ever-enthusiastic collaborator, a kind soul, and a very good egg.

Thanks to my agent, Ed Wilson, an excellent human and master of pep-talks. And to Hélène Butler, for her kind soul and poetic words. Huge hugs and thanks go to everyone at Johnson & Alcock for being endlessly lovely and kind at all times.

I'll always be thankful to my publisher, Angry Robot, for taking a chance on my genre-bending tales. Thank you to Eleanor Teasdale, for believing in me throughout this whole journey. To Rose Green, for your keen eye and editorial genius. To Travis Tynan, for his eagle-eyed ability to spot inconsistencies from a mile away. To Caroline Lambe, for sharing my stories in the most meaningful way (and for so many other email chats late at night, that only we know about!) Thank you to Sarah O'Flaherty for her incredible cover art and endless patience. And thank you to Amy Portsmouth for her endless enthusiasm, perseverance, and willingness to accept (and even nurture) my already over-excited nature. Everyone at Angry Robot has been wonderful and supportive. You're all brilliant. Thank you for everything you do.

And a final thank you to you, the one holding me in your hands. Thank you for believing in this story and letting it live on in your head.

ANGRY
ROBOT

We are Angry Robot

angryrobotbooks.com